A LOTUS PALACE MYSTERY

USA TODAY BESTSELLING AUTHOR
JEANNIE LIN

The Hidden Moon Copyright © 2020 by Jeannie Lin

ISBN: 978-0-9909462-8-1

This is a work of fiction. Names, characters, places and incidents are the product of the author's imagination or are used fictitiously. Any resemblance to actual events, locales, or persons, living or dead, is purely coincidental.

Cover design © Deranged Doctor Design (www.derangeddoctordesign.com)

Cover photographs © Linxi Photo (www.lx-photo.com)

Digital Edition 1.0

All rights reserved.

No part of this book may be reproduced in any form or by any electronic or mechanical means, including information storage and retrieval systems, without written permission from the author, except for the use of brief quotations in a book review.

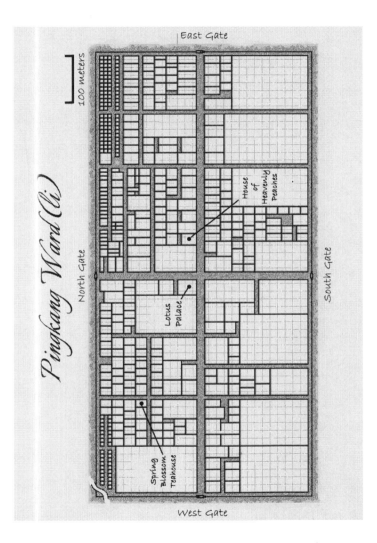

Pingkang Ward (li)

East Gate

100 meters

North Gate

South Gate

West Gate

House of Heavenly Peaches

Lotus Palace

Spring Blossom Teahouse

CAST OF CHARACTERS

Note: The family name comes first for characters who have both given and family names listed. I.e. Bai Huang has a given name of Huang and a family name of Bai.

- **Bai Wei-ling** - Known as Wei-wei. The only daughter of the Bai family. Protagonist of *The Liar's Dice* and *The Hidden Moon*.
- **Gao** - A street-smart informer who has worked with Bai Huang in the past. First appeared in *The Lotus Palace*.

SECONDARY CHARACTERS

- **Yue-ying** - Former servant in the Lotus Palace pleasure house. Bai Huang's wife and Mingyu's sister. Protagonist of *The Lotus Palace*.
- **Bai Huang** - Wealthy and handsome aristocrat, known for being a playboy. Yue-ying's husband and Wei-wei's elder brother. Protagonist of *The Lotus Palace*.
- **Mingyu** - Former courtesan in the Lotus Palace pleasure house. Married to Wu Kaifeng. Yue-ying's older sister. Protagonist of *The Jade Temptress*.
- **Wu Kaifeng** - Former head constable of Chang'an known for his exacting and intimidating demeanor. Mingyu's husband. Protagonist of *The Jade Temptress*.
- **Li Chen** - County magistrate responsible for investigating crimes and administering justice in

the eastern half of the capital. First appeared in *The Lotus Palace*.

- **Zhou Dan** - Servant in the Bai family mansion.
- **Bai Chang-min** - Wei-wei and Huang's seventeen-year-old half-brother.

PROLOGUE

Tang Dynasty China, 849 A.D.

At night, the imperial capital became a place of lanterns and shadows. A puzzle board of gated wards. The messenger rode through the streets, past dark alleys and crossroads. Crowds gathered in the night markets to seek out evening refreshment. He urged his horse past the street life to hurry toward the gates. Soon the lights died away.

Though he could not see his pursuers, he knew they were there. He was being hunted. If he could make it past these walls, and out to the main arteries of Chang'an where the city guards patrolled — if he could make it free of this maze, then he could deliver the message.

There was a bridge ahead. Just beyond that, a row of torches from a night patrol. Their appearance brought hope, and he dug in his heels to ride toward them. His horse's hooves clopped against the stones of the bridge and echoed out into the night. The water of the canal flowed below like a shimmer of glossy ink, reflecting the torchlight against its black depths.

The patrol turned at the sound of his approach to start toward him. As the circle closed in, the messenger realized it wasn't the guards coming to his aid after all.

There was no time for decision. No chance to flee or fight. An invisible force hit him in the back of his shoulder, lodging near his shoulder blade. The next impact struck him square in his chest, unseating him. He plummeted into the canal and his message was lost forever, swallowed by the murky water.

CHAPTER 1

Three things cannot be long hidden: the sun, the moon, and the truth. — Ancient Proverb

Wei-wei was dreaming of flight, the rush of wind, and the glare of sunlight when a rapping sound startled her awake. The dream tore away like paper and she opened her eyes to darkness. There was more knocking.

Feeling her way through the chamber, she reached for the door and opened it. Her brother stood there, framed by the moonlit courtyard.

"Huang." She was still foggy with sleep.

"It's time, Wei-wei," he said, calling her by the milk name that everyone still used. A faint worry line was etched between his eyes, disrupting the smoothly sculpted contours of his face.

She didn't need to ask time for what. Huang's wife was past the ninth month of her pregnancy. The entire household had been waiting — any day, any day now. But the tightness in her eldest brother's voice made her pulse quicken.

"What's wrong?" she asked. "Is Yue-ying alright?"

"She's asking for her sister. Can you take the carriage—"

"Of course. I'll get dressed."

He handed his lantern to her and closed the door. It was still so dark outside. Was it the middle of the night or close to morning? Something wasn't quite right. As Wei-wei reached into her dresser, a feeling of unease hovered over her.

She was worried about her sister-in-law and the baby, of course. She and Yue-ying had become close over the last year.

Wei-wei grabbed her simplest hanfu robe. The garment was fashioned of muted green silk and draped over her underclothes. She knotted a sash around her waist, then smoothed her hands through her hair, coiling it high into a knot. She fixed her hair in place with a wooden pin, hoping she didn't look too dreadful.

That was when she figured out what was bothering her. It was her brother's appearance. Huang didn't look as if he'd just been roused out of bed. He'd been in full uniform, dressed in his state robe and official headdress. Huang looked ready to report to the Imperial City.

He was gone from the courtyard when Wei-wei opened the door. The rest of the household had woken up by then. She could hear the servants' voices, and Yue-ying's bed chamber was lit. A startled cry pierced the night air, making Wei-wei jump. The midwife was urging Yue-ying to walk while Yue-ying was breathing hard, biting back sobs.

Wei-wei didn't know how long babies took to come, but she had a feeling she should hurry. Though she was twenty-five years of age, on the old side of marriageable, pregnancies and babies and motherhood were still somewhat a mystery to her. There were no books on the subject in their library. All she knew was childbirth had been painfully difficult for her own mother. So much that Mother wouldn't risk it again.

She had insisted Father take a concubine after Wei-wei was born.

One of their servants, Zhou Dan, was already at the gate leading out to the stable. He undid the latch and held the gate open for her before moving to ready the horse and carriage.

The Zhou family had attended hers for over a generation now. Zhou Dan had grown up in the household alongside her and Huang, having been born in the year between them. He was almost like another brother, though, unlike her actual brothers, Zhou Dan was supposed to oblige her.

He worked quickly while hitching up the horse, his lanky form casting shadows in the lantern light. Then he turned to help her up before climbing into the driver's seat in front.

"Take me to Pingkang li," she told him.

"I remember," Zhou Dan replied, urging the horse forward.

This wasn't the first time she'd taken the carriage out at night to go to the pleasure quarter. She'd done it without permission the other times. It was only a week ago that Huang had discovered what she was doing and tore up the ward pass she had forged. Zhou Dan still shot her the occasional cross look over dragging him into trouble.

She was glad that Huang had asked her to go now. At least there was something she could do to help.

As the carriage pulled around to the front of the mansion, Wei-wei could see a group of strangers assembled outside their gate. What business could they possibly have? It was hours before sunrise.

It was only when they moved past that she saw the men were flanked by the city guards. The guards were dressed in full armor, swords at their belts and spears in hand. A knot formed in her stomach at the sight of them.

Her brother held a minor administrative position in the Imperial City. He'd been called at odd hours before, but had never been given an armed escort. The men followed the carriage with their eyes as it rolled past.

～

IT WAS STILL dark outside and the roads empty by the time the carriage reached the ward gates. Morning was just peeking through the edges of the night sky. Yue-ying's baby had decided to come into the world before the city had fully awoken.

Chang'an was divided into over a hundred wards, each one walled and gated. Each ward was designed to be a stronghold unto itself during a siege, which wasn't as unlikely as one would think.

The carriage was stopped by a pair of guards at the southern gate. Zhou Dan produced a pass stamped with the Bai family seal, and the guardsman made a note in his logbook before waving them through. They emerged out onto a main thoroughfare and immediately headed south on the grid.

The Bai family mansion was located in the northeast section of the city, in the residential wards closest to the imperial palaces. Yue-ying's sister lived several wards away in the Pingkang quarter. The carriage moved past the East Market and several guard towers as the sky lightened overhead. It would take over an hour to bring Mingyu back.

Once they reached Pingkang li, Zhou Dan showed the pass again to enter. This neighborhood was markedly different from where Wei-wei and her family lived. The northeastern part of the city was characterized by wide lanes and large private residences. Here, the buildings were packed in tight, separated by narrow streets and alleyways.

Pingkang li was famous for its pleasure quarter, where scholars and noblemen came to drink and be entertained by specially trained courtesans. The most notorious courtesan houses were located in the center of the ward, while the northern section was home to a multitude of smaller drinking houses, shops, and laborers' tenements. It was definitely the seedier part of the ward, which, Wei-wei had to admit, she'd recently become familiar with.

Gambling dens were illegal in Chang'an, but they were tolerated as long as the owners paid off the right officials. Brothels, on the other hand, were perfectly legal, and they thrived here in the north side as well.

Mingyu and her husband had recently opened a teahouse in the area, garnering a steady stream of customers. Mingyu's former status as a celebrated courtesan had something to do with that. Even at this early hour, the teahouse already had patrons coming and going.

Zhou Dan pulled the carriage to the side of the establishment, and Wei-wei hurried up the steps to the entrance. She pulled aside the beaded curtain to peer inside. She immediately found Mingyu. Her silk robe was a vibrant spot of blue like a robin's egg in a gray nest. She breezed through the tea room as if walking on clouds.

Mingyu had been known as one of the Four Great Beauties of the pleasure district with her fine-boned features and ivory pale complexion. She continued to draw attention in the humbler setting of the northern section.

Mingyu's eyes widened when she saw Wei-wei.

"Is it Yue-ying?" she asked. "How is she? How is the baby?"

"Everyone is fine." At least Wei-wei hoped so. The whole affair seemed frightening even under the best of circumstances. "She's asking for you."

A towering shadow appeared beside Mingyu. Her husband, Wu Kaifeng, was also well-known but for different reasons. He took the tea tray from her hands and indicated that she should go with a curt nod. Wu was a man of few words and fewer social graces.

Wei-wei turned to go but stopped just short of colliding into a wall that had suddenly appeared. Not a wall, exactly. Someone was standing closer to her than courtesy allowed.

Wei-wei glanced up and was startled into silence by a familiar face, angled and hard at the edges, with a jaw roughened with stubble. She could feel her heartbeat coming awake to thump inside her chest.

"Gao," she said, her breath catching. He only went by the one name, which forced her into familiarity.

"Lady Bai."

Her chest flooded with warmth.

With his height and the sharpness of his features, Gao presented an intimidating figure, but he held himself with a sort of loose-limbed casualness that called that impression into question. He belonged here, and the people who walked these streets seemed to know it and bestow a measure of trust onto him because of it. Her brother certainly did.

Gao looked exactly as she remembered, exactly as she'd imagined him whenever she'd closed her eyes. He was spare of build, whipcord-lean, and dressed in a dark tunic. In the dimness of the morning, he could have disappeared into the shadows. Barely there, yet ever so present.

"It's been seven days," she ventured, then bit her lip. That made it sound like she'd been keeping count. Which she had.

His dark gaze held hers for a long moment. "It has been."

Gao wasn't smiling, but the corner of his mouth twisted upward as if curiously pleased. For her part, Wei-wei couldn't say what she was feeling. She'd considered that she might never see Gao again. Someone like Gao and someone like her. A desert and a stream — their paths were never meant to cross.

"My brother's wife is having her baby."

"Is that so?"

"Everyone else at home was occupied," she explained, for lack of other things to say.

"Right."

She searched for her next words. He seemed to be doing the same, brow furrowed. The last time they'd seen one another, there was tragedy and scandal involved. Gao had intervened in a potentially dangerous situation to help her and her brother. It seemed inadequate now to pleasantly inquire about his health.

A throat cleared loudly behind her. Mingyu stood there, staring impatiently at the two of them.

Mingyu was known for her sharp wit and clever conversation. She must have thought they were babbling like children.

"Should we be going, Lady Bai?"

"Yes. *Yes.*" She turned away from Gao, flustered. Zhou Dan was waiting right at the corner beside the carriage. She signaled him and he climbed into the driver's seat to pull the carriage closer to the teahouse.

"I have to go now," she told Gao hastily.

"Of course, Lady Bai."

Gao gave a slight bow as Wei-wei turned to rush down the steps. She caught Mingyu's pointed look as they climbed into the carriage. Zhou Dan urged the horse forward down the street.

"Be careful around that one," Mingyu warned, glancing back at the teahouse. "He's trouble."

Gao remained at the steps, his piercing eyes fixed on her.

"Why would you say that?" Wei-wei cringed at how her voice cracked. She was usually much better at claiming innocence.

"One hears things."

She still didn't know what to feel about Gao. Wei-wei

couldn't deny she was drawn to him, while the rational part of her reminded Wei-wei she had a habit of being too trusting. However, the last time she'd made that mistake, it had been Gao who had come to her aid.

Her mind could argue back and forth with itself forever. It had a habit of doing that.

Was it Gao's connections to criminal elements or his questionable morals that Mingyu had heard about? But Gao and her brother were associated in some way, so that must mean he could be trusted. Didn't it?

"Baseless rumors, I'm sure," she said hopefully.

"Lady Bai," Mingyu admonished. Her gaze remained fixed straight ahead as the carriage rolled toward the ward gates. "You don't need me to tell you these things."

Wei-wei released a drawn-out breath. The last time she'd encountered Gao, she'd nearly been abducted by the local crime lord. Maybe she did need to be told these things—and very firmly.

~

BAI HUANG HAD ENCOUNTERED death before in his position but not like this.

He'd been summoned to the northeast section of the city, the area closest to the imperial palace. The mansions there easily overshadowed his own family's residence. These wards were home to the most well-connected families in the capital. High officials of the upper ranks, aristocrats, even distant royalty.

Huang stood on one of the main roads outside the wards that led to the palace and stared at the cluster of bodies strewn in the center. The guards had formed a barricade around the area to keep civilians away. The wards would open soon and this street would be flooded with traffic.

Breathing deep, Huang tried to fortify himself before moving forward. He stepped carefully past a scattering of arrows and averted his gaze when he saw one embedded in a man's throat. The body lay rigid upon the ground with sightless eyes pointed heavenward. Four others had been with him, all dressed in similarly plain robes. They had been traveling early in the morning toward the palace section when arrows had rained down on them, ending their lives. He glanced up to the surrounding mansions. Someone had gotten onto the rooftops to launch this attack.

As tragic as these deaths were, he hadn't been summoned for them. They were attendants and servants. Their death was tragic nonetheless, but not his domain.

A gray-haired official with a long beard stood at the very center of the bloodshed, his spine stiff and straight. His silk robe was deep purple in color, signifying his status as a member of the first rank. His hands were folded behind him as he surveyed the scene impassively. Huang approached to greet him with a low bow.

"Chief Censor."

"Inspector Bai."

Zheng was the head of the Censorate, the investigative branch that provided oversight into the workings of the imperial court as well as local officials. Unlike the Six Ministries, which operated parallel to the Emperor, the Censorate reported directly to the Son of Heaven.

Bai Huang had been granted a position as a censor after passing the imperial exams, but in a different sort of role. Huang suspected he'd been recruited for his connections rather than his academic performance. Publicly, he held a minor position within the imperial records office, but his true jurisdiction was the lower officials who operated in the capital. He was a known playboy within the capital, which allowed him to move without raising suspicion through the banquets and pleasure houses where powerful men gathered.

Zheng stood over a sixth body. The tips of his boots were planted just beyond the pool of blood soaking into the road. Huang stared down and fought the sickness roiling in his stomach.

Huang could smell the blood. He smelled nothing but blood.

A dagger protruded from the victim's chest. The murderer hadn't even cared to collect his weapon, but more disturbing than that was how the victim was clothed. The man's state robe matched Zheng's in color. Also deep purple. Also first ranked.

"That can't be—" Huang began in a low voice.

"Chancellor Yao Yuan," Zheng confirmed soberly.

"On my grave."

Huang forced himself to look back over the carnage. The senior official had been on his way to see the Emperor when someone had stabbed him and left him to bleed out on the dirt road where everyone could see. Huang bowed his head and pressed the back of his hand against his mouth. His stomach lurched dangerously.

Chancellor Yao Yuan was second in power only to the Emperor. And he'd been murdered within view of the Yanxi Gate, a mere stone's throw away from the imperial palace.

CHAPTER 2

The northern section of the Pingkang ward was one of the crowded corners of Chang'an where the city had started to grow and sprout like weeds. A commotion of shops, boarding rooms and storehouses were packed side-by-side and on top of one another until even the walls could not contain the rising tide of the populace.

Commerce spilled out onto the streets. Vendor stalls cropped up wherever space allowed. Anyone with a commodity to sell could prop up a basket on a busy corner to do business.

Gao approached a stall where the weaver and his daughter were setting out baskets. It was far from a proper shop, just a makeshift stand hammered together from planks of wood set in front of an alley.

The weaver's shoulders sank when he saw Gao. The daughter looked at Gao with wide, wary eyes.

"It's the first of the month," Gao announced.

The man launched into a lament, the same one Gao heard last month. Business was slow. Customers were stingy. Oh, the price of rice and salt.

He begged. His daughter begged. Gao pressed his fingers to the bridge of his nose and looked down the lane at the other shops he needed to visit. If he could, he'd will himself back to that morning. For a moment, Wei-wei had been there, looking at him with those wide, dark, endlessly inquisitive eyes and the sun shone a little bit brighter. Then she was gone, and now he was here. The most hated man on the street that morning.

"Headman Hui doesn't need any more baskets," Gao asserted when the weaver held up his finest basket in lieu of payment.

In the end, Gao had to take a strip of red silk as payment. Silk was commonly accepted as currency in the marketplace, but its value shifted frequently. Scraps like the one he was holding were difficult to exchange and practically worthless. Some customer had foisted it on to the weaver, and now he had passed it on to Gao.

The next shop went quicker. The wine merchant handed him a pouch of coins along with a sour look.

Protection money, Hui called it, from gangs and thieves. Of course, there were those who said that Hui and his gang were the thieves. It was business as any other. And Gao knew what it was to go hungry. This was better.

The butcher paid his fee in cuts of meat which he delivered wrapped in paper and tied with twine. Gao deposited everything into a sack slung over his shoulder. The next stop should be an easy one. The pawn shop and Hui's operation fed into each other. Hui's gambling dens and paper lotteries created traffic for the pawn shop, while Hui's reputation for controlling the streets kept potential thieves away from the pawnbroker's cash. The only thing Gao had to worry about for this collection was counting the money to ensure the broker wasn't trying to gouge him.

"*Get out!*"

Some scamp stumbled backwards through the door of the pawn shop, landing on his backside in the dirt. He scrambled to his feet.

"Swindler!" the boy retorted, brushing off his clothes.

Gao recognized him. The boy had done a few menial jobs for Hui's crew here and there. At seventeen years, Fu Lin was one of the younger ones. The men teased him, calling him Fu Lin after the small lion dogs that wealthy families kept. The squat shape of his head and short nose did somewhat resemble the pampered creatures.

Fu Lin's face lit up when he spotted Gao, which was not a good sign.

"Brother Gao," he said, beckoning. "I have something for you."

Gao stayed where he was.

Fu looked furtively over his shoulder before shuffling forward. There were dark circles beneath his eyes. "Look, it's real jade."

He held out a carved block of green stone that fit across his palm. A dark vein ran through the stone.

"This pig of a broker won't take it. How about I give it to you for ten zhu? You know it's worth more. You can sell it and make a profit."

The youth looked disappointed when Gao didn't leap at his offer. "Feel it. It's heavy. Must be worth at least a tael, two taels of silver, right?"

"How did you get that?"

"I found it."

"Found it," Gao echoed hollowly.

Fu Lin lifted his chin and attempted to return Gao's stare, but he wavered. If Gao had to guess, he'd say the fellow had suffered a rough night at the dice tables. Fu Lin had that downtrodden and desperate look about him.

The jade seal had to belong to some wealthy nobleman or merchant. The man's cursed name was etched on it, after all.

"Wherever you *found* this, it's worthless," Gao said through his teeth.

He prayed Fu hadn't unknowingly robbed some drunken bureaucrat. Gao understood why the pawnbroker had chased the boy out of his shop. If Fu could find some stonecutter willing to grind the insignia off the seal, he might be able to sell the jade. But the truth was, that hunk of stone wasn't just worthless. It was trouble.

Fu wasn't ready to give up. "How about you give me just two or three zhus, Brother Gao? You can find someone to sell it to. You know people."

Gao spied a local constable in his midnight blue uniform walking at the end of the lane.

"Get rid of it. Fast," he said in a low tone, moving quickly away.

That last warning was more charitable than Fu Lin deserved. The boy was begging for trouble, and it would find him sooner or later. Gao walked away without looking back. Some of these fellows looked to him like an elder brother for the simple reason that he'd survived out here longer than they had.

Gao found Hui was sitting at the tea stand, surveying the intersection with greasy speculation like the gutter lord he was. He was a portly man, fatted and self-important. He stared across the road at the new teahouse which was over-flowing with customers.

"That teahouse has been running for six months now and we have yet to pay them a visit," Hui said, running a thoughtful hand over his bearded chin. "They make enough to afford it."

"Wu Kaifeng will cut your throat personally," Gao replied.

"He doesn't have a reputation for violence. He's a businessman now."

"As constable, he built a reputation that every thief on the street still fears. I suggest you leave him alone."

The crime boss looked annoyed. He reached for the sack Gao had laid between them. "I don't need business advice from you."

Gao kept his expression blank. There was value in being regarded as slightly brighter than the rest of Hui's minions, but not much brighter. To that end, it was useful to challenge a man like Hui occasionally, but not too often.

"Constables from the magistrate's office seem to be gathering," Gao said, turning to face the teahouse. "You may want to warn any of your crew out on collections today."

Hui scowled but he gestured to one of his lackeys hovering nearby and relayed instructions to him. The fellow ran off, presumably to carry out Hui's orders. Apparently, Hui did feel like taking Gao's advice today.

"Do you know what's going on?" Hui asked.

Gao shook his head. He wasn't under any obligation to report on Fu Lin or anything else. He was thinking even the simple collection job Hui had asked him to take on for "easy money" was not the beneficial arrangement he had hoped. The crime lord still held power over these alleyways. Gao had thought to get on Hui's good side after their last encounter hadn't ended the way Hui had planned.

Wei-wei and her brother, Huang had become entangled in a scandal involving a disgraced bureaucrat who was selling answers to the imperial exam. The bureaucrat had abducted Wei-wei to hand her over to Hui in a desperate attempt to pay off his debts, which had then dragged her brother into an ill-conceived rescue attempt. Gao had stepped in to untangle the whole lot of them from one another. He'd then convinced Hui that the high-born siblings weren't worth drawing the attention of imperial authorities. After all that, Gao had, of course, owed Hui a favor.

Apparently, Bai Huang hadn't learned enough from being in danger merely a week ago. The young nobleman was back now, talking to Wu Kaifeng just outside the door of his teahouse.

The young Lord Bai seemed to make a point of looking out of place whenever he came around. Usually it was with a garish choice of clothing, though no one ever ridiculed him about his manner of dress. Lord Bai was known for being a friendly fool who was free with his coin, and, thus, was well-liked in these parts.

Today his clothing set him apart for another reason. Bai was dressed in a blue-gray official court robe.

"What is this?" Hui interrupted, rummaging through the contents of the sack. He pulled out the strip of red silk and dangled it between his pudgy fingers.

"Weaver had a slow month," Gao remarked absently, continuing to study the exchange on the other side of the road. "The price of this and that went up."

Wu Kaifeng had his arms folded over his chest while Bai Huang looked to be explaining something in great detail. Occasionally Wu would give a slow, single nod.

Hui snorted. "Well, I should find out why the magistrate is sending men around."

Gao took that to be the end of their meeting. As he stood to go, Hui stopped him. "You're smarter than these other fools."

He regarded Hui with surprise, not certain what to make of the observation.

"Keep your eyes open for me, hmm?" As a parting gift, he held out the long scrap of silk. It fluttered like a kite's tail in the breeze. "Payment for your services today," he said with a smirk.

Gao reached out to take the silk without comment. Hui was an easy man to underestimate. He could be crass, greedy, and vindictive, but he was also cunning. One didn't rise in these streets without some measure of intelligence.

Across the road, the conversation between Wu and Bai had concluded. Wu Kaifeng had returned to his teahouse while the nobleman was headed down the steps into the streets. Huang spotted Gao's approach. They angled their paths to cross.

"I hear you should be congratulated on happy news," Gao ventured.

Huang's look was both surprise and confusion.

"On the start of your family. Your sister mentioned it."

Huang's expression was far from happy. His jaw locked and his spine grew rigid with tension. Quite far from the foolhardy, rich playboy persona he typically projected.

"Something happened this morning," the aristocrat said darkly. "Something that could mean disaster."

"No news of any sort here."

"The imperial court is keeping everything quiet, but it won't remain secret for long. If you hear of anything…" He paused, taking a breath that had the weight of mountains in it.

From what Gao knew, the aristocrat had finally passed the imperial exams and had been appointed to some minor bureaucratic position. Admittedly, Gao had become more curious since meeting the young Lord Bai's sister. Between the two, Wei-wei was much more interesting.

"What is it you're looking for?" Gao probed.

It wouldn't be uncommon for Bai Huang to come to him for information. Pingkang li was where the powerful mingled with the baser elements of society. There was also a drinking house on every corner. It was destined to be a place where things were overheard.

"I'm looking for recent newcomers to Chang'an. A group of people who don't appear to belong—who are where they shouldn't be."

Gao frowned. The imperial capital was home to over a million citizens and was inhabited by traders and merchants from lands far and wide. "No one belongs in Chang'an."

He wasn't trying to be difficult. Huang seemed unfocused.

"These men would be armed. They would be trained in weapons use, even archery. They're likely men-for-hire," Huang went on.

"Mercenaries?"

Huang met his gaze squarely. "Assassins," he corrected.

Gao glanced at the guards who trailed them at a distance. Typically, Huang walked these streets unprotected. This was even after he'd suffered a serious attack in the past, but today was different.

"Are these 'men-for-hire' why the magistrate has his constables about?" Gao asked.

"Even the magistrate's office hasn't been informed yet."

Which would explain why Huang would go to former constable Wu Kaifeng instead. There must have been another reason the magistrate had his men in the streets.

"I'll see what I can find out," Gao offered.

He was certain Hui or his spies had watched the entire exchange. Gao started to go when Huang stopped him.

"For your trouble." Huang pressed a string of coins into his palm.

Gao stared at the money, feeling the metal burn against his skin. Huang wasn't out of line. This was the nature of their association. Gao was a low-life street informer, and Lord Bai was rich enough to buy whoever he needed.

"Some would consider me a man-for-hire." Gao said, his voice tight.

Lately it seemed everyone he knew was trying to pay him

off in one way or another. He couldn't fault them when that was who he was. One needed to eat.

He suddenly saw Wei-wei before him, a ray of light and warmth in the gray of the morning. One needed other things too.

"The men I'm looking for are a different sort. What they did, what they're capable of doing—" Huang's expression darkened. "I'd wager this goes far beyond where you're willing to go."

CHAPTER 3

Wei-wei held the warm bundle in both hands, a sleeping swaddle of baby wrapped in linen, and prayed she didn't accidentally drop the little creature. Her sister-in-law, Yue-ying, was sleeping in the bed beside her. Over the last day, Wei-wei had learned that babies could act like they were ready to come out in the morning, but then hold back stubbornly until halfway through the night before being born.

The midwife had directed their maidservants to bathe the baby girl and brew medicinal teas for the new mother. Yue-ying had fallen asleep in exhaustion while the women of the household were busy feeding and fussing and passing the baby around. When morning came, the midwife was dismissed and it was everyone else's turn to rest. Wei-wei was left to attend to her new niece while her sister-in-law slept peacefully.

She had never held a baby before. Or even really seen one this close.

"Little one," Wei-wei whispered to her.

The baby didn't have a name yet. Yue-ying insisted that they wait for Huang to return before choosing one.

The little girl's eyes were closed tight, the lashes long against her tiny face. She was the size of a kitten and pink-skinned. Apparently, she was exhausted too.

Eventually Yue-ying stirred beneath her covers, squinting against the sunlight streaming in through the window.

"Oh, is it too bright? I can close the shutters."

Wei-wei stood before remembering her hands were full. She wasn't even sure how to safely set the baby down. Mingyu had planted the bundle into her arms with instructions to call her if Yue-ying wanted her. Then she'd left.

Yue-ying sat up groggily. She had the same fine bone structure that Mingyu was known for, but in Yue-ying the features were softer, warmer. What did distinguish her was a red birthmark that curved along the left side of her face from cheek to jaw.

Wei-wei had heard some ladies calling it a beauty mark, the way it framed her face and drew attention to her mouth. Of course, that was easy to say after Yue-ying had managed to marry one of the most sought-after young men in the city. Before joining their family, Yue-ying had been a servant in the pleasure quarter, far beneath their family in class and status. What she lacked in formal education, Yue-ying made up in practical knowledge and experience. It gave her a level-headed perspective that Wei-wei and Huang often lacked.

Yue-ying searched until she found her daughter in Wei-wei's hands. "Why are you holding her like that?"

Wei-wei looked down. Her arms were stiff from being stretched out in front of her. All of her concentration was directed to keeping the baby still. For such a small thing, she was getting kind of heavy.

"Lay her in the crook of your arms," Yue-ying said, yawning. "So you can rest her against you."

Wei-wei adjusted her hold and froze when the baby stirred, yawning just like her mother. Then the little creature settled back to sleep as Wei-wei cradled her close. This did work a lot better.

Wei-wei turned her attention back to her sister-in-law.

"How are you?" she asked, now that she was less concerned about dropping the baby. "Do you need anything?"

"Has Huang come home?"

Wei-wei let out a breath and shot a quick glance out into the courtyard. Huang had been gone for the entire day as well as last night.

"He'll be back soon, I'm certain."

Yue-ying nodded wearily. "He has important work to do."

Of course, her brother's job was important, but certainly the records office could manage without him. He knew that Yue-ying was about to deliver when he'd been summoned away. Even if he was caught up in something urgent, he should have at least sent word.

She looked down into her niece's little face. Huang didn't even know that he had a daughter now. It wasn't like him. He'd doted on Yue-ying over the last nine months.

"I should go look for him," Wei-wei resolved.

"That's not necessary." Yue-ying turned on her side, smiling as she looked at her daughter. "She looks like him."

Wei-wei glanced at the little wrinkly red face skeptically. Everyone kept saying she looked like either Huang or Yue-ying. Their Amah, the maidservant who had cared for Huang and Wei-wei when they were children, had even insisted the baby looked like Wei-wei. She couldn't say that she saw the resemblance.

"I can hold her," Yue-ying said. She stretched out her arms and Wei-wei gently laid her niece in her mother's arms before sitting back down beside the bed.

"You don't think—" Wei-wei started before biting her tongue.

"What?"

It was probably not the time to bring up anything worrisome. Yue-ying was still exhausted from childbirth and the household had gone through a big event with the coming of a new baby. But the Bai family was all too accustomed to biting their tongues. They looked the other way and let silences speak. The problem with silence was one could fill them with anything.

After Yue-ying had married her brother, Wei-wei finally had someone in the house to talk to. Someone she could confide in and share her opinions with. If something was wrong with Huang, Yue-ying should know about it.

Wei-wei lowered her voice. "Do you think it's possible Huang has gone back to his old habits?"

"No! Of course not," Yue-ying protested.

Her brother and his dice games would hang over him for the rest of his life. Something took hold of Huang whenever he started gambling.

Wei-wei regretted bringing it up. A sharp frown creased Yue-ying's brow. She pulled her little girl closer protectively. "Your eldest brother has changed, Wei-wei. He's very different now from what he was like even a year ago."

"I know he has," Wei-wei said hastily. "I shouldn't have said anything."

She had spent her entire life worrying about her family. Wei-wei had taken on the business of making peace and healing the rifts between all of them. She sealed the cracks before anyone noticed, before the damage grew though neglect. Their family was held together by silence so she'd become adept at working in those pockets of silence. Of dealing with the unspoken.

It was wrong to complain. She wasn't unhappy. As a

result of her efforts and schemes, direct and indirect, Huang was now married and had passed the civil exams. Her younger brother, Chang-min, was growing into adulthood and preparing to take those same exams. Everyone was growing and changing. It was only Wei-wei who stayed the same.

Her new sister-in-law didn't need to inherit this worry. She had her own family to look after, this little girl who should grow up full of laughter and free of care.

At that moment, the baby woke up and started to cry. It was a small sound, like the mewing of a cat, but insistent. This little girl certainly hadn't been silenced.

"She's hungry," Yue-ying said.

Wei-wei took the child so Yue-ying could sit up straighter. After giving the girl back, Wei-wei went to fetch Mother or Amah or someone with experience in these matters.

Even though Wei-wei was inexperienced when it came to babies, she could still be helpful. She would go find that brother of hers, and if she couldn't find him, she knew who might know where Huang had gone.

Gao.

Gao always seemed to know things. And he seemed willing to oblige her—or was he humoring her?

Her face flushed hot at just the thought of Gao and their adventures together. They were small, unspoken rebellions that she held close to her chest. She'd never spoken to anyone about her encounters with him which were, perhaps not outright scandalous, but certainly highly improper.

She hadn't confided in Yue-ying and certainly not Mother. Her brother knew, but Huang seemed to be avoiding that conversation lately.

She'd only go to Gao as a last resort, Wei-wei decided.

Only if she had tried everything else and Huang was still nowhere to be found. She was only trying to get information. It wasn't as if she was doing anything so inappropriate.

Yet.

~

Wei-wei constructed her story as she approached the entrance to the Imperial City where the administrative offices were located. She hadn't even needed to make up a tale. Huang's wife had given birth and Wei-wei was his sister and she needed to speak to him. Immediately. It was a personal and, yes, a highly private matter. Involving family.

It was true that Huang had worked through the night on occasion. He claimed that the Emperor slept very little and sometimes needed records and notices drawn up at odd hours, but how important could it be that Huang hadn't come home or sent word for two days?

What if he was caught up in something worse than a pressing assignment at the records office?

Wei-wei wondered if showing an unsightly display of emotion might help her cause. Or perhaps she could invoke her father's name, even though her father was away from Chang'an presently. The Bai family name certainly opened doors for them that would be closed to others, but she wasn't Lord Bai or young Lord Bai or even the youngest Lord Bai, her seventeen-year-old brother. She was young Lady Bai, the daughter — *just* the daughter.

Still, a lower-level clerk wouldn't dare be rude to her. If she didn't waver, if she didn't flinch, she would get herself into that office.

Huang had been appointed as the Assistant Collator of the Left Office shortly after passing the imperial exams. His department was located in the administrative section in the Imperial City. Wei-wei directed the hired sedan right up to the great archway at the front, but that was where her courage faltered. The towering doors were open at that time of day, but there were guards stationed in a row before the gate and it was clear she was not going to maneuver past them.

She dismounted from the carriage and climbed the stone steps. Then she relayed her message to the functionary at the entrance who took her message courteously enough before ducking back into the courtyard.

And then she waited.

Wei-wei tried not to fidget as she stood at the gate. Bureaucrats in state uniforms passed by on either side of her while she stood still like a boulder parting a river stream. Finally, a tall, distinguished looking man came to greet her. He had long gray hair and a trimmed beard that tapered down to a sharp point. The elder official looked down at her with his shoulders squared to block her passage through the gate.

Based on this robe, Wei-wei could tell he was someone important. It was made of dark purple silk. "May this servant ask who she is addressing?"

"Censor Zheng Shi," he replied courteously. "I most humbly apologize to the lady, but her brother is occupied with an important matter."

She was taken aback. Censors were supposed to provide oversight over imperial affairs. Why was a censor speaking for her brother?

"Our family has had a very momentous event. My brother's wife has just given birth—"

"Much happiness to your family, of course. I'm certain Lord Bai will contact you as soon as he is able."

"If I can just be permitted to speak to him."

"Unfortunately, he is not here."

"Perhaps I can leave a message for my brother."

"A message would be appropriate."

Wei-wei had written a note just in case something like this happened. She pulled the folded paper from her sleeve to hand to the censor. As he reached for it with long, spindly fingers, he paused.

"It is said Lady Bai is even more clever than her brother."

She flushed at the compliment. How did the censor know anything about her?

"Lord Bai's dedication to his family is well-known," the official continued. "As is your family's loyalty to the Emperor. Take comfort that any sacrifice you endure is for the sake of our empire."

With a final bow, he receded back into the Imperial City. The guards remained at their stations before the gate, impassive witnesses to the whole exchange.

That did not go as well as she'd hoped.

"You got further than I did, Lady Bai."

She turned around to see Gao at the foot of the steps with his lips curled in a sardonic smile. He started climbing toward her, his long legs closing the distance between them. There was something about his appearance that both unnerved and excited her. Even the way he moved, confident and with such purpose, seemed unusual to her. He moved without reservation, without courteous consideration.

His dark hair was pulled back and tied behind him, though a few untamed strands had escaped to fall around his face. Wei-wei realized, with some dismay, that the sharp cheekbones and hollows that distinguished Gao's appearance in her mind was due to scarcity. Everyone she was accustomed to seeing, even their servants, had a soft, well-kept roundness about their features.

Gao might not be hungry today, or yesterday, but there

was likely a time when he had been. And it was likely more than for a few days. There were other elements too that highlighted the undeniable differences between them. Vibrant silk for her, hemp and ramie, dyed dark, for him.

He was an element outside of her little compartments, the double-courtyards and the thick stone mansion walls that kept the world away—or her contained within. His very presence set her senses on alert and her mind on fire.

"You're also here for Huang?" she asked. "I was going to ask for your help to find him."

"I did see your brother recently."

"When?"

"Yesterday. Shortly after I saw you."

She bit her lip, considering the information. "How did he appear to you?"

"Tired. Worried."

Wei-wei looked downward. A lot had happened in the last day. "Armed guards came to take Huang yesterday morning, and he hasn't been home since. Now that bureaucrat made it sound as if he's been tasked with an important assignment."

"He asked me to watch for anything suspicious. I assumed he could be found here." He indicated the entranceway with a tilt of his head. "Maybe you can help since your brother isn't around."

He glanced at the guards before taking her arm and directing her down the steps. His hold was light, but she still felt the shock of warmth from his touch. They moved away from the administrative buildings to blend into the surrounding lanes. Once they were alone, Gao pulled in close.

"Someone was found beside the canal yesterday in Pingkang li."

She swallowed. "You mean...dead?"

Gao nodded, looking a lot less disturbed than she was. Wei-wei had always heard the lower market wards were dangerous places. She'd even encountered criminal elements once herself, but Gao remained so calm in the face of it. As if he'd seen all this and more.

"Why would Huang be asking you to search the streets? He works in the records office."

"I wondered the same. In the past, I never considered why your brother was so curious. It was his own affair, not mine. But yesterday he was different. Something had happened and he was shaken."

She remembered how Huang had appeared to her the morning Yue-ying had started experiencing birthing pains. Her brother had been distracted.

"I think this may have belonged to the man by the canal," Gao said, reaching into this belt. "It wasn't exactly what Huang had asked about, but he wanted to know if anything seemed out of place."

He held up a block of pale green jade, angling his palm between them to hide the object from prying eyes.

Her pulse skipped. "How did you get that?"

"I paid two zhus for it," he said. "Your brother's money."

She hadn't known Gao for very long, so she couldn't tell if he was lying. If he'd stolen the jade, she assumed he wouldn't show it to Huang or to her.

"It's a personal chop," she explained. "One that a nobleman might wear hanging on his belt. What does the insignia say?"

His lips drew tight. "I can't read it."

The confession left a heavy feeling in the air. Wei-wei took the seal from Gao's hand, eager to move past the sudden tension. She tried to inspect the carving on the face, but it was stained dark with ink and impossible to make out. Looking about, she found a small pool of muddy water on the side of the lane and bent to dip the seal into it. Then she straightened and pressed the seal against a paper bulletin that had been plastered to the wall.

"We should be able to see who this belongs to—"

She pulled the chop away, then gasped and nearly dropped the jade. Her pulse raced. She had to have read the characters wrong. Frantically, she scanned the impression again.

"What is it?" Gao asked behind her.

"Heaven and Earth."

Wei-wei tore the bulletin away and crumpled the paper into a ball. They needed to get out of here. Quick. She paced around in a hapless circle until she found a narrow alley to duck into. Gao followed in behind her.

She spun on him and held the jade up between them. "Where did you get this?" she demanded through her teeth.

What had she done? The carving was covered in mud. She scrubbed the carved face against her sleeve, not caring about the stain. Once it was as clean as she could make it, she held it up again.

"Where did you get this?" she whispered again.

Her hand trembled. Gao reached up to clasp it firmly between both of his. "Someone found it. I bought it from him," he repeated, his tone steady.

She fixed a hard stare at him. Wei-wei doubted Gao found her at all intimidating, but finally he yielded.

"I found it in the hands of a small-time thief in the Pingkang ward. Who does the jade belong to, Wei-wei?"

He was close enough for her to make out every line on his face. There was a pale scar running across the knuckles on his left hand.

"It's an official imperial seal," she said, looking directly into his eyes to be sure he understood. "A document stamped with this mark is as good as a command from the Emperor's mouth. The person they found dead by the canal—who was it?"

CHAPTER 4

Gao didn't know the answer, and he was beginning to think he didn't want to know. He had assumed the chop came from someone wealthy, but it seemed the owner was a lot more than just rich.

"It must be a forgery," Wei-wei insisted.

He nodded. "It must be."

"Or...or I could be horribly mistaken."

"You could be."

Gao was still holding her hand. Her wide, dark eyes fixed onto his, fathomless and inadvertently sensual. He felt Wei-wei's gaze deep in the pit of his stomach. Women in the pleasure houses drew and painted their eyes to have that elegantly curved shape. Peach blossom eyes, he'd heard them called. Gao wasn't one for poetic associations, but he'd make an exception for Wei-wei. Especially when she was this close and so, so pretty.

"I think the punishment must be death for forging an imperial seal," she despaired.

Easy. "Then let's get rid of it."

"No!" She shook free of his grasp. "We can't just throw it

away. What if it's real?" She paced away a step, then turned sharply back to him. "Why would someone have an imperial seal on him? How did he die?"

Wei-wei searched his face for answers, though Gao was pretty certain he revealed nothing in his expression. Fu Lin would have seen the body, but, in the way of scoundrels, Gao hadn't asked too many questions, and Fu Lin hadn't offered much information.

"If this was someone important, why didn't anyone report his death?" Wei-wei went on. "Why was he traveling alone with such an important treasure?"

More importantly, how long before the two of them were surrounded by city guards and thrown in prison?

"All things I intended to ask your brother," he replied calmly. "So, you no longer think the seal is a forgery."

She pressed her lips together as she inspected the inscription. "I don't think anyone would dare."

Wei-wei was truly frightened, and Gao's instinct was to trust her on this. He might dwell in the crowded alleys and tenements of the Pingkang li, but Wei-wei and her people lived in the shadow of the imperial palace. The Bai family held high-ranking government positions and cared about the comings and goings of the court. Though the Emperor was the heartbeat of Chang'an, he had little to do with Gao's day-to-day life.

"We should put that away then," he suggested gently, holding out his hand. Carefully, she placed the jade into his palm.

"My brother must be involved in this. He hasn't come home for two days. He's never even seen his daughter."

Gao tucked the chop back in his belt, cursing himself for getting involved as well. He didn't want to be caught in possession of an imperial relic any more than Wei-wei did, but he was the one who had taken it off of Fu Lin's hands. It didn't seem right to burden her with it.

"Where do we go now?" Gao prompted.

She considered the question for a long time. "The magistrate's office," she said finally.

"Your brother mentioned that the magistrate's office hadn't been informed."

"Informed of what?"

Gao shrugged.

She frowned at him. "My brother has confided in you."

"He hasn't told me anything," Gao denied.

She let out a breath. "Magistrate Li knows my brother. He'll know what to do."

The last thing Gao wanted to do was go before the magistrate, even if he wasn't dragged in with chains when it happened. But Wei-wei had no such reservations, and she was looking at him expectantly with pupils as deep and dark as wells. Fit for him to drown in. No wonder the Bais could get away with anything.

"Let's go then," he relented. "Together."

~

HE WAVED DOWN A SEDAN. If Wei-wei had any objections about being packed into the seat close beside him, she didn't voice them. She even took in stride the smelly gray mule that pulled the transport.

The magistrate's office was located several wards away. The morning traffic had thinned as they neared mid-day. Wei-wei opened a bamboo parasol and held it overhead to block the sun. For the moment, they were sheltered together, sectioned off from the city despite the crowded streets. The silk of her sleeve brushed against him, and she smelled impossibly like flowers.

"You're very quiet," she said after a while.

This was the longest period of time they'd ever spent together. That made it a good day, all death and conspiracy aside.

"I was thinking what a mismatched pair we make." He turned his head to see her reaction.

Wei-wei was watching him intently. She didn't avert her eyes or shy away.

"Not so mismatched," she protested.

"A proper lady like you riding alongside a vagabond like me?"

Wei-wei fidgeted. "You're not—I mean, you're a..."

He grinned, daring her to answer. "You're not afraid of being seen with me?"

"There are so many people on this road. No one would even recognize their own mother in this crowd," she argued.

Then, as if to prove a point, Wei-wei lowered her parasol and placed it between them on the seat. Her movements were less than confident as she looked out to the road, trying hard to look comfortable in her own skin.

"Scandal," he drawled, under his breath.

She slanted a cross look at him.

"What were you doing at the Imperial City alone and on foot anyway?" he asked. "As rich as you are?"

"Huang's wife just gave birth and the entire household is busy fussing over the baby," she explained. "Mother took the carriage to go to temple and the horse was hitched up to run to the market. With Father coming home, the family is planning a banquet at the end of the week. There's too much going on for anyone to notice where I was."

"I don't think that's true."

"It is. In our house, there's Huang, the favored son. Then there's Chang-min, my younger brother. One can hardly see me between them."

He could see her. Wei-wei was vibrant, and quick-thinking, and she demanded attention with her very presence. The first time they'd met, she was standing out in the street, wearing one of her brother's ridiculous outfits. Completely out of place, yet completely unbothered by it.

"I have something to ask you," Wei-wei said after a pause.

He waited.

"My brother says that the two of you aren't friends, but you're always helping us. Why is that?"

Wei-wei watched him expectantly with those wide and probing eyes, as black and deep as the still waters of a lotus pond.

"Because you two always need it," he replied crookedly.

"Come now," she scolded, annoyed. "You've helped us when there's no benefit to you. Like this matter now. You could have left it alone, but you came to find Huang."

"Who's to say there's no benefit for me." Gao ran a hand over the front of his tunic and looked out to the road.

What could he say? How else would he have an excuse to see her?

He didn't have any designs on Lady Bai Wei-ling. She'd given him her birth name once, but even that knowledge felt like a secret he wasn't meant to have. For a common street hood to have any intention toward someone like Wei-wei was madness. He was like a child vying for a sweet, imagining the phantom taste of sugar on his tongue. Unable to give up the quest because nothing else around was nearly so good.

He'd held Wei-wei in his arms once, a sensation he still remembered in his bones. The moment had been brief and brotherly. It was the first time she had encountered death and it had shaken her. At the time, he thought it was good she'd finally learned a lesson about the dangers of the capital. Wei-wei was too fearless, too eager to rush into danger.

Gao had thought she would stay safe in her gilded mansion surrounded by servants, where she belonged, and he would never see her again. He'd held her closer than he should have because of that. In farewell.

But it wasn't the last time.

"We're here," Wei-wei announced.

The magistrate's yamen loomed ahead. The administrative compound was not nearly foreboding as the Imperial City, but it was still a place Gao preferred not to be known. The mule driver brought the sedan to a stop and Gao paid him.

"You don't have to come inside," Wei-wei suggested, sensing his reluctance as he looked to the gate.

"We'll do this together," he reminded her

The magistrate would have questions about where the jade seal had come from. If Wei-wei couldn't answer, the finger would point back to him anyway. He also had a responsibility to shield poor Fu Lin from the magistrate as well. Gao had dragged the boy into this mess now, all for the paltry price of two zhus. Barely enough to purchase a cup of rice, but certainly enough to buy trouble.

In front of the gate was a brass gong mounted upon a stand. There was an old tradition that stated that anyone, rich or poor, could ring the gong to seek an audience with the magistrate. There was no reason to ring it that day. The gates stood open for their arrival.

Inside, Gao instinctively fell back two steps behind Wei-wei, both in a show of deference as well as to guard her back. There was a blur of activity in the offices. Armed constables and other functionaries hurried to and fro. A sense of urgency fueled the proceedings.

Wei-wei gave her name to the clerk in front and was invited into the inner chambers with little delay. He was always surprised at the places she was able to go on sheer boldness alone. Gao followed behind her, curious to see where this would lead.

To Gao's surprise, they were taken directly to a private office. The magistrate was at his desk. His rank was denoted by a forest green robe and fitted silk cap with a pair of cloth flaps that hung to his shoulders. It was said on the streets that Li Chen was young for such a high post. Gao would have placed Li as near the same age as him at twenty-eight — though Li did have the eternally youthful and softened look of the well-fed. He exerted an air of smooth polish and cultivation.

Magistrate Li stood from his desk to greet them, or specifically, to greet Wei-wei.

"Lady Bai," he said with surprise. "What brings you here?"

He spared Gao a questioning glance before turning his full attention back to Wei-wei.

"We have a very important matter to bring before you," she began, her fingers twisting nervously. "I didn't know where else to go."

Gao saw the magistrate's gaze flicker to Wei-wei's hands, taking note of her nervous gesture, before focusing back to her face. "Go on."

"My brother hasn't come home for two days."

"He must be busy in the records office," Li assured.

"No, there's something else." Wei-wei glanced toward Gao. "Magistrate Li may wish to close his door."

Gao waited until the door was closed before approaching the desk. He set the jade seal on top of it.

"It looks like an imperial seal," Wei-wei said in a whisper.

The magistrate stared at the cut stone in disbelief. Just as Wei-wei had done, he first inspected the carved insignia, then pressed it into a dish of red cinnabar paste before stamping it onto a clean sheet of paper. He stared at the imprint for a moment before folding the paper to hide the mark. Then he sat back in his chair, rubbing a hand over his chin thoughtfully. He really did appear too youthful to be a county magistrate. Gao imagined Li was the sort with powerful friends and connections.

Magistrate Li finally glanced up, looking first to Wei-wei then at Gao.

"We have not met before." It was the first time the magistrate had acknowledged him. Gao certainly wouldn't have been brought directly in to see the official had he shown up on his own.

"He's an associate of my brother's," Wei-wei chimed in. "His name is Gao."

"Gao," the magistrate echoed thoughtfully.

Gao hoped the man came across so many names in the course of the day that his own would soon be forgotten.

"How did this come into your possession?" Li asked.

"I found it in a pawn shop in Pingkang li."

Gao figured the further he was removed from the origins of the jade seal, the better. "It looked valuable, so I bought it."

"And brought it immediately to my brother," Wei-wei added hastily. Fortunately, she didn't contradict his story. "But Huang wasn't in his office. Is it genuine?"

"I can't be certain," the magistrate replied. "I must report it to the imperial authorities at once."

He set the jade seal into a box and tucked it away into a cabinet which he immediately locked. When he turned back to them, his look was serious. "I'm telling you both this news because we need as many people assisting the authorities as possible. A victim was found dead beside the canal at the northern end of the Pingkang ward. My constables couldn't identify the body, but they assumed from his clothes he was wealthy. His purse had been cut away and any other belongings lost or stolen." He took a deep, heavy breath. "This jade chop and that victim, both appearing in the ward. I don't think it's a coincidence."

The magistrate locked gazes with Gao. "As to you, Mister Gao, I will need your help to locate exactly in which pawn shop this was found. I would also ask that you come with me to see if you can identify the body."

"I don't know if that would be useful. I don't know many rich people."

"You seem well-acquainted with Lord Bai Huang and his sister," the magistrate pointed out.

Out of the corner of his eye, Gao could see Wei-wei watching him, waiting for his response. Gao's first instinct about the jade seal had been correct, but he'd failed to take his own advice. So here he was, with the county magistrate staring him down.

"This servant will happily assist in any way he can."

CHAPTER 5

Wei-wei was strongly discouraged from accompanying the magistrate and Gao back to Pingkang. Magistrate Li Chen warned her that it would be upsetting and unseemly for a young lady like her to be subjected to the unfortunate circumstances of his profession. In short, she was cut out and sent home.

"Is this case the reason my brother has been called away for the last two days?" she asked as Li ushered her into a sedan.

He shot her a confused look. "Why would Lord Bai Huang have anything to do with a criminal investigation? He's a collator in the records office."

Li then gave the order for the runner to be on his way. Wei-wei looked back over her shoulder just in time to see Magistrate Li departing with Gao's tall, lanky form beside him. A sudden thought came to her, forming a hollow pit in her stomach. Did Gao know more about the victim than he was admitting?

She had believed Gao's story without question. How could she not trust him? He'd saved her life and Huang's in the past, but Li Chen had been immediately suspicious of him. She'd thought it unfair. Gao didn't dress or speak well, or carry a lofty family name about. He had scars on his hands and everything about him was rough-edged with a hint, no, a promise of danger. He came from the streets and didn't hide it. Couldn't hide it.

As much as she wanted to deny it, she'd heard people refer to Gao and his knife. No one talked about knives that weren't dangerous in some way or another. Huang had warned her away and Mingyu had warned her away. Even Gao had tried to warn her away from himself.

No one said a thing when she returned home. The baby had everyone's attention now. She should be grateful for that.

"In a few months, once you get your strength back, you can try again," she heard Mother saying to Yue-ying as Wei-wei passed her chamber.

Because Yue-ying's first attempt had yielded nothing but a worthless girl.

Wei-wei walked through the courtyard to her own chamber. She felt unsettled and even more restless than usual. Maybe Magistrate Li was right. There was something unseemly about being connected in any way to death. It upset the harmony of things, calling the very balance of the universe into question.

Inside her room, Wei-wei removed her outer robe and draped it over the chair. Her maidservant would rub it with salt later to clean the mud stain from it. Wei-wei was too tired to take care of it at the moment. Her journey had taken her most of the day, and it had seemed like one dismissal after another.

Except for her encounter with Gao. At least he took her seriously, even if he did tease her about her manners and general inexperience about the world.

She didn't mind, Wei-wei thought as she sank into her bed. She even liked the teasing a little bit.

It was too bad that he was probably a criminal. Not guilty of these current crimes, but certainly of others in the past. She drifted off to sleep, thinking of how it felt to sit shoulder to shoulder with Gao, able to say whatever was on her mind. She wasn't expected to remain dutifully silent. Nor did she have to be sheltered from *unseemly* things.

She had to be woken up for the evening meal. Wei-wei took supper with Mother, who once again expressed mild joy, but also disappointment over Yue-ying's baby girl. Mother had so been looking forward to a grandson.

"What is there a boy can do that a girl can't?" Wei-wei countered, taking a slice of steamed bamboo between her chopsticks.

"I'm not saying my girl isn't clever," Mother soothed. She was dressed in a house robe for supper with her hair pulled back in a simple knot. "But tradition requires a son to carry on the family line and give offerings to our ancestors."

"Will the spirits just starve, refusing to eat rice from a woman's hand?" Wei-wei asked. "Which seems unreasonable, considering a woman probably cooked the rice."

The argument was rote by now.

"Be respectful," Mother said in a huff.

They ate the rest of the evening meal in silence, which is what her family was so good at. There was nothing to listen to but the faint scrape, scrape, scrape of chopsticks against porcelain bowls.

Afterward, Wei-wei returned to her room to read. She was still upset, having overheard her mother earlier.

Mother was a scholar's daughter, raised on principles of obedience and filial piety. She'd believed her daughters should be educated, but she also believed they shouldn't brag about it. If Wei-wei's learning was for any purpose, it was to serve her family.

Huang had been first-born in the family. She'd come two years later, but as a girl, Wei-wei had become nothing more than a placeholder. A sister between two brothers, destined to be forgotten once she was married to another family. She'd fought all her life not to disappear. To prove herself more useful to the family than just a temporary daughter to be married away.

She drifted off to sleep again. When she woke up, Wei-wei heard a deep voice carrying across the courtyard.

Huang. Her brother was home.

Her heart leapt. Wei-wei rose and flew across the courtyard to the chamber that Huang and Yue-ying shared. She could see her brother's silhouette through the paper panes of the window.

Inside, he and Yue-ying were speaking quietly to one another. Huang was holding his daughter, rocking back and forth gently, and Wei-wei's soul filled with happiness, realizing it was the first time. She couldn't bear to interrupt them. Instead she waited outside the chamber, even when the night air became chilled.

Huang saw her as soon as he came out an hour later. He paused, raised a hand to his lips to indicate quiet, then lifted one of the house lanterns and headed toward the front of the house to the outer courtyard. She followed him to his study where he lit the oil lamps before turning.

The words burst out of her. "Huang, I was so worried."

"Thank you for taking care of Yue-ying. For taking care of everything."

Now that she could finally see him, Huang looked tired. Worn. She knew Huang was thought of as handsome. In his Academy days, his fellow scholars had taunted him by calling him *miàn shǒu*, which she'd taken some time to figure out was a somewhat derisive compliment that meant he had a pretty face that wealthy women desired in a lover. At the moment, however, there were deep circles beneath his eyes, and when he sank into his chair, it was with his entire being. He collapsed like an abandoned theater puppet.

"It's been two days, Elder Brother."

She waited, watching him carefully. He scrubbed a hand over his face. For the first time, she noticed the stack of papers on his desk. When had those appeared?

"The morning when Yue-ying went into labor, I saw the men at our door. Imperial guards," she pressed.

Huang closed his eyes, shielding himself from her gaze. "These are state matters."

Something was happening in Chang'an, and he had been pulled into it. Huang had to tell her. Her brother told her everything because he knew she would find out eventually anyway. They'd been that way since they were children.

"A body was found beside the canal in the Pingkang li," she prompted.

He opened his eyes then and Wei-wei knew she'd hit upon something. She recounted her entire day to him, including the jade seal and the visit to Magistrate Li. And Gao.

"Gao?" he asked slowly. The name grated against his throat.

What was her brother's problem with Gao? Huang was the one who regularly sought him out for information.

"He came looking for you. *I* came looking for you."

Huang nodded slowly and rubbed a hand over his eyes again. "Wei-wei," he said finally. "There's something I have to tell you."

She seated herself across from him. She was reminded of childhood and sitting across from their father and the very same great wooden desk.

"I don't work in the records office. Or rather, I don't only work in the records office."

She glanced at the towers of paperwork rising beside him.

"I am officially a member of the Censorate."

The Censorate?

"You report directly to the Emperor!" she gasped.

"Well, I report to a senior official who reports to the Emperor. And I submit many reports."

How could he be so subdued about this? A censor held a very important position in the imperial government. Way more impressive than the Assistant Collator of the Left Office. "But you've seen him?" she asked. "You've been in the presence of the Emperor?"

"Only from the back of a huge assembly hall—"

Wei-wei sank back in her chair, overwhelmed. Proud. "You must have done very well in your exam."

Huang managed a chuckle, despite the lines of exhaustion in his face. "It's nothing. Instead of holding a minor bureaucratic position, I have a moderately more elevated bureaucratic position."

"When I came to look for you, a member of the Censorate came out to speak on your behalf. His name was Zheng Shi."

He seemed surprised by that. "Zheng is the censor-in-chief who oversees the entire Censorate."

All of the sudden, the last few weeks made sense. Huang's role was to investigate the conduct of other government officials and matters of corruption. It was why he would be summoned at odd hours.

"But why can't you tell anyone?" she asked.

"It's a special position. The Emperor wanted to have his own men who could operate without anyone else knowing."

Her mind was spinning. Her brother, not only a censor, but a secret censor.

"You can't tell anyone," he warned, seeing the expression on her face. "Not Mother or Father. Not even Yue-ying."

"Your wife doesn't even know?"

He shook his head. "There's no need to tell her. This is my duty to the empire."

"And Father?"

"He's a member of the Ministry of Defense."

Her eyes widened. "Surely he's not under investigation—"

"No," he said hastily. "Stop spinning wild stories, Wei-wei. But Father knows and interacts with many officials. It's beneficial to have those connections available with no one being aware."

"It seems so dishonest."

Huang shot her a pointed look with his eyebrow sharply raised. "Dishonest? Who has another forged ward pass under her pillow? And took my clothes to have them altered? Who's been bribing the matchmaker for years? *Years?*"

Wei-wei clamped her mouth shut. She didn't realize Huang knew about the matchmaker. It wasn't exactly a bribe. The woman just knew that if Wei-wei were to be married off, there would be no more visits and no more gifts.

"Why are you telling me now?" she asked him.

"I can't seem to keep any secrets from you," he admitted. "And this current case…"

He let out a long sigh as he shuffled through the papers.

"Is it related to the victim by the canal?" she asked again. "Or the jade chop?"

"I don't know, but it's possible." He sat back again, his gaze wandering helplessly over the stacks of documents. "There was an assassination near the imperial palace. You'll hear of it soon—everyone will hear of it soon. The Chancellor who was killed was a powerful man who wielded considerable influence in the imperial court. The Censorate has been given ten days to solve this case; that's why I haven't come home. Tomorrow I'll go out again."

"Why ten days?"

When her brother met her eyes, it was the most serious she'd ever seen him. "The Emperor suspects conspiracy. A murder like this rarely stands on its own. If the Chancellor's death is part of a larger plot, the co-conspirators will need to act fast. A ten day deadline holds us all responsible." He placed a hand over the stack of papers, his fingers curling into a fist. "It's a common tactic for flushing out the disloyal from within."

~

WHEN WEI-WEI and Huang were young, they had both learned how to read and write. When the family had hired a tutor for Huang, he was instructed to teach the Classics to both of the Bai children. It was accepted within the household that Wei-wei was more focused, had the better memory, loved learning more. But it wouldn't matter. Huang was the one who would take the imperial exams.

"Help your brother," Mother would urge her when Huang fell behind in his studies.

And so she did, from when they were still children to the present. On Huang's final attempt to pass the imperial exam, Wei-wei had frequently stayed up half the night with him. When Huang had finally passed, she'd felt in some part it was her triumph as well. It was the closest she could come to realizing any accomplishment of her own—through her brothers.

This night felt very much the same. They stayed awake late into the night to sort through documents that had belonged to Chancellor Yao.

"We make stacks," she instructed. "Petitions, notices,

letters. Catalog and date everything. Also note any names mentioned." Details were her strength.

"We'll start from the most recent and work back," Huang added. "I need to find anyone who might have reason to seek revenge. Or a rival of the Chancellor's."

As they worked, Huang told her the details of the case. The Chancellor had been killed on the way to an early morning meeting with the Emperor. He'd been surrounded by his own servants and functionaries.

"The meeting was on the Chancellor's itinerary as well as the Emperor's. The Chancellor's secretary would have known as well as his attendants. Same with the Emperor. The palace eunuchs, the guards. The guardsmen in the nearby lookout tower claimed to have been summoned away at that very moment. They failed to detect anything unusual down below, even once it was over."

"How many were there?"

"There were two in the lookout tower. They've both been imprisoned for questioning."

A chill went down her spine. Given the seriousness of the crime, the two guardsmen might be assigned blame and executed regardless. In that situation, it would make sense to her to tell the truth and hope for leniency. Huang's job had some very grim aspects to it.

"The arrows came from on high. The assassins were likely perched on the rooftops and shooting downward at the attendants. They killed the servants first. Then someone approached the Chancellor on foot and dragged him from his horse."

A lump formed in the back of her throat. Huang paused when he saw her expression. "I'm sorry, this is frightening you."

She remembered being sent away by Magistrate Li to protect her frail femininity. "I'll be fine. Go on."

"Then…Actually, you don't need to know what happened then—"

She shot him a look.

"They stabbed him in the heart."

She regretted giving him that look.

"This had to have been done by more than one killer," Huang concluded. "And someone powerful had to give the order. Whoever he was, he remained far away from the bloodshed." Huang gestured towards the papers. "I believe it was someone Chancellor Yao had made an enemy of."

"What was Chancellor Yao going to meet with the Emperor about?" she asked. "Maybe the traitor wanted to stop that meeting."

"That part is for someone who holds a higher rank than I do. For me, it's the records."

Despite the grimness of the situation, he managed a grin.

They worked beside each other for the next hour until she could see that her brother could no longer keep his head up.

"How long has it been since you last slept?" Wei-wei asked.

"I don't remember what sleep feels like."

"Go to bed. You're more likely to miss something if you're too tired."

He nodded groggily and stood. "I'm grateful to have your help on this, Wei-wei."

"Anything for my Elder Brother."

Anything to feel valued and useful. Huang left to go to his wife for what few hours of sleep were left, and Wei-wei kept on working.

CHAPTER 6

Gao found Fu Lin hunched over a dice table. It was late in the evening, deep into the Rat Hour, and the gambling den was full of desperate souls searching for a change of luck. Gao recognized Fu Lin by his prominent forehead, his brow furrowed deep in thought as if he could will the dice to obey. The rascal's eyes grew large when he spotted Gao. He scooped up his remaining coins—there weren't many—into his palm before turning to go.

"Don't worry." Gao hooked a hand into the collar of Fu Lin's tunic just as he started to tear away. "I'm not here for your money."

"I-I gave you a good deal on that jade, Brother Gao!"

"Yes, about that—"

He directed Fu Lin into the alley outside, all while the boy stammered and begged and apologized. Gao took this to mean he still owed money to Hui after pawning all his ill-gotten gains.

"Tell me more about how you got that chop, Fu Lin."

"I found it. Someone had dropped it."

Gao shook his head slowly, and Fu Lin sank back against the wall. "Truly, I just found it."

"By the canal?"

Fu Lin paled. "Brother Gao, I don't know anything else."

"Fool, the magistrate has plastered up notices on every street. Tell me what you know or you'll be talking to the constables."

That afternoon, Magistrate Li had taken him to the constable station house where the body was being kept. Gao suspected it was to see his reaction. To see if he flinched or revealed any sign of guilt.

Gao had known there would be trouble when he bought the seal from Fu. He just hadn't realized how much.

"The body was found lying beside the canal according to the magistrate's report. I know you didn't kill him," Gao said. "Tell me everything you remember. I won't tell the magistrate."

"I...I saw him floating down the canal. At first I thought someone had fallen in."

"When did you see him?"

"Yesterday morning. I'd spent all night playing tai sai and then the dice turned on me halfway through the third hour. Tiger Hour. That hour is always unlucky for me."

"Why were you at the canal in the middle of the night?" It would have been several hours before sunup.

"I had lost all my money," he confessed. "I was wandering around, trying to think of some way out of everything I owed."

"Then you saw a man," Gao prompted.

"I saw someone floating through the water. I shouted to him, but there was no answer so I waded into the canal. He was so heavy! He had on an expensive robe and it was soaked through. The water was pushing against me and it took all my strength to drag him onto the bank. I nearly got killed myself dragging him out!" Fu Lin added indignantly.

"And the only thing you found on him was the jade seal."

"There was a very small amount of money in his purse," he admitted. "He was already dead and his family must be rich. They wouldn't need it."

"When you pulled him out, you discovered he had drowned?"

"No, I didn't say that."

Gao halted. He had been prepared to ask a whole series of questions about strangulation or other injuries. Magistrate Li had only revealed the body to Gao for a matter of seconds before ushering him out of the room.

"He didn't drown," Gao posed. "But he was already gone when you found him?"

"He'd been pierced from the front and back. One of the shafts had broken off, but I could see the arrow through his chest when I dragged him ashore. It was awful."

An arrow. The man had been shot, but the magistrate had led him to believe the victim had drowned.

Magistrate Li had a barrage of questions for him earlier that day. Had Gao seen this man in the area? Did he frequent the gambling dens, the brothels? Had he seen him in the streets?

There were mansions within the ward interspersed between the pleasure houses and common dwellings. The magistrate must have checked first with those households. If one of the wealthy residents of the ward were missing, he would have been discovered quickly. Instead, no one had reported him missing and no one was looking for him.

The victim must be an outsider. Pingkang li was the pleasure district. There were many reasons people would come from outside the ward.

Suddenly, Gao recalled something that Fu Lin had said.

"The water was pushing against you," Gao said.

"Yes, when I went in."

The current. There was a current flowing through the canal.

Gao envisioned what must have happened. Fu Lin had pulled the victim out of the water, perhaps believing he was saving a drowning man. When he'd found the man was already dead, Fu Lin had dragged him onto the bank to search his belongings before scurrying off. It was hours later, late in the morning, before the body was discovered. Whoever the man was, he'd first been shot before falling into the water. Then he'd been dragged along by the current.

"Get up," Gao instructed. "And take a break from losing for one night. I have some work for you."

Fu nodded, though Gao doubted he'd be able to stop gambling. Not while there was anything in his possession he had left to lose.

Magistrate Li and his constables were searching the Pingkang li for information about the victim. They didn't know how long the body would have floated in the water or when it had been taken out. Only Fu Lin knew those details, and Gao was going to put that knowledge to use.

~

A BOWL of tea at Mingyu and Wu Kaifeng's teahouse cost more than it did at the stand across the street. Gao assumed it was because you had the luxury of drinking with a roof over your head, while sitting in chairs that weren't buckled and splintered. He was surprised the tea was recognizably better, even to his unrefined tastes.

"What did you think?" The smooth voice pierced his thoughts. A pale hand appeared over the table to tip more hot water into his bowl. "That you would come and sit here and *she* would just appear?"

Gao glanced up only to be skewered by a pair of exquisitely shaped eyes. Pretty, like two jeweled daggers.

"Lady Mingyu," he greeted. The title was honorary. More a street name, much like how he was sometimes called the Knife.

"I didn't realize you had such imagination." She tapped an elegantly manicured fingertip against the table. "To dream such dreams."

"I have no such dreams."

Gao thought about telling her his plan had worked at least once. He'd been hovering around Mingyu's teahouse for an entire week now, and hadn't Wei-wei shown up the other day, just as he'd hoped?

Her gaze slid over him, taking in his every measure. Mingyu knew the power of silence as well as the effectiveness of words. He lifted his tea and took a drink as an appeal for peace. There was no need to make an enemy of her, especially when he was there to speak to her husband.

Mingyu narrowed her eyes just so at him before turning to tend to other business.

It wasn't long before the formidable Wu Kaifeng arrived. He appeared from the backroom, his expression severe, and walked directly over to where Gao was sitting. That, in itself, should have been worrisome.

"You won't be conducting any business here."

Wu cast an imposing shadow. The former constable towered over most people, in physical height as well as demeanor. If Gao were standing, he'd be close in stature to Wu Kaifeng. At least tall enough to see eye to eye, but he remained seated with his posture relaxed and neutral.

"I'm not here to cause any trouble. I've come to ask your opinion."

He'd avoided dealing with Wu Kaifeng until now. When Wu was head constable of the county, outlaws knew to stay out of his way. Fortunately, their paths had never crossed.

"What do you want to know?"

"It's rumored that you could look at a victim and tell when he had died."

"That is only occasionally true."

It was an unusual conversation to have with the former lawman, but Gao sensed there was an answer to his question out there.

"There's a strong current in the canal that runs through the city," Gao began. "If a body is found floating in the canal in this ward at the Tiger Hour, can we determine where it fell in?"

Wu stared at him without expression for a long time. So long that Gao wondered whether Wu had heard the question.

"There are many factors to consider," Wu said finally. "The speed of the current, the weight of the body."

To his surprise, Wu pulled a chair over and sat down at the table. "You're talking about the man who was found just yesterday."

Gao nodded.

"Are you working for the crime lord, Hui?" Wu inquired.

"Not on this matter," Gao replied honestly.

Once again, Wu was silent for a long time. Whatever he was calculating in his head, he was taking his own time with it. Let the world be damned.

"Are you looking to collect the bounty?"

"Bounty?"

"A hundred taels of silver."

Gao hadn't known about that. Had that amount been set after he and Wei-wei had shown the jade seal to the magistrate?

"I have no interest in the bounty," Wu continued. "But I do want to see justice done."

"I wouldn't mind some silver," Gao admitted with a shrug. One bought things with money.

"I will assume, for now, since you've come to ask, that you did not have anything to do with this man's death."

"Not this one," Gao agreed.

There was a flicker behind Wu's eyes at that, but he went on. "My wife does not like me being pulled in whenever a body is found. There are many unresolved deaths in this city."

Gao recalled Bai Huang had come to speak to Wu Kaifeng yesterday as well. It seemed no one had forgotten that Wu Kaifeng had been head constable not long ago. He'd been involved in solving several notorious cases in the capital.

"This is what I would do," Wu began.

Gao leaned in close to listen.

~

GAO WOKE up early the next morning in his bunk. The space was smaller than a monk's cell, which suited him fine. He had few belongings and most of his days were spent on his feet out on the streets. His nights as well.

He drew water from the public well and completed his morning routine before leaving the tenement to walk down the street. The building where Fu Lin lived with his family was just at the corner. They were packed on the second floor into two rooms that were not that much larger than Gao's bunk.

Gao was fortunate. Fu Lin was there, which meant he'd gone home the night before like Gao told him to.

The boy shuffled out from the hovel, looking disheveled as he pulled his cap on. "What is it, Brother Gao?"

Something to be said for Fu Lin, he was always eager to work. He was just too eager to spend as well.

"Come on."

Gao led them to the walls of the East Market. The gates wouldn't open until noon, but discarded refuse tended to collect in the shadow of the market. It was a paradise for beggars and scavengers. He and Fu picked through the junk, searching for discarded rags and clothing.

Fu didn't ask too many questions. He trudged behind Gao with an armload of junk as Gao haggled for a few lengths of bamboo. Then they loaded their findings into a handcart and started pushing.

"Where are we going?" asked Fu.

"We're following the river," Gao replied.

The waterway led them out of Pingkang li and into the neighboring ward where it continued to wind south. After an hour, they stopped beneath the shade of a bridge and set to work.

"What are we making?" Fu Lin asked as Gao instructed him to tie the bamboo poles together with two cross-pieces.

"A dummy."

It didn't have to look life-like, just be of approximate size and weight. And it had to float. By noontime, it looked more like a beggar's raft than anything that resembled a person.

"This is a lot of work for a dummy. Is this a religious thing?" Fu Lin asked.

Gao blinked. "Do I seem devout to you?"

The boy shrugged.

He was right though. It was a lot of work for a whim. Gao usually preferred the easy route when it came to money.

"We're trying to find out who murdered your nobleman," he told Fu.

"He's not mine!"

Fu looked warily at the dummy, as if it had suddenly

become possessed with the spirit of the dead man he had robbed. Maybe Fu Lin was the superstitious one.

"Well, he was very important. Big bounty for anyone who captures the killer. Better hope some constable doesn't think it's you."

"No, Brother! I would never kill anyone. He was just floating there in the water."

They finished stuffing the dummy with empty coconut husks and secured everything with cord. How did Wu Kaifeng think of this trick?

It was close to lunch time. Gao bought some rice cake wrapped in banana leaf from a street vendor and tossed one over to Fu. Then he leaned back against the foot of the bridge, enjoying the shade and the movement of the water as it flowed by.

The boy took a healthy bite. "You didn't tell the magistrate about me?" he asked around a mouthful of sticky rice.

Gao shook his head.

"How much is the bounty anyway?"

He finished chewing before answering. "A hundred taels of silver."

"Waaaa…." Fu's eyes popped wide open. He let out a little laugh. "No wonder you decided to turn thief-catcher. A hundred taels!"

The little gutter rat was enchanted by the lure of the money now, completely blind at how important someone had to be for the magistrate to offer such a reward. People like him and Fu could get knifed in the streets while constables walked by without even slowing. In contrast, a death like this couldn't be ignored.

"Are you going to eat that last rice cake, Brother Gao?"

Gao tossed it to him. "Feel free."

Fu Lin gave him a toothy grin before unwrapping the

parcel. "Do you know what I'd do with that much money? I'd host a huge feast. Invite everybody."

He wasn't a bad fellow. Gao was actually enjoying the time. It was better than bullying some poor shopkeeper for coins.

While he waited for the boy to finish, Gao took out the strip of red silk from his pocket. Rolling the length into a cord, he started looping it into a decorative knot.

"What would you do with the reward?" Fu Lin asked.

The knot formed a leaf-like pattern, interweaving and braiding together. "I'd change my life," he said absently.

Fu gave a snort. "But how?"

Gao knotted one end and formed a loop in the other, hooking them together to form a bracelet before stuffing the silk back into his pocket. He wasn't doing all this for anything as rational as silver. He just wanted something to talk about so a pretty girl might pay attention to him for a little longer than he deserved.

Wei-wei was clever and educated and endlessly curious. Maybe that was why he was so taken with her. She spoke to him as if what he said carried weight, as if she wanted to know what he had to say. She could ask him all the questions she wanted. Wei-wei would never have to pay him to provide information. She'd never need to pay him for anything

"Let's go before it gets too late," Gao said.

Together they dragged the dummy onto the top of the bridge, first looking out for any patrols, before dropping it over the arch. The bamboo figure plunked into the water where it sank a little before bobbing to the surface. Then it started moving downstream along the current. Gao was keep pace at a fast walk.

Fu Lin had to rush to match Gao's longer stride. "What are we doing?"

Gao hushed him. "Counting."

They retraced their same steps, walking at a brisk pace along the canal through the ward. This was how they would get an estimate of the speed of the river. There were variations along the way, such as if the body became caught on the river bank or some other debris. If it hit a slow spot where the water pooled and swirled before smoothing out.

"Just a rough estimate," Wu Kaifeng had reminded him, jotting down example calculations.

Gao had a firmer grasp of numbers than he did characters, though he would have never dreamed up such calculations in a hundred years. He barely knew what a hundred taels of silver could buy. The only thing he was sure of was that Wei-wei would still be far beyond his reach. Even if he had a thousand taels to his name.

CHAPTER 7

Wei-wei yawned twice during her younger brother's morning lesson. Chang-min was too focused on his studies to notice, but once he finished his recitation, he was met with a long silence. She had started to nod off.

"I'll get tea," she said, shaking herself awake. "Recite the Analects next."

It was fifteen chapters. Dutifully, Chang-min started from the first passage, word for word.

She'd been up late into the night sorting through Huang's collection of papers. Then her elder brother had gone to meet with Magistrate Li that morning while she continued with her tutoring duties at home.

She had seen to her younger brother's education from the time he was eight years old. Women weren't allowed to sit for the exams, but she could bring honor to the family name by helping her brothers.

Chang-min was seventeen now and growing quickly like a bamboo shoot, his limbs taking on an elongated look. Chang-min's resemblance to their father was becoming more pronounced as he grew. Wei-wei could see it in the shape of his chin, but it was said he favored his mother in his eyes. Wei-wei wouldn't know. Chang-min's mother was her father's concubine whom she'd never met.

Her younger brother had been brought into the household when he was two years old and put under Mother's care to be raised. Wei-wei had been only ten at the time. It wasn't until she was sixteen that she'd taken over his instruction. Mother's headaches had been getting worse, and she needed to rest frequently. Father was away for long stretches of time, and Huang had started his first course of study the Academy. That was also the start of his dark road to the gambling dens. It just seemed to work out better for everyone for Wei-wei to step in.

Wei-wei knew that Chang-min occasionally wrote to his birth mother who stayed with their father. Wei-wei planned for Chang-min to take the provincial exams in two years. Two years after that, he'd be ready to take the palace exams. Perhaps once his studies were over, he could see his mother more often.

On the way to the kitchen, she noticed Mother and a guest were seated in the front courtyard. Amah had brought out the baby to them. She lay swaddled in a carrier between Mother and a middle-aged woman that Wei-wei didn't recognize.

"The fortune-teller was convinced she would be a boy," Mother was saying. Did she have to always sound so disappointed when she told this story?

"No, Bai *Furen*. Your family carries its talent in its girls."

Wei-wei slowed her step to listen. At that moment, both women looked up and spotted her.

"She has such a bright face," the woman said, smiling broadly.

"Daughter, come greet Madame Li."

Li? Where was she supposed to know a Madame Li from?

She approached carefully, taking in the woman's embroidered silk robe. Her hair was pulled up and coiled over her head like a crown.

She bowed, "Li *Furen*. I hope you're in good health."

"Yes, yes, very good, my darling." Her eyes sparkled as she looked Wei-wei over.

Why was this woman being so friendly? And why was she acting so familiar? Li was such a common name.

"What are you doing right now, dear? Can you come join your mother and I?" their guest asked.

"Wei-wei is tutoring her younger brother," Mother answered on her behalf.

"We have always heard of how well-educated she is. A credit to her family."

Wei-wei should have been overjoyed to receive such praise and attention for once. Instead it made the hairs on the back of her neck rise up.

"I must return to the study," she demurred, making the strategic decision to forego the tea and escape to safety. She bowed and made a quick retreat.

Back at the study, Chang-min was in the middle of his recitation. She wondered if he was really that dedicated. She and Huang used to pause so they could chatter amongst themselves, only to start up once the tutor was back in earshot.

He did stop when she turned to peer out the door. "What are you doing, Elder Sister?"

"There is someone in the outer courtyard. I'm trying to see when she leaves."

"Why are you acting like you're hiding?"

"Analects," she reminded him. "Keep reciting."

Madame Li didn't stay much longer. As soon as she left, Wei-wei hunted her mother down. Mother had gone to her own chamber. As Wei-wei entered, she sat at her dressing table, removing some of her jewelry. Her mother had put on the adornments for the distinct purpose of the visit.

"Who was that, Mother?" Wei-wei helped free the jade pin from her mother's hair. Mother had gone through the trouble to style her hair that morning. Now the hairs on the back of Wei-wei's neck were really standing up.

"Why, that was Madame Li." Her Mother's tone was light, almost sing-song. "Li Chen's mother."

"Magistrate Li Chen?"

Mother nodded, smiling. "She came to send good wishes to our family and see the baby."

Wei-wei's stomach sank. This was uncalled for. It was all too…all too overly polite. "But we're not even close to their family."

She had never heard Mother speak of the Li family. They didn't live in the neighborhood. The only interaction they'd had with the magistrate was official business.

"You are twenty-five years of age this year, Wei-wei."

No, no, no, no, no.

"Well past time to start a family."

Not this conversation again.

"And Li Chen is educated, accomplished. From very good family."

There was nothing materially *wrong* with the magistrate. He wasn't unpleasant to look at. His features were smoother and a touch paler than…some. And he was physically less imposing compared to certain individuals she had been in recent company with. In the past, she might have considered that a good quality. Now all she could think of was that the magistrate would never, ever approve of his wife speaking to questionable past acquaintances.

It was marriage itself Wei-wei objected to. The restrictions and the loss of everything she'd built for herself within the family. Mother would never understand that. It was a mother's singular goal to plan for the future of her children.

This was the sort of fight where Mother would only dig her claws in deeper if Wei-wei resisted. So, she said nothing but, "Yes, Mother" until she could extract herself.

And then she fled.

~

WEI-WEI HAD MADE it out of the front gate and started down the street when a voice stopped her.

"Do you want to know what I found out?"

She spun around and started, blinking. Gao was there. He had one shoulder propped casually against the wall while a half-smile played over his lips.

"Come with me," she said.

His smile disappeared behind a look of astonishment.

"Quickly."

She hurried down the lane. He followed, catching up to her easily in a few long strides. "Lady Bai."

"Mister Gao. Are you well?" The hurried pace left her slightly breathless, but that was no reason to be impolite.

He laughed. "I'm well. Has something frightened you?"

Yes. A pair of matchmaking mothers. She couldn't explain exactly why the urge to flee had overtaken her, but it had. She wanted to be anywhere else talking about anything else. Under normal circumstances, she would have been thrilled to see Gao. He was unexpected and exciting. Today, he was a much-needed distraction.

There was a small temple at the end of the lane dedicated to the Great Buddha. They entered into the garden and she went inside to stand before the altar. There were no statues or relics on display, just a small clay figurine and modest offerings of flowers and fruit.

The temple was swept daily by an old monk who lived there. Wei-we dropped a coin into the alms bowl. In return, she could stand there quietly for a while, hidden from view.

Li Chen. She knew what was happening here. Her younger brother would soon be off to an academy, and she'd be left without purpose. Her hopes of remaining respectfully unwed were fading. Yue-ying's daughter was too young to need a tutor.

After a few minutes, Wei-wei hadn't managed to come up with a solution, but at least she felt less rattled. She left the sanctuary to find Gao waiting.

"Did you ask Great Buddha for anything?" he asked once they returned to the street. His tone was only mildly mocking.

"No," she admitted. How does one pray for something not to happen? For something not to happen was a non-state. It didn't exist.

"Then why go to temple?"

"There are only so many places I can go." She continued walking down the lane and he fell into step beside her. It was pleasant, as if his presence gave her a reason to be there rather than wandering alone.

"I go to the temple, then to the market. Then from the market, back to the temple. That's all there is most days," she explained. "There is nowhere else where I can be alone. Other than our home. It feels so confining sometimes."

"Your home is a palace," he interjected.

"You've never been inside."

"I've been all around it. I circled the walls twice today, wondering how to call on you. A palace," he concluded with a lofty grin.

She regarded him, torn between returning home to her confining palace or staying out here without a reasonable excuse to justify it. Mother would ask her where she'd been for so long and she would say...She didn't know what she'd say.

The only thing she did know was that the farther she walked from home, the less she thought about what was waiting for her back there. If she were alone, she would have had little choice but to return.

"There's a polo match," she told Gao, her stomach tight with nerves.

"Polo," he echoed.

She nodded.

"Polo," he assented.

She started toward the fields with Gao by her side. Just having him so close made her heart beat faster. It was an act of defiance being out here with him, so close to home. She tried to look at him out of the corner of her eye as they walked.

Gao wasn't what she would consider handsome, but his look was striking. His features were distinctive and hard to overlook. "Chiseled" was the word that came to mind. Cut from stone and left rough.

What would her mother think if she saw her walking beside Gao? Wei-wei never had to wonder about such things because she made sure not to get caught. She thought of it now, while the threat of betrothal hung over her. What would her mother think of Gao?

Mother might like that Gao was tall, and that would be the end of what she found favorable. Every other trait was unacceptable. A vagabond and drifter. No name with a dark reputation.

Gao must have had similarly judgmental thoughts about her. She was willful, stubborn, naive. Spoiled.

"Do you think I'm spoiled?" she asked all the sudden.

"Yes," he answered without pause.

He glanced at her, smirking. Gao's look entirely changed

when he smiled. She managed a smile back, her heartbeat skipping.

The field was on public ground and was frequently used by the surrounding households for matches. The dirt had been sifted through and then tamped down with oil to control the clouds of dust that were kicked up by the horses. That gave the surface a glossy, stone-like appearance.

As they neared, Wei-wei could see the game was already well underway. She'd forgotten her parasol and the sun was high, beating down upon the riders. She and Gao found a sliver of shade just to the right of the field. They stood side by side beneath the tree to watch.

"Choose a team," she said.

"Red."

"Mine is green."

The players were marked by a colored band wrapped over their upper arms. They soared down the field, and she could feel the thundering of hooves over the ground. Her pulse answered the rhythm, beating faster.

"Do you know how to play?" she asked him.

He snorted. "With my stable of horses?"

Wei-wei turned her attention back to the match. She kept on forgetting how different their lives were. Their paths wouldn't have crossed if not for her brother's scandalous past and his associations in the pleasure quarter.

"I bet you'd be a fearsome player," he said.

"I would be."

"You'd be like that one."

A player on the green team wove his horse between two opponents to strike the ball down the field.

"Fearless," Gao concluded.

"Invincible," she concurred, wishing it were true. She'd never played before in her life.

Another player from the green team hit the ball into the end gate and a cheer went up from the crowd.

"We learned how to ride from my father," she told him. "There was a time when he'd taken my brother and I with him to an appointment in the north, to the open grassland. My mother says that's why my brother and I are so wild. Too much freedom as children."

His lips quirked. "Yet some would say you can do no wrong."

"What do you mean?"

"I've seen you outside your home, and you weren't at the market or the temple," he pointed out.

"I'm obediently wild," she countered.

Gao conceded with a laugh. She liked talking to Gao. She never knew where the conversation would take her. The truth was she was bolder around him. She liked that too.

"Is your father still in the north?" he asked.

"He's stationed closer now, in the region between Hedong protectorate and the capital. The Ministry of Defense is concerned about a *jiedushi* operating so close to Chang'an."

"Your father is there as a safeguard then."

The *jiedushi* were generals who acted as military governors over semi-autonomous protectorates . They swore loyalty to the Emperor but commanded their own independent armies.

"His command is too small to defend against Hedong's governor should he move against the capital. Father always says his job is to prevent war and keep the region stable. The imperial court is in constant fear of uprising from its own generals."

She realized Gao was watching her and not the match.

"The things you say," he marveled.

She blushed. Whatever Gao thought of her, she wasn't

insignificant. Someone who needed to be hidden away and sheltered.

"One can't grow up in our household without hearing this sort of talk over tea," she dismissed.

"It's not just talk, Wei-wei. Anyone can see you've studied for a long time."

She blushed even harder. "Have you been out of the city?" she asked, trying to shift the focus.

"I was born in Chang'an, left, came back."

Wei-wei frowned. "What a disappointing story."

"My story would certainly be disappointing."

"I don't think so."

Gao was one of the most interesting people she'd met. There was a layer of mystery to him. Or maybe she found him fascinating for all the reasons he thought her amusing.

"Why did you come back?" she asked.

"I remembered life being different here," he replied slowly. "Easier. But when I came back, it wasn't better or easier. Everything had changed."

"There's a story of a man who helped rescue a young maiden," she began. "He escorted her home safely and her father invited him to a feast to thank him. But everything seemed different there. The food and drink were all things he'd never seen before. When he woke the next morning, he returned to the road to find that a hundred years had passed. It turned out that the maiden's father was the Dragon King and dragon time is different from our time."

"See, that's an interesting story."

"I always thought it was sad. The dragons thought they were rewarding him, but they just couldn't see the world the way he did. When he came back, everything he knew was gone."

Gao found a spot in the grass so they could sit. The actual spectators were on the other side of the field, seated beneath an awning. They looked like smudges of paint in the distance.

"Did you ever have a name besides Gao?"

"I've forgotten it."

"How can one forget his own name?" she asked, incredulous. She regretted her tone when she saw his flat expression. "Oh, I'm sorry. Some people don't have...I mean, are not attached to family—"

She felt a pang of sadness as she said it. Her family was everything to her.

"I had family."

There was a quietness in his voice she'd never heard before. She didn't dare say anything more. They both fell silent, eyes fixed on the polo match though neither paid any attention to it.

"My father was imprisoned for taking bribes," Gao said. "He didn't hold any high office. He was just a tax collector."

Wei-wei stiffened. Her skin flushed with shame on his behalf. She wanted to apologize for asking such intrusive questions and prying into his life.

"Gao is my family name," he told her. "It's the only thing I kept...from before."

A cheer went up in the stands on the other side of the field. Someone had scored a goal. It gave them something to focus their attention on momentarily.

"I'm sor—"

"Don't apologize," he cut her off. "You don't need to worry about politeness around me. I don't have any manners anyway. It's so rare that we see one another, better not to waste time."

She couldn't help but feel chastised, but she knew Gao didn't want her to act wounded. Still, it was a pause before she could find something to say.

"You do have some manners," she observed, as a matter-of-fact.

A muscle ticked along his jaw. "Do I?"

"Your diction. I always wondered about that."

He turned to her. His crooked smile was a peace offering. "I don't even know what that means, Wei-wei."

"Your manner of speaking. Your phrasing is, at times, very formal. It confused me at first."

"Because you couldn't figure out how to treat me?"

She ignored his challenge...for now.

He glanced upward, as if considering her words. Then he nodded slightly. She wasn't sure if it was agreement.

"It's why we have such unusual conversations," she concluded. "Neither one of us knows what's proper."

"I like our conversations," he admitted.

A ball of warmth grew in her chest.

Another roar came from the crowd. The match had come to an end.

"My team won," she declared.

"You chose well." He reached into his tunic and pulled out a coil of red silk. He paused then, running his teeth over his bottom lip. It was the first time she'd seen any sign of awkwardness from him.

"Your prize," he said.

To her astonishment, he handed her the red silk, his palm lingering over hers. She smoothed the coil out with shaking fingers and discovered it was a bracelet.

"It's so pretty," she said, admiring the intricate knot looped into it.

"We should go. The crowd is leaving."

He helped her to her feet, his hand firm over her arm. Unexpectedly she felt tears forming in her eyes as soon as he let go.

"I should tell you what I found out yesterday," he said, starting to walk. "It really took a long time to work out."

She was grateful he hadn't noticed anything. A tear spilled over her cheek and she swiped it away roughly. The bracelet was crushed in her fist--she was afraid to let it go. It was such a simple gesture. Why was she falling apart?

Beside her Gao was talking about current and calculations and time tables. She didn't hear half of it and didn't understand the half she did hear. She fell back a step, hoping he wouldn't see the tears on her face as she struggled to compose herself.

Gao stopped when she did. Wei-wei hastily pressed her sleeve to her eyes.

"Lady Bai?" he stepped close, his voice filled with concern.

She was grateful for the current fashion of oversized sleeves. She tried to hide behind hers now. It wasn't subtle, but she'd lost any hope of subtlety.

"Wei-wei, what's wrong?"

Gently, he tried to lower her arm while she fought him stubbornly. It was comical, if she could separate herself from her body to watch the show.

"I used to bribe the matchmaker!" she blurted out.

"Wh—what?"

"I knew all it would take was for that gossipy old auntie to say, the Bai family has a daughter who's this and that—and then it would be out of my hands. So, I paid her not to mention me."

"Alright." He didn't understand.

"I was so certain I had nothing to worry about. I'm twenty-five years old. You would think that would be beyond marriageable."

"Yes. Way beyond marriage," he agreed, pressing his lips together as they threatened to curve upward.

"A spinster," she emphasized with a sob.

How could she ever make Gao understand? He went wherever he pleased. Wei-wei was just beginning to enjoy the taste of freedom. Mother had stopped trying to seek out suitable sons for her. She had taken an important role tutoring her brother, and now Huang wanted her to help him with his important work as well. Their family had not one, but two male children to carry on the family line. And they had enough wealth to feed a sister consigned to spinsterhood.

"I'm certain my mother wants to make a match between me and—" She sniffed loudly. This was so awful, but she couldn't stop. Not until she explained to him how awful today was. "A match between me and Li Chen!"

"Who's Li Chen?"

"The magistrate. Li Chen. *Magistrate Li*," she choked out, at once frustrated and heart-broken.

Gao was standing so, so close. Close enough that she could press her forehead to his chest if she dared. But she didn't dare.

"I know I'm not making any sense."

"No, you are. You are," he said quietly.

Her face was so flooded with tears that Gao was only a dark blur through them. His hands curved over her shoulders, steadying her, trying to soothe her. But everything he did was only making it worse. The bracelet, the way he was being so kind to her now.

"You don't understand," she insisted in desperation.

"I do," he said, cradling her face between calloused hands before he kissed her.

He tasted of salt. It was from her own tears. She could barely see him, but she could feel his mouth against hers, touching lightly. The world tilted and spun.

She pressed her lips back against his, not knowing the

way of this. It was like their conversations — awkward and unwieldy, yet still the best thing in the world.

Which made everything worse.

"Stop—"

His mouth still caressed hers even as she tore away. She ran to hide just on the other side of the tree and squeezed her eyes shut. Her heart beat furiously.

She was thinking of too many things at once. How long she'd been away from home. Her mother looking so happy. The loneliness inside her. It was always there, this loneliness. Happiness only came from wanting her family to be happy.

Wei-wei breathed deep, trying to force back the swell of emotion rising in her chest. Threatening to burst out of her.

She'd just lost her first kiss to someone who was unsuitable, and now she had to go home and pretend that heaven and earth hadn't changed places.

CHAPTER 8

Wei-wei was on the other side of the tree where he couldn't see her. He leaned his head back against the wood and closed his eyes.

"Wei-wei," he began gently.

"Please don't speak."

He fell immediately silent. Just like he'd stopped kissing her when she'd asked. Just like he'd remained ridiculously hidden behind this tree when she'd said she needed to calm herself, and she couldn't as long as she could see him. He'd done all this even though he needed to touch her more than he needed to breathe. Could Wei-wei feel his heart beat through the wood? It was pounding so hard.

He did all this and everything she asked, no matter how foolish. He'd been compelled to indulge her every whim from the first moment he'd seen her. She had a way of convincing people — at least of convincing him. She had a way of rushing headlong into things, though maybe this time he was the one who'd acted before thinking.

Wei-wei was not the sort of girl he was allowed to kiss.

"I didn't plan to do that," he said.

Her reply came from the other side of the tree. "I thought we weren't going to apologize." She still sounded choked up. There was a long pause. "Why did you do it then?"

"I don't know. I must like spinsters."

He could hear muffled laughter.

Wei-wei.

"What was it that you were saying before? About the body by the canal?" she asked, sounding a little steadier.

"It was nothing."

"You said you're working with former Constable Wu?"

"Not exactly. He helpd with some calculations. Made a list of times."

"Times?"

"Like a schedule. A map of where the crime could have occurred along the river and when."

Moments ago, they had been kissing and now they were talking about death and crime. And it was still wonderful. A wonderful madness.

"Do you think it's possible—" she stopped herself.

"What?" He peeked around just enough to catch her wiping at her eyes.

Wei-wei bit her lower lip, her brow furrowed in thought. "What did my brother tell you the last time you saw him?"

Gao shrugged. "That something had happened. Something big and that he suspected someone had been hired from outside the city."

She nodded slowly. Her nose was red and her eyes swollen. Wei-wei worried her teeth against her lower lip as she pondered something, and he was unreasonably, unbearably tempted to kiss her again.

"The time table is brilliant," she said absently. "The magistrate can focus his investigation."

The magnificent Magistrate Li. Gao had already decided

he hated the man. "I was going to go to him, but I have another idea."

"What is it?"

Catch the killer and be a hero. Why not? "I'm still thinking on it."

He really didn't have any plan yet, but whatever it was, he was going to do it without going to Li Chen, if he could help it.

When Wei-wei finally came around, he caught a glimpse of the red cord around her wrist before she pulled her sleeve over it. They kept an arm's length between them as they returned to the streets. He was painfully aware of every inch between them.

"We should say farewell here," Wei-wei said when they reached the front of the temple.

The Bai mansion was at the end of the avenue. She turned to face him. "Tell me how your plan works out, once you... think on it."

"I will."

Their gazes locked for a devastating moment. Her pupils were dark and endless, and he could already feel himself falling into them. Thinking things, dreaming things. He would slay tigers for her if she asked.

"I've been away a long time. My family will wonder what I've been doing."

Her expression said she knew there would be trouble, but she didn't care. He waited for the very last glimpse of her as she disappeared down the street before he turned to go.

~

As MUCH AS Gao hated it, he did need to enlist Magistrate Li after all.

He went to the magistrate's yamen and provided the

timetable he had drawn up with a suggestion to look for disturbances along the canal on the night of the murder. He'd expected Li would scoff at his suggestion, but the man was actually reasonable.

The official pulled out the reports from that night himself. He sat at his desk flipping through the pages while Gao stood, feeling outclassed and outmatched because the small inked characters actually meant something to this man.

"Here." Magistrate Li planted a finger on top of an entry in the logbook. "A horse was reported loose in Xingan ward that night. No one claimed him. That's valuable property for no one to come forward."

"Good. Now you just need to make two arrests in that ward," Gao proposed.

"On what evidence?" Li asked.

Gao made a face. "You require evidence to make an arrest?"

The magistrate went to pull the door shut.

That night, Magistrate Li insisted Gao come along as he and his constables carried out the plan. As he crowded into the wagon, Gao had to begrudgingly admit that, though Li looked pampered and proper, he was apparently the sort of magistrate who joined the ranks of his men.

He had to respect an official who voluntarily stayed up half the night if it meant catching an outlaw.

Even though Gao would be considered an outlaw.

Even though Gao really didn't like the man.

"It's night time," Li observed. "Most of the streets are empty. How will anyone know of this?"

"All it takes is some gossipy street urchin to say an army of constables stormed in and did this and that," Gao said.

They needed a spectacle and the magistrate appeared ready to deliver. They rode in a wagon along with eight men armed with swords, clubs and pikes. All in all, it was a strange turn of events: Gao the Knife riding alongside so many uniformed constables with swords at their side. Luckily there were no bulletins with Gao's likeness posted on the walls.

The wards had been locked down since sun down, but they were on official business. The guards pulled the gates open and the wagon rolled down the center of the ward toward the canal. The constables stationed themselves near the bridge and then waited.

The pair arrived within the half hour, with the lead man ringing a bell to warn people of the coming of the night soil collectors so innocent bystanders could dart out of the way. The warning was unnecessary. The night soil men had the unsavory job of collecting waste from chamber pots throughout the city. They'd then sell the night soil to farmers in the southern part of the capital to fertilize their crops. You could smell the night soil collectors from a hundred paces away and, if an unfortunate breeze happened to blow the wrong way while they were near, you couldn't run fast enough.

Gao felt a bit guilty for targeting the collectors, but they were known to work throughout the night and their routes took them past every house. If anyone could be witness to this crime, it would be the night soil collectors.

The constables advanced on the pair and shouted for them to halt.

Lawmen liked to say that only the guilty run, but that wasn't true. The younger of the two men took one look at the armed horde and flung his bucket of shit at them before turning to run.

Luckily, Gao had remained a safe distance away. Magistrate Li had wisely done the same, leaving his constables to take the brunt of the attack.

Amidst cries of disgust, a team of constables chased down

the night soil collector, who immediately wailed he was innocent the moment the constables had him in chains. A few spectators peered out of their windows, wondering what was going on. Gao exchanged a knowing look with the magistrate, who took out a handkerchief to press over his nose as they loaded the shackled collector into the wagon.

The older of the two night soil men bowed to the magistrate and did everything he could to be accommodating. He was escorted to the wagon without the need for shackles. Afterward, Magistrate Li directed the wagon to head to Pingkang li before returning to the magistrate's yamen. Every man had his face pressed against his sleeve as the wagon traveled through the streets.

"Eh, you get used to it," the older night soil man said.

The younger collector scowled at him, the chains of this shackles clanking together with every movement.

The wagon took them to the center of Pingkang li, where the most popular pleasure houses were open for business. It was generous of the magistrate to return him home. Unlike the constables, Gao wasn't earning anything for his time.

They came to a stop within view of the illustrious Lotus Palace.

"Well, this will certainly breed gossip," Gao said, hopping off the wagon.

He was surprised when Magistrate Li also climbed down.

"I have some business to attend to in the vicinity," Li explained.

Business. In the pleasure district well past midnight?

Gao said nothing. Instead, he took his first clean breath in a long time. "What happens now?"

"They'll be given a bed, food. I'll see they are well taken care of for their trouble."

"Give it two days," Gao suggested. "Enough time for someone to start getting anxious."

The magistrate nodded. "Good plan, Mister Gao."

That was that. He started to go, but Li stopped him. "You seem well-acquainted with the Bai family."

His pulse skipped. "Somewhat," he replied warily.

Magistrate Li regarded him with a steady look. Gao had the impression he was being taken apart bit by bit by that gaze.

"And Lady Bai, how do you know her?"

Gao's hands clenched involuntarily. He forced them loose. "Young Lord Bai hired me for her protection."

The magistrate considered the answer and seemed satisfied. It made perfect sense that Gao would be a man-for-hire. A servant.

"With all those criminals roaming the streets," Gao added in a stealth attack. "Things can get dangerous, right, Magistrate?"

"Right," Li echoed slowly. The official kept eye contact longer than necessary before taking his leave.

CHAPTER 9

C onquerors are kings, the beaten are bandits.
The old proverb came to her as Wei-wei was flying over vast lands and mountains. She was a bird, able to see everything below. There were two armies in red and green facing a larger one in gold.

Not a bird. She was a dragon and one hundred years had passed. Wei-wei was suddenly sad that Gao had grown old while she was away living another life. How was he supposed to know that she was a dragon?

The armies were fighting and the red army fell, leaving only the green against the gold. Gold was the Emperor's army.

"My team won," she said.

Gao was there, waiting just outside her door. She went to him, but he moved farther away like the moon.

Oh, this was just a dream, she realized, still dreaming. The visions devolved into fragments and she woke up with her face against a stack of petitions.

She'd fallen asleep reading through them for her brother. Her hand rested on top of one report. The sight of the red silk looped around her wrist sent a little jolt of happiness through her. Joy and sadness, at once.

She reached out to run a finger along the bracelet. Her gaze strayed down to the petition once more. She'd pulled this one out last night for a reason. It was a reminder to read it again when she was more clear-headed.

Sitting up, she rubbed a knuckle over her eyes and opened the paper.

It was a judgment regarding a general who had raised several large armies in the northeastern part of the empire. A year ago, he had signed a treaty conceding control of two of his six territories in Pinglu circuit.

Six territories. These warlords were practically kings themselves. Her father had said that. Those were the sorts of conversations they had in their family. Lectures about duty and politics and military philosophy. The talks were meant for her brother Huang, but Wei-wei always listened in her quest to be the perfect student. Mother told her a proper lady didn't need to know such things, but Gao had seemed impressed when she'd spoken of the military governors and the balance of power.

The beaten are bandits...

General Lin Shidao surrendering lands to the Emperor.

Wei-wei grabbed the report and ran out of her room excitedly. Outside, she encountered Yue-ying sitting in the courtyard with Mother.

"Is Huang home?" she asked.

"He didn't come home again last night," Yue-ying said, looking sullen.

"I'm sure he's doing very important work," Wei-wei assured.

The family still didn't know about her brother's secret appointment and she couldn't tell them.

"Wei-wei!" her mother reprimanded. Mother looked her

over, from her disheveled appearance to the paper clutched in her hand. "How are you going to make a proper bride like this? Go get dressed!"

Wei-wei ducked back into her room. "Wild," she heard her mother mutter as she pulled the doors closed.

Huang had said the Emperor had given him ten days to solve the murder because a crime this grave meant treason was brewing. The Emperor was right.

She splashed water over her face and ran a comb through her hair. After a brief glance in the brass mirror, she opened her door to call for a maidservant. She was going to have to go to the Imperial City to find Huang and should look more presentable and less…wild. She made sure the silk bracelet was hidden as her maidservant entered to help her dress.

An hour later, her hair was carefully combed, looped, and pinned and she was outfitted in layers of lavender and rose silk. She straightened a shawl around her shoulders and once again headed out. This time, Mother was no longer there to judge her appearance. She had disappeared into the kitchen to oversee the making of her special dumplings. Mother's special dumplings meant special guests.

"I'm going to see Huang," she called out as she moved past the kitchen door. "He's expecting me."

Mother called out something in protest, and Wei-wei made sure to be too far away to hear.

Zhou Dan had the carriage hitched up quickly.

"So pretty today," he remarked as she seated herself.

Her spirits lifted.

"For her future husband," he added with wicked glee, and her spirits sank.

Zhou Dan knew how she loathed the thought of getting married. Marriage meant less freedom, more duties. Giving herself over to a man who was practically a stranger. Zhou probably knew about her secrets more than anyone else in the house, just as she knew his.

"Is there an official invitation?" she asked as he maneuvered the carriage down the lane. "Are we entertaining a special guest today?

"Oh, no, not at all, young Lady Bai," he crowed. "We're just supposed to be ready just in case someone happens to stop by. Like maybe during the Monkey hour when business is slow. I'm supposed to bring you back before that, by the way."

"My mother," she snapped, which also conveniently doubled as a curse. She'd played into her mother's matchmaking plans by dressing nicely to visit her brother.

The carriage took her to the gates of the Imperial City where she noticed something had changed.

"More guards," she breathed.

Additional sentries had been placed around the wall. As the carriage approached, she could see the guards in the watchtower had their bows raised and arrows trained onto them. A chill ran down her spine.

"Our young lord works in a fortress," Zhou Dan whispered, impressed. "Is the Emperor inside?"

"There are at least two more fortifications before one could conceivably be in the presence of our Celestial Emperor," she asserted.

The northernmost part of Chang'an was a series of palaces within palaces as rulers for the last thousand years had vacated one home for another, building a more magnificent monument each time. Each shell a successive layer of armor shielding the imperial and aristocratic families from the rest of the populace.

The only armor she had was expensively tailored clothing and layers of etiquette. She lowered her eyes from the archers in the towers. Stare at them too long and they might think she looked suspicious.

The carriage came to a halt. When she stood, her sleeves nearly swept the ground. It was a status symbol, all that extra silk they could afford. The climb up the stairs leading to the gate was more of an ordeal this time. Small steps, lifting the hem of her robe, making the movements appear graceful.

Every eye was trained on her as she came to the gate. Even the structure itself seemed more imposing than she remembered, with spiked studs jutting out from it in a grid pattern. She was very much entering a fortress, but this time she was determined to be allowed inside.

She pulled the letter from the folds of her sleeve to present to the head guard. "Honorable Sirs, I have received a summons from Lord Bai Huang."

Her brother had given her the letter so she could get to him if she needed. Wei-wei figured this errand was warranted. There were only six days left before the Emperor demanded results.

The guard returned the letter, bowed, and then directed that the door be opened. It was a heavy affair, with two men taking hold of it from outside and another two from inside that were only revealed once she set foot into the complex. Her business was relayed to a runner and a functionary arrived shortly to escort her to Lord Bai.

This sight was common to her father and brother, but it was her first time inside the Imperial City. Formerly a palace, the complex now housed the most important administrative offices and bureaus of the Six Ministries. Her grandfather and her great-grandfather had worked here. Their family came from a long line of bureaucrats.

And now she was here as well, even if she couldn't sit for the civil exams or be placed in the Ministries.

The functionary brought her into the halls of the Secretariat. The department was responsible for drafting all imperial decrees. It was a highly revered function and required an entire bureau of scholars. Her brother supposedly held a minor position within the department in the records office.

She followed the attendant through a series of cells and studios until she saw Huang sitting behind his desk. Her Elder Brother, bureaucrat and secret censor. The attendant left her there with a final bow.

Now she could finally tell Huang what she'd discovered. She hurried forward, excitedly.

"General Lin Shidao," she declared, storming the confines of the office. "He has motive to move against Chancellor Yao. A year ago, Chancellor Yao oversaw the general's concession of two of his territories to imperial rule. Since then, there have been skirmishes in those areas. Thought to be bandits, but maybe they aren't lowly thieves—"

Why did Huang keep glancing behind her?

She turned and started at the sight of the gray-haired bureaucrat seated in the corner. She recognized the jutting chin and the long, groomed beard. Mortified, Wei-wei effected a hasty bow. "Chief Censor."

Zheng Shi tapped one long, well-manicured finger over his lips. "It's sound advice to lower one's voice"—he dropped to a whisper—"when accusing a military governor of treason."

She bowed once more. "Forgive this humble servant, Chief Censor. She does not yet know her proper place."

"Perhaps that is not a bad thing." Zheng slid a look over to Huang. "Young Lord Bai tells me you are assisting him as his secretary."

"Yes, Honorable Sir."

"The venerable Ban Zhao assisted her brother, the historian Ban Gu, in his scholarship. You follow in an exalted tradition."

She blushed. To be compared to female scholar Ban Zhao was the highest praise. "The Chief Censor is overly kind."

"Now, young Lady Bai was describing a fascinating theory. Perhaps she can speak further on it." He held up his hand to stop her before she began. "In more private quarters."

Zheng rose to his full, stately height. The first time she had met him, she'd assumed he had the advantage of looking down at her from atop the steps at the gate. Now she could see how he'd present an authorial figure speaking in front of an audience. He was dressed in dark burgundy and black, his rank denoted by the embroidered insignia around his belt. She would have to study up on those, the indicators of rank, if she were to spend more time in the imperial offices.

But that wouldn't be possible once she was married, she reminded herself. It was barely possible now. She feared she'd done irreparable damage to her brother with her accusations.

Zheng led the way while she and Huang filed in behind him.

"I'm sorry," she mouthed to Huang as they crossed paths into the hallway. She didn't know he was conversing with a superior.

He gave her a look that assured her there was nothing to worry about. She wasn't so sure. She watched the rigid wall of the chief censor's back as he took them to what seemed like an even deeper recess of the building. Not a word was spoken until they were enclosed inside the inner chamber. The space was sparsely furnished, with a woven mat in the center of the floor and several stools around a low table.

Zheng gestured toward the seats with a stretched hand. "Please."

She and Huang seated themselves beside one another while Zheng settled in across from them. Wei-wei waited for the bureaucrat to start the conversation. Now that he was involved, etiquette demanded that he control the exchange, but she was eager to continue revealing what she'd found.

"I would surmise that the young Lady Bai is aware of your position as a censor," he said to Huang.

"My sister is trustworthy. There is no one more loyal and dependable—"

Zheng stopped him. "You are in an unusual position, young Lord Bai. It would be expected that you will need to make decisions that are—shall we say—not in quite the usual order of things. The Emperor trusts your judgment in this matter and so must I."

Huang dipped his head to acknowledge the senior official's largess. She did the same, though inside her mind was racing. Could she have caused Huang to be dismissed? She had never considered the possibility — she was Bai Huang's younger sister who was nothing and nobody to the men he worked for. She'd have to be more careful from now on. It was harder to wander freely when one wasn't invisible.

"Now," Zheng went on pleasantly. "Young Lady Bai should continue."

She took a breath and pulled out the stack of papers tied with string from the pocket in her sleeve. "Chancellor Yao received many notices over the last year about skirmishes along the Huai river. There are many mentions of 'supply raids' and dismissed as the work of common thieves. The raids border General Lin's remaining commanderies. There's even a petition that insinuates the attacks are being sent from the general's lands."

"All this is true," Zheng confirmed. "However, one must remember that General Lin Shidao has openly declared his loyalty to the Emperor. He surrendered control of his commanderies as evidence of this. Though Chancellor Yao has been vocal about the growing power of the jiedushi, he had been very effective in negotiating a compromise."

"If compromise means surrendering land," she replied.

Huang jabbed her with his elbow. The chief censor raised his eyebrows at that.

"Still, young Lady Bai's conjectures have merit. Considering she has little exposure to the imperial court, her observations are quite astute." Zheng looked to Huang. "A shame that women are not allowed to take the civil exams. Once in a while, an exception certainly arises."

Wei-wei blushed. She never imagined a senior official would feel this way.

Zheng turned his attention back to her with a spark glinting in his eye. "The plot Lady Bai lays out is artfully constructed. Something I have spoken to young Lord Bai about extensively. When we investigate corruption, it is tempting to slot the pieces into something that is ordered and interlocking. The mind strives for harmony, does it not? But motives and actions are not always harmonious. When we seek out order, we may force inherently misshapen pieces together to enforce our own sense of well-being. And yet be no closer to the truth. This is why good scholars do not often make good censors. Too much poetry and worship of the social order."

Again, he looked to Huang. "I hear that Lord Bai Huang was a very poor scholar."

Huang ducked his head to hide his grin. Wei-wei was shocked to see that the chief censor truly liked her brother. He saw something in Huang, even with his imperfections and inconsistencies, that others, like their father, had always dismissed.

"This humble student recognizes the flaws in her theory," Wei-wei said, realizing she was probably speaking out of turn. "She had only hoped to provide a seed for more experienced persons to cultivate."

"Now there is the poet in the family," Zheng mused, wagging his finger at her.

She smiled, though it was forced politeness. Zheng Shi wasn't what she expected, but he was an imperial censor. He had to be watching and assessing every detail. If Huang was recruited as a censor because of his ability to get people to let down their guard, then it made sense that the chief censor might use the same approach. Zheng was steady and patient throughout the exchange, in contrast to her impertinence and eagerness.

The chief censor was akin to a spider. He didn't need to outwit or outmaneuver his foes. He just needed to wait them out.

Maybe Huang could learn from him. Maybe she could as well.

"If I may?" Zheng reached for the packet of papers as Huang gave his assent. She'd nearly spoken over her brother, forgetting the rules of status that governed her out in public. As her elder brother, Huang held the authority and would speak for her.

"I will leave brother and sister to say their farewells. Lord Bai, we shall discuss this shortly."

He rose and left the room so that it was only the two of them together.

"I'm so sorry," she said again. Wei-wei had been excited to have found something useful, but now she doubted herself after Zheng's lecture.

"The chief censor seems to respect your opinion, which is

good," Huang told her. "I've been looking inside, among the Emperor's advisers and inner council. I'm certain there was someone who knew of the Emperor and Chancellor Yao's meeting in order to coordinate the attack. There was a changing of the tower guard at an unusual time that morning. Not at the start of the hour. This is the work of someone close, maybe even within the imperial court."

"Do you think my suspicions of Lin Shidao are far-fetched then? Pinglu circuit is a long distance away from Chang'an and imperial politics."

"No one who wields that much power is ever that far away," Huang countered, sounding entirely unlike the brother she knew. She was starting to see him with new eyes. "But there's something that Zheng didn't tell you. In addition to surrendering two of his commanderies, General Lin also sent one of his sons as hostage to the imperial court as a sign of loyalty."

She was aghast. "His own child? How barbaric!"

"It's a common practice. Princes and lords come to stay at the imperial court under the Emperor's charge as assurance against rebellion. They're treated quite well."

She still didn't understand the practice. "If the General refuses to obey him, the Emperor will have the child executed?"

"I don't think it's ever occurred. It's just a formality. And Lin Shidao's son isn't a child. Yijin is his third son. He must be nineteen, maybe twenty by now. And he's not truly a prisoner. He goes around the city with an armed guard detail."

"How do you know all this?"

Huang shrugged. "We used to drink together. Lin Yijin likes his Ancient Well Liquor probably a little too much. Expensive, high quality stuff. If you get too close to him, his guards will hassle you."

Wei-wei stared at her brother, unblinking.

"My one talent," he reminded her with a half grin.

Her theory was looking weaker by the moment. What man would move against the empire when his own son was in danger? A third son was still flesh and blood. "I'll keep looking through Chancellor Yao's papers," she said, trying not to sound defeated.

"We will look closely at General Lin," Huang assured. "We'll look at everyone. We have to. There are only six days left."

What would happen then? Punishments, demotions? Or worse—Huang predicted that there would be another move against the empire. If the first target had been Chancellor Yao, then the next could very well be the Emperor. She didn't even dare say it aloud.

There had been no official proclamation about the Chancellor's assassination. Even the rumors were muted. More guards patrolling the streets. News of some kind of unrest outside on the Yanxi gate that was quickly contained, even though that was far from the truth. Her neighbors hadn't heard of it, and even Gao was unaware.

Gao. He had been looking into the death by the canal without knowing there was another, more shocking murder looming over the city. She'd considered bringing up the chancellor's assassination to Gao when they'd last spoken, but Huang had insisted that his position as a censor remain secret. After that, she…

She had been distracted. Gao had kissed her. She'd kissed him back and had promptly forgotten everything about jade seals and dark conspiracies. The only thing she'd been clear on was that she absolutely did not want to married off to Li Chen.

A gong sounded the hour—the Hour of the Goat. Next would be the Monkey Hour which meant it was time for her to go home to prepare for special guests that evening.

"There's one other thing," she brought up.

Huang waited.

Wei-wei blew out a breath. "Elder Brother, I need your assistance in a small matter regarding a betrothal."

Huang straightened. "What do you need?"

"I would like for it not to happen."

A pained look flickered across her brother's face and her stomach sank. "Mother's already convinced you?"

His look of pain intensified. So did the knots in her stomach. "Huang, you didn't—"

"I was trying to help you, Wei-wei. You helped arranged my marriage to Yue-ying. I thought, as your brother, I should do the same."

"But you love Yue-ying!" she protested. "You were pining for her."

He didn't deny it. "And Li Chen is a good match for you."

"You don't—" She stopped, lowering her voice. "You don't even like Magistrate Li."

"He passed the palace exams at eighteen years—"

"You think he's smug and superior."

"He was appointed magistrate of eastern Chang'an at twenty-seven years of age."

"You know I don't want to get married!"

Huang sighed but continued listing what he considered to be Li Chen's qualities.

"He's not too old. He lives close. You wouldn't have to move far away from our family. He's the best choice."

Oh, she could hit her brother. "I helped you so you could marry the woman that *you* chose, Huang."

He exhaled, looking defeated. "Wei-wei, you would have never chosen anyone. All you wanted was to have your way, no matter what. It can't be that way forever."

She touched her hand to her wrist. She could feel the

bracelet that Gao had given her, hidden beneath her sleeve. That's where it would have to remain. Hidden.

She had never had a suitor or even an admirer before. Her life had been devoted to bringing honor to her family. She'd never had a choice—so how could she ever have chosen?

CHAPTER 10

Wei-wei sat on the chaise in the salon with her hands folded neatly in her lap. Opposite her, an extremely long arm's length away, sat Magistrate Li Chen. He was in a dark robe the color of cherrywood with his topknot fixed with a silver pin. She'd never seen Li in anything besides his official uniform. The everyday clothing made him appear younger.

Mother and Madame Li were chattering away in the next room. She could hear them bantering about as if they were old friends. Wei-wei and Li Chen had been purposefully left alone, with the onerous task of becoming acquainted.

"Lady Bai."

She glanced up expectantly.

"It has been a while since we last spoke," Li said.

"It's only been two days," she pointed out.

Wei-wei half expected him to say something to the effect of how two days had been an eternity, but he didn't. This wasn't a romantic courtship. An arranged marriage was more between their families than the two of them.

She took consolation that this couldn't be the official

engagement party. Her brother was still at his office and Father wasn't scheduled to be home until the end of the week. Surely, as the head of their family, Father would need to be present. It would involve tradition and ceremony and the exchanging of gifts. An astrologer would be consulted in order to assign an auspicious date for a betrothal.

Wei-wei considered bribing the astrologer to select a day a long way out.

Li Chen picked up the tea bowl from the side table and took a sip, then set it down. All with very deliberate, very methodical movements while biding time.

They both spoke at once:

"I hear you enjoy poetry."

"Did you identify the victim?"

Li blinked at her. "Umm, the victim," he began uncertainly.

"The one who was carrying the jade seal."

"Well, uh…it's not appropriate to discuss such matters—"

"I was the one who brought in the seal," she reminded him.

Madame Li's laughter rang out from the other room. The mothers would have a fit if they knew what was being discussed in here.

Wei-wei waited, refusing to waver.

Li scrubbed a hand along the side of his neck. "I submitted the chop to imperial authorities for examination. It wasn't genuine after all."

"It was a forgery?"

"Yes. Correct."

He took another drink of tea. A long drink this time, glancing quickly toward the other room as if searching for a rescue.

"Did you identify who the victim was?" she pressed.

"Likely a counterfeiter. Certainly, a serious crime, but there are many cases that require greater attention."

He was lying and he was bad at it. She would think that a magistrate such as Li Chen, who spent his days reading others and discerning truth from falsehoods, would be better at hiding the truth. Two days ago, he had acted as if the case was critical. Now he seemed no longer interested in even investigating the crime.

"Forging an imperial seal is a high crime, is it not?"

He shifted uncomfortably. "Perhaps we should speak of other things, Lady Bai."

They fell silent once more. Mother had spent the previous hour drowning Wei-wei with praise for Li Chen. His rise through the ranks of the imperial bureaucracy, his good family name. He was a distant relation of the Emperor even. All of this was very important to her family, but all Wei-wei could think of were the long stretches of silence between them. Days and the nights of civil nothingness. It was possible to eventually find some semblance of harmony. She'd seen her mother and father move quietly around one another, shaping the landscape of their marriage gradually like wind and water over rock.

"Once you are married," she began carefully, "would you discuss such matters with your wife?"

"When I take a wife..." He licked his lips, swallowing nervously. The mention of marriage appeared to be as uncomfortable for him as it was for her. "I imagine such talk would not foster harmony in the home. It's important to keep such things separated, public duty and private matters."

It all sounded like duty to her, public or private.

"More tea?" she asked.

"Yes."

She called for one of the servants to bring tea. Then they sat, marking the minutes.

Li Chen was highly educated and an accomplished imperial scholar. She was well-read in history, poetry and philosophy. Certainly, they both had plenty of things to say.

Just not to one another.

She breathed a sigh of relief when it was time for their families to sit down for supper.

"Poor Magistrate Li, stuck here with a bunch of women," Mother teased as she directed Madame Li and her son to the dining salon.

"Not at all," he said with a small laugh. "It's an honor."

"My husband is expected back in the city by the end of this week," Mother continued, more by way of appointment than apology.

"Not so long then." Madame Li exchanged a knowing glance with Mother while Wei-wei hid a scowl.

Mother shot her a warning look, which meant her scowl was not hidden well enough.

Huang was conspicuously absent and Chang-min was deemed too young to stand in for his older brother. This left only Yue-ying and Mother along with Wei-wei herself to entertain the Li family. Mother had placed Yue-ying immediately next to the magistrate at the circular table with Wei-wei beside her. She was grateful that her sister-in-law was there to provide a buffer as the servants brought out individual plates of leek dumplings and goose stew with radishes.

"My eldest son couldn't be with us," Mother apologized. "Unfortunately, he is occupied with his duties in the records office."

"Oh, this one too," Madame Li said. "He is barely home. Even at night."

"There have been many urgent cases recently," Li Chen murmured. He lifted his gaze to meet Wei-wei's.

She looked away quickly, remembering how surprised he'd been to see her at his office. She lifted her porcelain spoon to poke at a boiled radish. Li had probably known about his mother's matchmaking intentions at that time.

"It has been quite a change living here in the northeastern quadrant," Yue-ying admitted. Her marriage to Huang had brought her into their household over a year ago. "It's so much quieter here. In Pingkang, there was always something happening late into the evening."

"And not good things," Madame Li chimed in with a frown.

"Mother," Li Chen admonished beneath his breath. He left the sentiment unfinished.

"I wish you didn't spend so much time there."

"My responsibilities require it," he replied.

"The dumplings are quite delicious," Yue-ying interjected, not with quite the grace or training of her sister.

"And the goose is infused with ginseng root," Mother said pleasantly. "Very warming for the circulation."

Wei-wei rarely saw her Mother in such a charming mood. The prospect of her stubborn daughter finally being matched seemed to lift her spirits. Wei-wei didn't want to begrudge her mother that happiness. If only she didn't actually have to get married to make Mother happy.

The rest of the meal finished amiably enough. The two mothers bantered back and forth. Wei-wei and Li Chen answered when spoken to. Mother expounded upon Li Chen's accomplishments as the county magistrate. Madame Li had nothing but compliments for Wei-wei.

The inevitability of the betrothal pressed down like an iron weight. The mothers had already decided. The rest was a mere formality. Wei-wei counted the days left before her father was to return. Was he returning specifically for this? Her formal engagement? She had only days of freedom left.

Unless his party was beset upon by brigands.

No, what an unhappy thought! She loved her father.

After the meal was done, Li Chen apologized for having to depart so early. Evening was just starting to come, but he had some case work to get back to.

"How very commendable," Mother said.

Wei-wei made some excuse to retire to her room, which was the reason she was the only one around when Madame Li and her son stepped outside to the courtyard garden. She ducked into the study to avoid having to carry on any awkward conversation.

"Again?" Madame Li scolded under her breath. "Three nights now. You're to be married soon."

Married. That word again. Wei-wei felt it like a rock in the pit of her stomach.

"It's not that," Li Chen replied in an uncharacteristically harsh tone which told Wei-wei immediately what "that" was. She was also convinced that it was indeed "that".

"What will our new relations think...?"

She couldn't hear the rest. The two had moved away. When Wei-wei peeked out from the study, Mother was leading them to the front gate to see them off. Wei-wei waited until they were clearly gone before going to seek out Zhou Dan. He was in the kitchen and looked to have just finished his evening meal.

"Did you speak to their servant?" she asked.

"We spoke for a while," he replied with a grin that indicated Li's carriage driver might have had a few things to say.

$\sim$

THE STREET WAS DIMLY LIT, a lone lantern hanging from a post at the corner. Gao was stationed at the corner with no particular purpose other than to watch the doors. He knew which ones opened into the illicit gambling dens and brothels of the northern lanes. The night patrols likely knew as well, but Hui bribed them to move along.

Gao was expecting an uneventful night. He'd lend an imposing presence around Hui's establishments, listen for any gossip around the night soil collectors who had been detained. It was all going to be routine—

Until a young aristocrat in a garishly lavish robe appeared before him.

"Heavenly Peaches," stated Wei-wei, or rather, stated Wei-wei dressed in men's clothing.

It was an outfit her elder brother Huang had worn when he frequented the pleasure quarter. With the bright blue and green pattern, it was reminiscent of a strutting peacock, which Bai Huang had done a good job of emulating in his day. Wei-wei brought her own sort of assertiveness to the costume. The Bais truly were shameless. They walked the street as if they owned it, which certainly lent to Wei-wei's disguise as a young lord out on the town.

Gao remained where he was, arms folded over his chest as he leaned against the wall. "What are you doing out here alone?"

"I'm not alone," she said impatiently. "You're here."

"How did you get here?"

"I took the horse from our stable."

He'd encountered her out in the quarter after dark before, exploring the forbidden reaches of the night city, but he was surprised at the frequency. Her brother had a gambling habit. Perhaps Wei-wei had her own form of addiction.

"No one notices?" he questioned. "Your family won't cry thief or call the city patrols?"

"Everyone's asleep."

"Really?"

"Zhou Dan takes care of the stable and he has a girl he's in love with he likes to visit. I cover for him; he covers for me."

One had to admire her resourcefulness. "Hui should hire you to extort money for him. You might be good at it."

Wei-wei gave him an impatient look. "The House of Heavenly Peaches," she reminded.

"I know of it."

She pulled away, confident that he would follow. Gao pushed off the wall a moment later. Of course, he was going with her. Wei-wei grew bolder every time she ventured out, but she was far from knowledgeable about the city. Hui's gambling den would have to survive without his presence for the night.

"I'm afraid of you, Wei-wei," he said, catching up to her. It was a way of saying he admired her—and maybe a little fear was warranted. "The House of Heavenly Peaches is a pleasure house."

"I thought so from the name."

"One of the big ones."

"Like the Lotus Palace?"

"They're rivals."

She had pulled her hair up into a tight topknot which accentuated the contours of her chin and jawline. He could see the resemblances between brother and sister very clearly, in both appearance and manner. Gao had called her pretty, but really, she was beautiful. There was a proud confidence in how she held herself. She truly believed that roads would clear for her and doors would open.

"Why are we going there?" he asked.

"Li Chen." Her lips tightened around the name.

"Popular man."

"You've seen him?"

"He was here in the pleasure quarter last night."

Gao hadn't yet told her of his arrangement with Magistrate Li and how they had set up the night soil collectors.

Something he'd mentioned seemed to strengthen her resolve. She moved quicker.

They reached the main square with the House of Heavenly Peaches standing at the far end. Wei-wei ducked into the soup stand across from the courtesan house and took a seat on a wooden bench. The soup seller started toward them but Gao warded him away with a look before sitting down beside her. They were facing the doors of the pleasure house.

"It appears there's some sort of gathering there tonight," Wei-wei observed.

Across the lane, the lanterns were lit and every window thrown open. Soft, warm light and music drifted out into the street.

"It's not unusual for a man like the magistrate to frequent Pingkang li," he said. "You know, he asked about you."

Her head turned sharply. "Magistrate Li? What did he say?"

"He asked how I knew you."

"What did you say?"

He shrugged. "I don't remember."

Wei-wei appeared skeptical, but he didn't want to recount how Li Chen thought of him as her servant. That rankled more than it should have.

"Li should be here soon," she said, turning her attention back to the Heavenly Peaches. "He left right before me, but he would have had to return home first."

"You followed him here?"

"Magistrate Li is hiding something and I don't trust him," she insisted, her eyes flashing. "He came to our house as a guest and lied about the jade seal."

Magistrate Li dining at the Bai mansion. The thought was a punch to the gut. "What did he say?"

"That the seal was fake and he was too busy to be bothered with that case any longer."

Gao snorted. "A hundred taels of silver tells a different story."

She stared at him. "A hundred taels?"

"That's the bounty for whoever catches the killer. Li also enlisted an army of constables to take two witnesses into custody last night."

"How do you know that?"

"Because I was with him."

She fell silent, pondering the information. He found her even more intriguing dressed in men's clothing. Maybe it was sentimentality on his part. This was how Wei-wei had looked the first time he'd seen her.

Gao was tempted to speak ill of Li Chen, as if that would give him any chance, but in the end, he needed to be honest with her. And with himself.

"Wei-wei, Li Chen is working hard on this case. He's dedicated to solving it—so much so that he'd listen to a scoundrel like me. I have a feeling he lied to try to shield you from unpleasantness. That's the proper thing to do. That's what I should do."

She looked downward. Her lashes appeared impossibly long in the shadows. When had he ever noticed a thing like eyelashes before?

"When are we going to talk about it?" she asked softly.

"Talk about what?"

"Yesterday. That was the first time I've ever...done that."

He knew what she was speaking of and his body knew, tightening at the mere memory. Her eyes had been red and swollen and he'd still found her tempting. Her lips had been so warm.

"The second time," he argued. "The first time you were sitting on a crate, by a street vendor selling pastries." He could still smell the warm honey.

She did not like being contradicted. "That wasn't the first time. That was only an attempt. A failed one."

"I didn't think you remembered."

Wei-wei fell silent.

He wanted very much for the next time to be right now, even if it was only an attempt. He swallowed, his chest ready to burst. From the corner of his eye, he saw Li Chen entering the pleasure house.

"There he is," he said with a tilt of his head.

She turned to look, leaving him with the graceful curve of her neck and he was awash with regret. He wanted to go on this adventure with her, just for the sake of being with her, but that would be foolish.

"Wei-wei, you're out here alone, and it's after curfew. You need to get home."

"I have a ward pass," she insisted.

"The streets here are not a safe place at night. You know that."

She let out a breath. "I don't trust him, Gao. He's hiding something."

"Or you're overly eager to see something sinister in his motives because you don't want to be married."

Her jaw set stubbornly. "That's not true."

She really didn't like not getting her way.

"I don't like the man either, but at least I know why."

"Why?" she demanded.

He locked eyes with her. "Because I wish I could be him."

"No, you don't."

"And you know why."

She blinked back sudden tears. "This has nothing to do with all that."

"It's not the worst thing in the world, marrying a rich and powerful man." He meant to sound reasonable, but it came out bitter. "You'll be cared for. Li probably has a thousand books. You'll have all the things you desire."

"Not all the things," she said quietly.

Whenever she needed to act out, she always came running here. Running to him. This is why the wealthy were drawn to the Pingkang li. To throw themselves into oblivion. And the scavengers in the pleasure houses and gambling dens were waiting to profit. Scavengers like him.

"I'll take you home, Wei-wei."

She looked to the upper floors of the pleasure house where Magistrate Li had disappeared. Red lanterns swung invitingly from the eaves and laughter rang from inside. Patrons continued to stream in.

"This is a chance to find out who Li Chen really is," she insisted, her jaw set.

"Wei-wei—" he warned.

"We can go in together."

He barked out a laugh.

Her eyes flashed with anger. "*Fine*. I'll go in alone."

She sprang to her feet and marched toward the House of Heavenly Peaches. Gao watched as she crossed the courtyard with an impressively cocksure stride. But she still didn't look remotely like a man. At least not to his eyes. On top of that, her name wasn't known there. She didn't have an introduction. He waited for her to be turned away.

Wei-wei reached the entrance. A hostess greeted her at the door. She would be coming back any moment now.

On the other hand, she had the clothes. She certainly had the attitude. The pleasant manners.

He shook his head and swore as the conversation went on. Then the hostess smiled brightly and beckoned Wei-wei inside.

CHAPTER 11

Wei-wei tried not to look too wide-eyed as she passed through the curtains into the pleasure house. It was like passing through clouds into another realm. The interior was lit as bright as day with rosy lanterns in every corner. Across from the entrance, a brush painting spanned the entire wall depicting the Peach Blossom Spring, an idyllic land where the ground was covered with petals. As the fable went, a forest of peach trees hid the mythical heaven on earth from the outside world.

She was taken in by the opulence. The sitting room was decorated with lacquered wood and pink curtains. It was a place of perpetual song and beauty, just like the story went.

A courtesan immediately took her arm. "Sparrow hasn't seen you here before, my lord," she cooed, settling in comfortably against Wei-wei's side.

The girl, presumably Sparrow, was younger than Wei-wei. Maybe sixteen years of age. She was dressed in a soft yellow silk with green accents and her lips were painted into a red cherry blossom-shaped pout. She looked like a painting herself.

"The Peach Blossom Spring is famously difficult to find," Wei-wei replied. She thought the analogy clever enough. As a young scholar, she would be trying to impress, right?

Sparrow laughed, emitting a sound like the tinkling of bells. "What's your name, my lord?"

"I'm called Bai Chang-min, Pretty Sparrow."

Guilt pricked at her like little needles. Hopefully her younger brother would never find out how she was misusing his name.

The girl affected a blush. Wei-wei didn't know why Gao was so worried. This was easy so far.

"Let's explore," she suggested to Sparrow.

Sparrow had taken full possession of her. Arm-in-arm, the young courtesan led her up to the second level of the pleasure house. The ascent up the stairs gave Wei-wei a chance to search through the crowd.

"Is young Lord Bai visiting the capital?"

"Oh no, Chang'an is my home."

"Then why haven't you come to visit me?" she scolded.

"I'll be certain to come more often."

Not so hard once one got the rhythm of it. It was easy— all wordplay and no real meaning. No wonder scholars liked this place.

"Are you looking for someone?" Sparrow noticed how she was looking about.

"A friend," Wei-wei said. "He drinks here frequently."

"What is this friend's name? Perhaps I can find him for you."

"But we're having such a pleasant conversation here."

Wei-wei thought against volunteering too much information. She needed to stay somewhat hidden if she wanted to find out more information about Magistrate Li. Wei-wei managed to maneuver them to a seat in the corner. Sparrow called for wine to be brought.

The banquet was gathering around the center of the second floor where several large parties clustered together. Wei-wei searched through them, but still no sight of Li.

"We should play a game," Sparrow said, sensing that Wei-wei's interest was starting to wander.

"What game?" she replied absently. She'd finally found Li. He'd claimed to have a gathering to attend tonight, but he had moved to an adjoining salon for a private sitting. She spied him through an open doorway, speaking to a woman. Unlike the other courtesans who seemed to favor bright colors, Li's companion presented a starkly elegant figure in black, interlaced with a leaf pattern in silver thread. A bright vermilion sash accented her waist.

Wei-wei started as Sparrow ran a manicured finger down her arm.

"It's a guessing game," Sparrow explained. The wine had arrived and she filled a cup for Wei-wei. "I get three chances to guess a secret about you."

Wei-wei's pulse pounded. Had she been discovered? "I have no secrets."

In the salon, the courtesan had risen to face Li. Her demeanor held a cool detachment.

"We'll see," Sparrow teased. "You are afraid of spiders."

"No."

Little Sparrow really was charming and easy to be around. And extremely self-assured for someone so young. Wei-wei could see how Lady Mingyu became who she was after being trained in a house such as this one.

Sparrow was certainly making an effort of it. Unfortunately, Wei-wei had other motives. She looked around the room at the gathering banquet. Scholars and officials visited houses like these for entertainment, but also to make connections and feed their own reputations. The courtesans facilitated the exchange while singing and dancing around them.

"You have ten brothers."

"No, only two."

Wei-wei glanced again toward Li Chen and his courtesan to find that they had pulled the curtain completely closed.

"I only have one try left. What could I possibly guess now?"

While she was distracted, Sparrow had inched closer. "You're ticklish!" she guessed, pouncing.

Wei-wei managed to catch the courtesan by the wrists, but Sparrow had no intention of backing down. Wei-wei struggled to escape while the girl laughed at the sport of it.

"Alright, you win," Wei-wei said, working to keep her at arm's length.

"Don't you like me?" Sparrow asked, pouting.

These games no longer suited her. "Yes, I like you. Now here's my game. You tell me a secret."

Sparrow narrowed her eyes craftily. "*We* don't tell secrets."

"Then tell me something everyone knows but me. That gentleman in the salon over there. Has he been here before?"

"Do I get a reward for winning our last game?"

"You didn't win."

"I did. You *are* ticklish."

Brat. "Fine. What do you want?"

"Promise to come see me again."

"I promise."

Sparrow batted her eyes. "And bring a gift."

Wei-wei was beginning to see what it might have been like if she had a younger sister. "Of course, a gift."

Sparrow sat back on the seat, smoothing out her hair. "He's been here several times this week, but if you want to be introduced, it will be difficult. He only speaks to Song Yi and he pays not to be disturbed. They'll talk for exactly one hour and then he leaves. He doesn't even want to hear her play a song or anything else."

Her potential future husband was having an affair with a courtesan. Was that enough reason to convince her family to decry the match? Of course not. It was barely even scandalous.

Wei-wei regretted their situation even more. Maybe Li Chen held some genuine feeling for this woman. He didn't want to marry Wei-wei any more than she wanted to marry him.

Maybe Gao was right. She wanted so desperately to find some way to escape that she'd run here, to the pleasure quarter, looking to catch Li Chen in some bit of scandal.

She was spoiled. Used to having her way. Wei-wei had even managed to make things work out for Huang. Her brother had been betrothed to someone else, but Wei-wei still found a way for him to marry Yue-ying. The sun rose and set for her, but not this time.

"Lord Bai, you look so sad all of the sudden. Are you in love with Song Yi as well?"

Wei-wei blinked at her. "As well?"

"The magistrate isn't the only admirer who has been demanding her time lately."

"Who's the other admirer?"

Suddenly, she straightened. "A courtesan must always be discreet."

Wei-wei frowned. Something must have clipped Sparrow's wings. The girl made an excuse about fetching more wine before rising to hurry away.

"Don't be too disappointed. I hear a courtesan's interest can be fickle."

She looked up to see Gao standing over her, a hawk hunting among the chickens.

"You scared her away," she accused.

Gao lowered himself beside her, his long legs jutting awkwardly from the low padded seat. His head arched slowly from left to right, taking in the surroundings.

"How did you get in?"

"I just walked in."

His reception was probably not as welcoming as it had been for her, given he didn't have a courtesan hanging on his arm.

"Have you uncovered some sinister plot?" he asked wryly.

Now that Gao was here, she remembered half the reason she'd stormed inside. He'd made her angry with his entirely rational outlook on the situation.

"Sinister indeed. The magistrate is enamored with a beautiful courtesan who he longs to spend time with. But because of his upbringing and class, he's fated to marry someone like me."

"You are well-matched for one another," he remarked, his voice strained.

She slumped down, defeated. "Don't say that."

Gao leaned forward, bringing him eye to eye with her. "Are you hoping to get caught?"

Was she? She looked downward, staring at her hands. "Everyone in our house has been trained to look the other way because of my brother. Huang was always getting into so much trouble, but servants aren't supposed to question their young lord. Meanwhile, Wei-wei was the dutiful daughter. She never did anything out of place."

"She was just too clever to get caught," Gao countered.

Wei-wei glanced up to see his half-smile. Something lifted inside her. Gao knew all her secrets. With him, she couldn't hide. She didn't have to.

"We should go before Magistrate Li recognizes you," he suggested. "I have a feeling he won't look the other way."

Maybe that was exactly what she wanted. To be just as unsuitable for Magistrate Li as Gao was for her. But it was thoughtless and reckless and wouldn't free her in the way she wanted. Mother would stop turning a blind eye. It would hasten Huang's need to see her married off, now that the bad son had become the good son.

Suddenly, everything was wrong and out of place. She was wearing her brother's garish robe while surrounded by perfume and pink curtains. Gao was the only part that made sense, his solid, silent and disapproving presence. He was the only one who dared to tell her she was on the wrong path. And he was right—she needed to go.

She nodded to Gao, and they stood to head for the stairs. They'd almost made it there when a very sharp, very drunk voice cut through the din of the banquet hall.

"Ancient Well Baijiu!" the drunkard railed. "Nothing else is worth drinking. Go fetch…go fetch some from the palace if they're out."

"Ancient Well," she murmured.

"What is it?" Gao asked.

A large banquet had gathered at the center of the room. There was a young man of around twenty years; top-knot disheveled, and swaying slightly on his feet. Two bodyguards stood on either side of him. They weren't outfitted in imperial armor, but they carried swords and certainly had the menacing look of hardened men. Most of the courtesans of the House of Heavenly Peaches had attached themselves to the party while the bodyguards stood apart, keeping a watchful eye on their charge.

"Friend!" the drunken nobleman cried out. "You, over there."

She tried to shrink back, but there was nowhere to hide.

"I know you!"

Wei-wei considered running away. Reluctantly, she

turned around and sensed Gao doing the same behind her. His hand settled between her shoulder blades, but she didn't know if it was in reassurance or a warning.

"You look familiar," the young man drawled, beckoning her forward. "Come on over here."

What choice did they have?

"Who is this?" Gao asked beneath his breath as they moved forward.

The distinctive choice of drink. The pair of armed guards.

"It's Lin Yijin," she muttered.

The feast Magistrate Li Chen had been invited to was hosted by the hostage son of General Lin Shidao.

~

BY THE TIME they joined the party, someone had brought a jug of the Ancient Well spirits. Two serving girls were making the rounds to fill everyone's cups, and Wei-wei was at a loss for how they could courteously remove themselves.

Lin Yijin craned his neck upward, staring at Gao.

"Your bodyguard keeps a pretty close watch, eh? I've got a pair myself." He indicated the two stone-faced warrior figures flanking him. "Hard to have a good time with them around."

Yet he seemed to manage. The two guards were outfitted with leather armor and an assortment of swords and daggers in their belts. Weapons aside, they looked large enough to crush a man with their bare hands.

"My elder brother used to drink with you," Wei-wei offered, hoping that would clear things up quickly so they could go.

"Who's your brother?"

"Bai Huang."

"Ah, the flower prince himself!" Yijin gushed. He staggered forward to slap her on the back. The two guardsmen straightened, coming to attention. Huang had warned her about how watchful they were.

"The flower prince," she echoed. "That sounds like my brother."

"What's your name, friend?"

"Bai Chang-min," she replied, hoping her younger brother's reputation was still intact when it was his turn to frequent the Pingkang li.

Yijin hooked an arm around her neck to drag her close. "It's fate that we should meet like this."

She staggered as he hung his full weight on her. Gao moved to separate her from his grasp, which made Lin Yijin's guards start forward. She shot a look at Gao to urge him back.

"That wolf would steal all the girls with that face of his," Yijin recalled with a laugh. "You know, you're even prettier than him—"

Even in his less than flattering drunken state, the young nobleman was startlingly handsome. So much that Wei-wei found him uncomfortable to look at. It was impossible not to stare. She found it even more uncomfortable that the young man was draped around her while Gao stood beside them. Gao's expression darkened with each passing moment.

Yijin pressed his face so close that he became one large eye in her field of view. "So, what did you come here to tell me?"

She was at a loss. "You invited us over—"

"Come now, don't be like this. What's the message?"

One of the bodyguards had tolerated Lin Yijin's antics for long enough. He came forward and wedged a leather-clad arm between the two of them. "You! Stand back!"

Wei-wei stumbled backward into Gao. His hands tightened over her shoulders to steady her, and she could feel the tension coiled within him, ready to spring.

"It's nothing," she insisted, bracing against Gao to hold him back.

He froze as their bodies pressed close. Wei-wei's heart was suddenly beating too hard, too fast.

"Don't be such a grouch to our new friends," Lin Yijin complained to the bodyguard. "Here, peace offering."

He reached for a cup and held it out to her, sloshing half of the contents out as he did so. Wei-wei took it warily. This caper had gotten completely out of hand. Was this the sort of crowd her brother had consorted with in his student days?

Lin grabbed another cup and was about to drink before he saw how Gao was empty-handed. With a great show of generosity, the general's son handed over his own cup, presenting it to Gao with two hands. He then searched through the crowd to procure another one.

"All in!" he toasted, raising his cup.

Wei-wei looked to Gao. He met her gaze before draining the spirits in one swallow. She went through the motions, but opted to toss the spirits over her shoulder. She wasn't going to drink some unknown liquor just because it had been handed to her.

Lin Yijin downed his drink, then started gesturing dramatically with the empty cup. "What is freedom, but a dream? These walls? A cage..."

Gao stared at him as if the young man had gone mad. "What is he doing?" Gao asked out of the corner of his mouth.

Wei-wei backed them up a few steps so Yijin wouldn't overhear.

"He's composing poetry," she said, cringing.

Gao pressed a hand to his face. "This is what rich people do?"

This was, indeed, what rich people did.

She tried to explain. "At some point someone is supposed to take over and compose the next verse. It's like a...a competition."

"Every breath, a price!" Lin Yijin lamented.

Over Lin's shoulder, Wei-wei caught sight of a tall gray-haired figure emerging from the stairway.

"The death of me," she muttered.

She spun away and hastily buried herself behind a pink curtain. Maybe Chief Censor Zheng hadn't seen her.

Someone approached while she flattened herself against the wall. She peered through the opening in the gauze to see Gao watching her.

"I can't fit behind that, Lord Bai," he said dryly.

She hushed him. "Don't use my name."

"I assume your old friend is someone we need to avoid."

Gao must have seen Zheng speaking to her at the gates of the Imperial City.

"Zheng Shi is a censor. Actually, he's the Chief Censor. I can't let him see me. Do you think he's seen me?"

"No, which is quite remarkable"—he looked her up and down through the part of the curtain—"considering."

"Where is he?" she asked, feeling something akin to panic.

"At the other side of the room and paying attention to the banquet."

The chief censor might have come to investigate Lin Yijin after Wei-wei had cast suspicion on his father.

"Walk to the stairs," she instructed Gao. "I'll stay close and hide behind you."

Gao did so with an easy stride and a sense of calm that she envied. She, on the other hand, scurried beside him while using Gao as a shield. They reached the stairs, and she descended quickly, holding her breath until she was clear of the pleasure house. The night air surrounded them.

"Strange night," Gao remarked.

How did he stay so calm? His face didn't register any sign of fear or even worry. Nothing fazed him, while her entire body shook from the nerves. She dragged Gao into the nearest alleyway.

"Very strange night," he repeated, his voice catching.

She glanced up at him to see him watching her, his look dark and unreadable. The sky overhead glowed with the pale light of the moon, and the silent lane was a soothing contrast to the noisy and brightly lit pleasure house. They were alone now, cocooned in darkness. A wave swelled up inside her, lifting her.

Rising onto her toes, she reached for Gao, her hands finding purchase against his shoulders. He was solid and unyielding as she leaned against him. For just a moment, fear pierced into her thoughts, but she fought past it. With her heart pounding hard, she pressed her lips to his.

It was both a second and an eternity before Gao returned her kiss. She sank against him, surrendering herself.

She'd lost her first kiss to him and now her second. She would gladly lose all the kisses if this was how it would feel each time. It wasn't merely the touching of lips, of mouths. Inside she was soaring. A hundred years swept by in seconds.

Suddenly she remembered she was wearing men's clothes. She plucked at the robe. "Does this feel very strange?"

"No." They were kissing again, his hands circling the small of her back.

Wei-wei was unschooled when it came to matters between men and women. She wouldn't have believed there could be anything more than this, anything better until Gao urged her lips apart with his own. And then his tongue was inside her mouth, hungry. A tendril of pleasure snaked down to the pit of her stomach. She could taste him too, and the sharp bite of liquor from an ancient well.

Her knees trembled, but Gao held her. She was vibrating. So restless, like she would jump out of her skin and the only thing that could keep her together was Gao's arms around her. Holding on to her as tight as he could.

"How can you be like this yet say things like Li and I are well-matched for one another?" she asked desperately. Just echoing his words sent pain to her heart.

"Because our bodies are made to do this." He pressed closer. "This is meant to confuse you."

Her shoulder blades came up against the wall as Gao pinned himself to her. She knew this was impossible. Because of birth and class. Who she was and who he wasn't. Wei-wei wrapped her arms around his neck to keep him there and she kissed him again, hungry. It wouldn't be like this with anyone else, her heart insisted. Not Li Chen, not anyone.

Gao sensed the rising urgency within her and groaned, a low sound deep in his throat.

He broke away. "Wei-wei." His voice was strained. "Look at where we are."

She could only look up at him. In the darkness, he was pure shape and shadow. She would know the angled contours of his face anywhere.

"Are you confused about this?" she challenged.

He didn't answer. Only shook his head once, not looking at her.

"Then why do you insist I am?"

If he said because she was young, because she was a woman, because she was *innocent,* she didn't know what she'd do. Maybe hit him. As if never kissing someone made one suddenly *so* innocent. And she wasn't that young anymore either.

He didn't say any of those things. His arms tightened around her for a long time before he pressed a kiss to the center of her forehead.

"Please let me see you home," he said.

She did let him. Gao so rarely asked her for anything.

CHAPTER 12

Gao accompanied Wei-we back to her ward. The horse was strong enough to carry both of them at a slow, steady gait. Wei-wei rode behind him in the saddle, her ear pressed against his back. His voice sounded deep, vibrating from within him as he told her more about his life.

He'd grown up near the wall of the East Market. His family had lived in a decent house with five rooms and a small courtyard. Then his crooked father had been arrested for taking bribes. The magistrate had handed down the harshest sentence, stripping Gao's father of his appointment and banishing him from the capital. And that had been the end of everything.

"Another magistrate, of course. Not the Magistrate Li we know."

At the mention of Li Chen, gloom fell over her.

It was as if Gao was trying to tell her—see, see how bad I am, from bad blood? But she was so hungry to know more about him. Was she truly so good? Or from good blood?

They spoke of other things too, taking their time as the

horse carried them back to the mansions of the northeastern section.

They reached the gate of the Bai mansion while it was still dark. The city was under mandatory curfew, and she'd asked him where he'd go, where'd he'd sleep. He told her not to worry. Among all the other things they could talk about during the ride back, it seemed a waste to go on about particulars. So she'd listened to him, and didn't worry.

Gao wished her farewell at the gate, fingers grazing hers before slipping into the night. There was no way for him to return to Pingkang until the morning.

After Wei-wei returned the horse to the stable, she snuck back in through the side entrance and slipped into bed. All was still and silent in the house.

She'd fallen asleep thinking of Gao. She'd always known she didn't quite fit in her surroundings. He didn't quite fit in his either, but that didn't mean they fit together.

In this world, servants married servants. Lords married lords. Her brother had caused a scandal by marrying Yue-ying, but he had survived. Their name had provided enough armor to protect him.

Wei-wei knew it wasn't the same for her. A broken reputation was irreparable for a woman. Yet she was all but begging scandal to come for her, which was reckless. Thankfully, she hadn't been caught.

At least she had assumed so until she woke up to a new day and wandered into the study. Instead of her younger brother waiting there for lessons, it was her elder brother.

"Huang, you're home!"

Her excitement faded when she saw the logbook he was flipping through. It wasn't one of the books from their library.

"Wei-wei," he said with a sigh. "You know there's a record of everything that happens in Chang'an."

Her stomach dropped. It couldn't be—

"A log is entered every time someone comes or goes through the gate after curfew." Huang turned the page. "It appears you've been coming and going quite a bit. Or rather, our younger brother has been coming and going."

She squeezed her eyes shut. She supposed it wouldn't help to point out that she had only gone out at night the one time since the baby was born. Huang already knew about the other times before that.

"Have you told Mother?" she asked.

"I don't need to tell Mother," he scoffed. "We're not children anymore."

Wei-wei opened her eyes. She could handle things if it was just Huang.

"If we're to speak of misbehavior in this family."

Her brother shot to his feet. "Not another word." He could anticipate where she was going. "That was all in the past. And I had a purpose for many of those 'misbehaviors'."

Their younger brother Chang-min did show up then, peeking his head into the library.

"Out!" Huang chased him away with a pointed finger. Chang-min disappeared as quickly as he came.

She and Huang were far from done.

"What noble purpose did all your adventures serve?" Wei-wei demanded.

"There is no comparison between you and I—"

"All the drinking and the gambling and getting stabbed in an alleyway?"

It was the sharpest, most jagged weapon Wei-wei could brandish. She had been backed into a corner. The threat of losing her freedom to an arranged marriage, Gao and the new feelings he brought forth, then the threat of losing even that small glimmer of light, for however long she could have it.

Huang stared at her, livid. Wei-wei regretted bringing up their family's darkest moment immediately. Years ago, her brother had incurred too much debt at the gambling dens and was too ashamed to go to Father to resolve it. The den boss had sent someone to collect payment and had left him bleeding in the streets when he refused.

At first, they'd been afraid of losing Huang, but once he survived, what happened afterward was even more difficult. Father had wanted to disown Huang for the disgrace he'd brought upon their family. Mother had pleaded with him. Wei-wei had pleaded. It had taken years for Huang to repair the damage with their father. They rarely spoke of that time, until Wei-wei had torn the wound apart just now.

Huang's jaw was locked so tight, he looked ready to explode. But he didn't yell or raise his voice. He looked so much like Father then, this quiet, overly calm anger. It chilled her to the bone.

Huang walked back to the logbook and turned to the last entry.

"Someone accompanied you back to our ward last night."

Wei-wei fell silent. The guards had taken both of their names and she hadn't thought twice of it.

"Did you ever wonder who it was that stabbed me in that alleyway?" her brother asked.

Her heart stopped. No.

He pointed to a single character on the page where Gao's name was written.

"That's impossible."

But she knew. All the threads started to untangle. All the troubling questions about Gao she'd recklessly dismissed. Everyone had warned her about Gao. He and her brother were long time associates of some questionable nature. Gao worked for the gambling den boss. Gao was feared in the Pingkang li.

Her brother had owed money and Gao was some sort of enforcer. It had to have been Gao.

And she'd been foolishly drawn to him for all the wrong reasons.

~

GAO HAD REMAINED awake for the rest of the night wandering the streets and avoiding the patrols in Wei-wei's wealthy neighborhood. Here the streets were wide and empty of the night markets and street vendors that cluttered the lower wards. The houses were walled and gated. Individual wealthy families dwelt with a handful of servants in the same amount of space where, in other parts of the city, hundreds of laborers would be packed on top of one another in the tenements.

The contrast between this ward and Pingkang where palpable. Even the air tasted different.

Dawn came after a few hours and the ward gates opened to let him out for the long walk back to Pingkang. Then he was down for a scant hour of sleep before it was time to rise again.

Magistrate Li was to release the precious witnesses today at noon. The night soil collectors had spent two comfortable days as guests of the magistrate's, well-fed and well-rested. Magistrate Li had probably given them a cursory interrogation, but their true value wasn't in what they had witnessed. Their value was in what someone *thought* they had witnessed.

Gao joined the constables' wagon in front of the yamen. He hadn't exactly been invited, even though it had originally been his plan. Head Constable Ma had called for volunteers to assist in the arrest. Sending in his constables first thing would draw too much attention.

Given the bounty was still a hundred taels of silver, there

were plenty of would-be thief-catchers who showed up. Gao spotted Fu Lin at the far end of the wagon as he climbed onto it. The boy squeezed through to the back.

"Change our lives, right?" Fu Lin said, bright-eyed.

Gao managed a nod. He hadn't yet recovered from his long, strange night wandering from the pleasure houses to the mansions.

The head constable started relaying instructions in a booming voice. The wagon would take them just outside the stakeout area where they were told to scatter. They would be there an hour before the witnesses were released. Their aim was to blend in and watch for anyone who approached the night soil men.

"Detain anyone who comes to talk to them," the head constable instructed. "Then the constables will come in to make the arrest."

"What if it's just someone passing by?" someone asked.

"They're night soil men. They stink. No one's coming by just for friendly talk. Twenty coppers for a capture today—if we take them in."

The wagon started to move. The ramshackle crew all jostled together as the wheels rolled over the dirt road.

"A lot of people to catch one criminal," Fu remarked.

He'd brought a bamboo rod as a weapon. Fu Lin was so short in stature Gao doubted he'd be able to hold anyone down, but maybe the boy had hidden talents.

Gao gave the lot in the wagon another look. Why did the magistrate need so many hands to apprehend a suspect? When they'd gone to apprehend the night soil collectors, it had been staged. They wanted the spectacle, but in this situation, it was arguably more effective to go out with a small, more concealable crew. One that could hide easily to stake out the area.

The magistrate was anticipating a greater need for

force. Why? The victim had been a lone nobleman, shot in the back with an arrow before falling, or being pushed, into the river. Unless Magistrate Li suspected more than one killer was involved. Maybe a gang of thieves, attacking in a pack.

The wagon released them outside the ward gates and left them to disperse on foot. The men all separated as instructed, though Fu Lin hovered close to Gao as they entered the ward. Gao wandered back to the bridge where the arrest had been made. Most likely the head constable would return the night soil men somewhere around there.

He searched out a tea stand with some shade and sat down. The tea woke him up a bit, even if it was watered down. It wasn't long before Fu Lin sauntered over and plopped himself down on the stool.

"All this trouble for only twenty coppers."

Gao's bones dragged as if they were made of lead and his head throbbed. The lack of sleep was catching up to him.

"I'll give you a zhu to keep watch," he proposed.

"Deal."

Gao handed over the money and proceeded to lean his head back against the post behind him, closing his eyes. It would be an hour before the witnesses were released. With his eyes shut, he could think of Wei-wei. The sound of her voice, her fearlessness, her laughter. The soft weight against his back as they'd ridden home. The taste of her on his tongue. Better than honey. A man could live for that.

He'd only known her for the span of a few weeks. At first, they'd only met briefly before she'd disappeared back to her land of mansions and gardens and polo matches. Those few memories had burned bright in his imagination while they were apart. Now, just from the last few days, he had so many memories of her that she filled his thoughts.

That was what happened when everything else in life was

drudgery. Bright memories burned brighter. Wei-wei was a vibrant red flower in the midst of a gray, rainy day.

"Hey, is that them?"

Gao opened his eyes to the sight of the two night soil collectors making their way over the bridge. The magistrate had returned them with their collection buckets, albeit empty. The older one had his shovel. They were deep in conversation, probably wondering why the crazy magistrate had grabbed them in the first place.

Gao nodded to Fu Lin. As soon as the collectors had put some distance between them, he stood to follow. Fu did the same.

It didn't take long. They had only been tailing the night soil men for minutes before two strangers appeared from the shadows to intercept them. The night soil men were directed into a laundry yard where they disappeared behind the draped sheets. A perfect place to hide a crime and the bodies...

Gao broke into a run, reaching a hand into his tunic to take hold of his knife.

"Brother Gao!" Fu called out behind him, panting as he struggled to keep up. "They took them into that yard over there!"

So much for stealth.

Gao reached the laundry yard and immediately swept the large sheet in front of him to the ground to clear his view. The night soil men were backed into the corner while two men loomed over them.

"What did you tell the magistrate?" one of the men demanded as the senior night soil man held up his shovel in defense.

The interrogators turned around as Gao tore through the hanging clothes with Fu Lin at his side. The taller of them unsheathed a machete from his belt. The blade was longer than a dagger, shorter than a sword. The perfect weapon for these close quarters.

The two separated, the machete facing off against Gao while his companion lunged toward the night soil men.

Machete Man swung his blade. Gao responded by throwing a pair of trousers at him. Then he switched his grip on his knife and used the moment to attack. The man dodged away from the thrust and re-centered himself, which told Gao two things.

This was a trained fighter.

Gao was in trouble.

A strangled snarl came from behind him, ringing more of fear than a battle cry. The night soil men fled while Fu Lin flew at the other man, swinging his bamboo rod wildly against the man's double knives.

Double knives meant more trouble.

Instinctively, Gao knew what he needed to do and it was run. They were outmatched.

He threw more clothes and maneuvered his way closer to Fu Lin. "Get help."

Fu took orders well, definitely one of his best traits. He ran off as Gao engaged the double-knife wielder.

Seeing it was now two against one, the pair exchanged a look and adjusted their approach. They circled, trying to pin Gao between them. Gao shifted to prevent exactly that. Machete Man grew impatient. He charged, and Gao jumped back as the blade swept at his ribs. Double Knives came next. Gao knocked away the first thrust, then evaded a swipe that came too close to his throat.

He'd had enough. Gao backed out of the laundry yard and took to the streets. The two men followed.

Gao's heart was pumping hard now, chasing away any trace of drowsiness. He raced back toward the market area, and had nearly reached the intersection when a team of constables poured into the lane. Fu was at the lead.

"There!" Fu shouted.

Gao spun around to see his pursuers coming to a halt. He locked eyes with Machete Man who took one look at the constables before fleeing. The two suspects split apart as they took off, veering off into the alleys.

Now Gao was the pursuer. He kept his focus on Machete Man, turning left to chase him down an alleyway. Machete Man was stockier than Gas was, but Gao had him on speed. He gained on him, prepared to tackle his legs, but Machete Man side-stepped. He swiveled around with blade flashing, leaving Gao with no time to do anything but throw up his hands in defense. The slash stung across his palm.

He'd been cut a few times before, which was a good thing. It kept him from being shocked by the minor wound. This cut was nothing. The pain hadn't fully set in yet, and his knife hand was still good.

Gao dived in to retaliate. The sudden movement was enough to make his opponent jump back, but Machete Man was experienced. He countered immediately. His elbow connected against Gao's breastbone. Sharp pain stole his breath, but Gao stayed close. The only way he was going to win against a machete was if he stayed close. Gao lunged again.

The man had him in size and weight, but Gao had height and enough momentum to stagger the larger man momentarily. He struck at the man's kidneys with a short punch, taking a blinding hit to the eye in return. It wasn't a full swing—they were too close for that. The machete was no good now, but neither was Gao's knife. The larger man dropped his weapon as they grappled.

Gao had him. It was a street brawl now.

Constable Ma was the one who ended it. The posse had

arrived to surround them. The men dragged them apart and one after another they pressed his opponent into the ground, clamping irons around his wrists. Gao assumed he was next, but the constables set him to his feet instead.

"Good work," Head Constable Ma said gruffly.

Gao ran his tongue along the front of his teeth, tasting the coppery tang of blood. This was a lot messier of a job than he preferred. "Did you catch the other one?"

"We're still looking."

Gao didn't respond, but he considered the second man gone. These were not common street thugs. They were trained and coordinated. If there were two, then there were four. The nobleman hadn't been killed by a random attack.

On the way back through the streets, he grabbed a cloth from the ransacked laundry yard to wrap around his hand. The cut wasn't deep and had just started to burn. It would hurt more later. The blood was still rushing through him, his spirits elevated from the fight.

As the prisoner was loaded onto the wagon, Constable Ma counted out twenty coins and handed them to Gao unceremoniously.

"Where are you taking him?"

"There's a jailhouse in this ward. We'll keep him there while we look for his friend. You still in?"

Gao held up his injured hand and shook his head. Truth was, he was more interested in the man they'd caught. The constables could scour the streets for hours for the other guy only to come up empty-handed.

"Where's Magistrate Li?" he asked.

"He'll be summoned to the jailhouse."

"Can I ride with them?" Gao asked, indicating the wagon.

Ma gave a gruff nod. Gao climbed aboard and the head constable waved them off before turning to direct the others to continue the search. Fu Lin flashed him a grin, brandishing his rod in a sign of triumph, and went to join the search party for Double Knives. Gao gripped the pouch of coins. He'd probably split his earnings with the boy. Fu Lin had done well.

As the wagon started off, Gao turned his attention to the prisoner. Not long ago they had been locked in battle. Now Machete Man was without weapon and chained. The chains formed a crisscross pattern over his chest locking his arms in place with his hands behind him. His face was a mask, but his eyes flashed fire as he looked at Gao.

One of the constables in the wagon had collected the machete. Gao asked to look at it.

The blade was forged steel and wickedly sharp. Gao had experienced the edge directly—the cut in his hand was clean. He was lucky the gash wasn't deep enough to hit bone; the blade was that sharp. Most importantly, the machete had been forged as a fighter's weapon, not a workmen's tool that had been re-purposed.

"Paid job?" Gao asked.

The prisoner didn't answer. He flashed Gao one last dangerous look before turning away.

CHAPTER 13

Magistrate Li didn't take long to arrive at the jailhouse. He appeared shortly after the constables had locked the suspect into a cell in the back. Gao was waiting just outside the door, and Li paused to stare at the sight of him. Gao imagined he was looking much worse than he had that morning. His eye had swollen over the course of the wagon ride and half his face was probably bruised beyond recognition.

"I heard you captured the suspect," Li said, still staring at him with barely restrained horror.

"There were two of them." Gao looked at the magistrate through one swollen eye and one good one. "Did you know there would be more than one? You sent your entire force."

He'd also attached an extravagant bounty and recruited volunteers, luring thief-catchers from far and wide.

"It's best to overplan," Li said in a controlled tone.

Gao had become familiar with the magistrate's perpetually thoughtful, perpetually worried look. It was clear Li was occupied with important administrative matters. He didn't want to be speaking to Gao at the moment, but he was too polite to cut him off. Perhaps Li Chen felt some sense of gratitude since Gao had been the one to come up with the plan to draw out the perpetrators. He'd also managed to catch one of the suspects, even if he'd gotten himself beaten to a pulp in the process.

"Are you going to question him now?" Gao asked.

"You're bleeding."

Gao looked down at his hand which he'd tied with a makeshift bandage.

"No, your other arm."

Surprised, Gao pressed his fingers to his forearm. He'd been cut just above the elbow. Blood had soaked through his sleeve, but the stain was hidden by the dark color of his tunic. Gao could feel the pain radiating from the wound now that his attention was focused on it. Before, the cut had been just one of many other aches and pains.

"You should have that seen to."

"It's nothing—"

"There's a physician nearby. Really, this is important. You must take care of your injuries."

Magistrate Li's tone insisted, quite clearly, that civilized people did not stand there bleeding openly in polite company.

Leaving no room for protest, Li gave him the address of the physician, and Gao left the jailhouse reluctantly. He'd wanted to see if he could be present for the questioning, but it wasn't his place. Magistrate Li was willing to indulge him so far, but Gao wasn't going to make any progress unless he cooperated.

The address Li had given him was only a few lanes away. The physician examined and cleaned his wounds, and determined Gao wouldn't need to be sewn back together. As Gao had been wounded aiding the magistrate, the physician refused payment.

"I hear there's a lot of activity out in the streets today," the man said. "Hopefully no one else gets hurt."

An hour had passed by the time he returned to the jail-house. A familiar-looking official in an indigo-colored robe was entering the building. Gao recognized the long gray beard as well as the robe from the House of Heavenly Peaches just last night. The chief imperial censor, as Wei-wei had explained. Gao watched as Chief Censor Zheng spoke to the clerk before being led inside.

Constable Ma came up behind Gao. "This case seems to be getting bigger by the minute."

"Do imperial censors typically come to see prisoners?"

The lawman snorted. "Not in my experience. You know, you're not so bad," he continued, almost companionably. "Are you looking for work?"

Gao stared at him.

"Steadier pay than thief-catching," the constable offered with a shrug.

Was there much difference between being an enforcer for the local crime boss as opposed to the county magistrate? Not that he was considering it. Gao preferred to stay unnamed and unknown.

"Did you find the partner?" he asked.

The constable shook his head in disgust. "He's gone. Maybe the magistrate will be able to find out something during the interrogation."

Which usually meant torture. Li Chen seemed pretty mild-mannered for interrogation, but maybe he had a cold-blooded streak to him. On the other hand, Gao had no doubts about the chief imperial censor. Zheng had the calm, steely-eyed look of a seasoned professional. From what Gao knew of censors, they were the Emperor's men and held authority over other men of power.

Shouting came from back in the jailhouse. "Guards! Guards, come quick!"

Constable Ma hurried forward, and Gao followed him back into the jailhouse. They wound through the corridor to the row of cells where prisoners were kept.

The imperial censor stood outside one of the cells with a look of alarm on his face. "Open this door immediately," he commanded.

"Only the ward chief has the key," Ma explained.

"Magistrate Li took the key!" protested another man, presumably the ward chief.

"Where is the magistrate?"

Apparently gone. The constables looked from one man to another, unable to answer. Zheng appeared ready to have all their heads.

"Break the door down," he ordered through clenched teeth.

Whoever this Zheng was, he was certainly feared. The constables leapt to do his bidding.

"And find the magistrate," the official added, storming off.

Constable Ma rushed off to find Magistrate Li, and Gao was momentarily left alone. There was a small opening in each cell door, allowing the keepers to peer inside. Gao walked over to inspect the prisoner's cell.

Machete Man was on the ground, face down and unmoving. His hands were still shackled behind him.

On his grave. What was Li Chen thinking, leaving this prisoner alone? And where had Li gone?

The ward chief returned with a pickax and hatchet, ready to break down the door. He prepared to swing at the hinges when Gao stopped him.

"Wait. I can do that faster."

He inspected the lock on the door. It was a brass box lock.

"I need something small and thin. A pin or an awl.

Carving tools—engraving tools," Gao demanded, inspiration striking him.

The ward chief stared at Gao, trying to decide whether to take his lead. In the streets, among laborers and workmen, no one claimed class or rank. Taking charge was a matter of standing a little taller, speaking a little louder than the rest. And standing firm. It was something Gao knew how to do— be just a touch smarter and bolder than everyone else around him.

"His death will be on your hands," Gao warned.

The ward chief turned and ordered the clerk to fetch some tools. Minutes later, the clerk returned and shoved a bundle into Gao's hands. Gao selected a long, flat tool that seemed most suited for the job and inserted it into the keyhole. He tried to get a feel for the mechanism inside, searching for the ward spring. It had been years since he'd done this.

Blowing out a breath, he slowed his movements. It was in there. He couldn't see inside, but he could sense it by touch if he knew what he was searching for. Finally, he found the spring that prevented the lock from turning and used the tool to push it back. At the same time, he pulled the lock open and then the door.

Gao slipped inside and then paused, hand ready for his knife. The prisoner didn't move as he approached. Still, Gao remained on alert as he reached out to turn the prisoner over. Machete Man's face was pale and bloodless. Gao already knew the verdict long before he bent his ear near the man's face to listen for breath. His pulse was also still.

Gao stepped back. The sight of death no longer unnerved him, but it was still unsettling.

The prisoner's mouth gaped open, as if he had gasped for breath as the last bit of life left him. A stream of spittle ran down his chin.

The ward chief came to stand beside him. "Poison?"

The man must have had it hidden on him.

Chief Censor Zheng had returned as well. He took in the scene from the door of the cell. "Dead?" he asked.

Gao nodded. He cared nothing for the prisoner. They'd fought and the man with the machete had tried to kill him. Still, he pressed the prisoner's eyes closed as a courtesy.

Zheng came forward to feel the man's pulse himself. Once he was convinced of the answer, he let out a breath, shaking his head. Then he looked to Gao. "Who are you?"

Before Gao could answer, Magistrate Li appeared at the door. He was out of breath. "How did this happen?"

The senior official glanced up from the corpse to fix his cold stare onto Li Chen. "I was wondering the same myself."

~

GAO WAS TRAPPED at the jailhouse for the next four hours while the imperial censor insisted on questioning everyone. Gao, in turn, insisted he was no one and knew nothing until Li Chen ruined things by coming to his defense. The magistrate attested that he'd sent Gao away when the prisoner had been poisoned, which suddenly had the chief censor very interested in how Magistrate Li was associated with the likes of someone like Gao.

At that point, Gao regretted teaming up with Li Chen. He regretted his attempt at being a hero.

He particularly regretted picking the lock, which of course highlighted that he had a questionable set of skills. And he'd done this all in a jailhouse under the scrutiny of county and imperial authorities. That was a particular lack of judgment.

Despite all his misgivings, the imperial censor didn't have Gao searched or his knife removed before questioning him.

It was all very civil. Zheng stood over him while Gao was made to kneel in the ward chief's office. It was a stark reminder of his position relative to the chief censor's. Gao was a nobody.

It didn't bother him. It couldn't bother him. He showed the appropriate level of humility when he needed to. Gao knew when to be invisible.

"Why did you join the search party?" Zheng asked once again.

"I was there for the thief-catching bounty."

"For twenty coins?"

Gao kept his gaze forward as Zheng circled. "That's a lot of money," he replied. And it was.

"You were nearly killed," the censor pointed out.

That wasn't entirely true. Being struck with a fist a few times in the face wasn't going to kill him, and the cuts barely scratched the surface.

"Then you came back to jailhouse. That is considerable dedication. For twenty pieces of copper."

"I thought the head constable might have more work for me."

Zheng stared at him while Gao kept his head lowered.

"You say your name is Gao?"

"Yes."

"Just Gao."

"Yes."

There were other questions. Why did he pick the lock? What did he know about the prisoner? Did the man say anything before or after his capture?

To all those questions, Gao knew nothing.

He was the first person to be dismissed.

Li Chen escorted Gao out to the front of the jailhouse.

"This is disappointing," Li said, deep creases lining his forehead. "He was the only evidence we had."

And he'd been killed when the magistrate had left on his own to wander away.

"Where were you?" Gao asked.

"I heard the constables had captured the second suspect."

Gao waited.

"It wasn't the right man," Li concluded.

"Well, I hope you find him," Gao remarked dryly. "One more thing," he called out as Magistrate Li turned to go.

"Yes, Mister Gao."

"Did you tell the censor about the jade seal? He would know if it was real, wouldn't he?"

"That seal was a forgery."

"Forgery? Wei—Lady Bai was fairly certain."

"It seems Lady Bai was mistaken."

The same story Li Chen had told to Wei-wei. Now a suspect had just died under his watch while another suspect slipped away. Magistrate Li had a reputation on the street for being a thorough and just administrator. Neither seemed to hold true in this case.

Wei-wei had been right about the chop as well as about Li Chen. The magistrate couldn't be trusted. It seemed the chief censor would agree.

The sun was setting soon, but Gao couldn't wait. He hurried to the northeastern quadrant, paying a coin for a carriage ride to get there quicker.

The sky was beginning to darken by the time he arrived. Gao ignored the front gate and went around to the side entrance near the stable, where he knocked on the gate and waited. It was the young groomsman who answered.

"You're Zhou Dan," Gao said.

"Yeah, I know you too," the servant retorted.

"I'm here to see Lady Bai."

Zhou Dan looked him up and down disdainfully. Even

the servants of the wealthy considered themselves above him.

"Would you tell her Gao is here?"

The servant didn't respond. He kept his gaze warily fixed on Gao as he closed the gate. A long time passed, and the sky grew darker still. A gong sounded in the distance, signaling it was time for the wards all over the city to close. Curfew.

"Demon dogs," Gao swore. Another night out on the streets.

When the gate opened again, it wasn't Wei-wei as Gao had hoped. Instead it was Zhou Dan once more. He held out a folded envelope through the entranceway, refusing to set foot outside.

"From the lady."

Puzzled, Gao reached for the envelope. As soon as he handed the packet over, Zhou Dan retreated inside and shut the gate.

Gao carefully unfolded the paper to reveal a red silk bracelet, tied into an eternity knot.

CHAPTER 14

Someone was pounding on the front gate.

Wei-wei was mortified. Gao had always been reasonable and even overly courteous. Perhaps that's why she'd thought the best of him, ignoring the obvious fact that he was a scoundrel. Possibly a murderous scoundrel.

The pounding came again. "I need to speak to Bai Huang," he called from outside.

"Who is that?" Mother asked wandering out from the inner courtyard.

Yue-ying came out beside Mother while cradling little Huiyin. She and Huang had finally chosen a name for their daughter. Her sister-in-law looked to Wei-wei worriedly as the pounding continued.

The whole household was stirred up now. Gao was causing a scene which wasn't like him. Gao was cautious. He was discreet. The last time she'd seen him he'd faded away like mist when she'd wanted desperately for him to stay.

Now she never wanted to see him again.

"Don't let him in," she instructed Zhou Dan. "He's a madman," she muttered beneath her breath.

Zhou Dan and his father, the groundskeeper, moved warily toward the gate. The elder Zhou gripped his rake in hand, ready to use it if needed. How would Gao react to being attacked by a rake?

The pounding grew louder, and Wei-wei wanted to crawl out of her skin. What could Gao possibly be thinking?

She turned toward Mother and Yue-ying. "Go back inside," she assured. "He's an associate of Huang's. Everything will be fine."

"Should we call for the city guards?" Mother asked.

"Everything will be fine," Wei-wei repeated. She mouthed the name "Gao" to Yue-ying.

Gao had taken part in rescuing Yue-ying from danger once. Another one of the many reasons Wei-wei had been misled about him. Hero and villain. But more villain, she reminded herself acidly.

Yue-ying assisted in ushering Mother back to her private quarters. "The loud noise is scaring my baby," she said gently.

Wei-wei was grateful to have an ally in their household now. She turned and came face-to-face with Huang. He'd emerged from his study looking less than pleased. They'd spoken little since that morning and only in short, terse exchanges out of so-called politeness.

"I didn't summon him," she insisted.

"But we know exactly why he's here," Huang retorted.

"He claims to want to speak to you."

Huang strode to the door. She was stricken, once again, by how much he had changed. It seemed he stood taller, commanded more respect and attention than he did in the past. This new presence had seeped into his bones. Her brother was growing into their father's place as head of their household.

Wei-wei followed five paces behind. As Zhou Dan and his father stepped aside, Wei-wei wondered whether she herself should be carrying some sort of weapon, but that was ridiculous. Gao wasn't like that.

She reminded herself that she didn't know what Gao was like at all. Sadly, she'd refused to see when it came to him.

When Huang opened the gate, she couldn't stop herself from peering through just to catch a glimpse. The sight of Gao stole her breath—he looked awful. His eye was swollen and purple. His hand was bandaged. She fought the urge to push past her brother to go to him.

Her heart sank. *Never again*, she reminded herself.

Gao searched for her over Huang's shoulder as well, his gaze connecting with hers and holding there for several heartbeats before turning his attention back to Huang.

"You said something big had happened. You told me to keep watch for anyone suspicious."

"I know you're not here for me, Gao," said her brother.

"I won't deny it."

Gao met her eyes again. He was taller than Huang. Perhaps not stronger, but certainly fiercer. She couldn't believe this man had tried to kill her brother and had nearly succeeded. And yet here they were, conversing in front of their house. Gao might have momentarily captured her attention, but there was no doubt in her heart where her loyalty lay when it came to protecting her family. She would call for the city guards herself.

"What do you have?" Huang asked.

"The drowning in Pingkang li and the men you were looking for are connected," Gao began.

Huang stilled. For a long moment, the two men stood apart, each taking measure of the other.

"You asked for my services that morning," Gao reminded him.

Huang pushed the gate open wider but only a little. "Come in."

She stared at her brother in astonishment. Wasn't he the one who had insisted that Gao was dangerous and unpredictable? That she shouldn't go near him? Huang ignored her as he directed Gao to the study, artfully positioning himself to keep her at bay. The servants hovered closer, curious at what was transpiring.

"Bring tea," she said to their housekeeper.

No need to abandon proper courtesy.

Huang and Gao disappeared into her brother's study with the door shut firmly behind them. Fear wormed its way into her. Gao was dangerous. He'd hurt her brother before. Was he any different now?

The housekeeper brought tea on a tray which Wei-wei promptly intercepted. She brought it to the study only to have Huang snatch it from her, and shut the door firmly once more.

How ungracious.

Wei-wei didn't press her ear to the door. She and Huang had discovered in their childhood years that there was a spot beneath a window that was the best place to listen. It was closer to Father's desk—now Huang's desk. She went there now, seated herself on the same flat rock she'd used so many years ago, and pressed her ear to the wooden panel.

"—Li said the seal was fake. It was a false lead." It was Huang's voice.

"He's lying." Gao's deeper, more gravelly voice. So, he agreed with her now.

"How do you know this?"

"Because I know when someone's lying."

The next part was too muddled for her to make out. She pressed closer.

"You were looking for weapons or fighting skills that were unusual for the street. For hired…" Garbled. "…mercenaries. I found them."

She listened breathlessly as Gao recounted an incredible tale involving subterfuge and a gang of constables and thief-catchers. A chase through the streets. As removed as she was, it was easy to forget that this had happened to him. It was as fantastic as the strange tales she liked to read about dragons and magical creatures.

Huang's reply was muffled again. She blew out a breath in frustration and shifted her position, desperate to find a better spot.

"The same official came to the courtesan house the night before. Tall, gray-haired."

"Chief Censor Zheng?"

The rest was a jumble of words. She was convinced Huang was doing this on purpose.

"Murder and conspiracy aside," Huang was saying. "There's something more important we need to discuss."

The death of her. Wei-wei straightened. If she were a cat, her ears would be perked up.

"Family is everything to me," her brother declared.

"Family is everything to Wei-wei as well." Gao. Would the sound of his voice ever not do this to her insides? "I would never hurt her. I've done everything to protect her. You know your sister can be reckless."

She seethed. As if Gao wasn't reckless. Look at what had happened to his face since she saw him last.

"I never lied to Wei-wei about who I was. Tell her for me, if she'll listen."

"She's listening now—"

Wei-wei jumped as Huang knocked loudly on the other side of the wall. *Demon.*

Straightening, she hurried back to the entrance and attempted to compose herself.

Her brother emerged alone from the study. She frowned at him, puzzled.

"I told Gao about the chancellor's assassination," he reported.

That was not what she cared about at the moment.

"And I asked Gao to stay."

Her eyes grew wide with shock. Huang called Zhou Dan over and instructed him to bring bedding and to see to their guest.

"He stabbed you and left you for dead," Wei-wei pointed out when it was just the two of them. "And you're letting him sleep in our home?"

"It's after curfew. What would you have me do? Send him out into the cold?"

She looked away guiltily. That was exactly what she had done last night. Sent Gao away after he'd made sure she had gotten home. She had assumed Gao knew how to take care of himself and that nothing could harm him. Seeing him today, bandaged and bruised, reminded her of how wrong she was.

"He's dangerous. You said so yourself," she reminded him. "Why do you continue to associate with him after what happened?"

Now that she had finally heeded his warning, Huang had turned completely around.

"Some might say I have poor judgment," he said sheepishly. "It's hard to explain."

She shot him a cross look.

"Gao didn't exactly leave me for dead. In his mind, he was saving my life."

That didn't make any sense. "You nearly bled to death in the street."

"It's complicated. Gao had warned me earlier that if I didn't pay my debts, I better not return or else someone was going to put a knife in me. I could have stayed away then, but

I didn't listen. I thought somehow I would find a way out of it."

"Huang," she admonished.

"I know. I had a lot of time to think of this, a whole year, remember? Well, the next time I came back to the dice tables, Gao took me outside before I could even start playing. I thought he was trying to be helpful, but he stuck a knife in me, just like he'd warned."

Her hand flew to her mouth.

"Wait." Huang closed his eyes and sighed. "Then he shoved my hand against the wound and told me to keep it there, pressed hard to slow the bleeding. He said the city guards were coming, and then he disappeared. After that incident, once I'd recovered, well—I figured he was the only informant on the street I could be sure didn't want me dead."

She was so angry she could barely breathe. This was madness. Gao was mad and so was Huang. They were all mad. "I should throw him out of here myself."

She needed to be done with Gao. Just yesterday she'd floated on clouds. They'd kissed and she'd dreamed stubbornly wild dreams of happiness. Now just the thought of him reminded her of how foolish she was.

"He *tried to kill you*," she insisted. Huang was like that boy who picked up the snake thinking maybe it wouldn't bite him.

"Little Sister." Huang rarely called her that. He took hold of her shoulders and looked her squarely in the eyes. "None of this is anger on my behalf. You're mourning over what can never be."

Huang had never looked at her so earnestly. He and Yue-ying had an impossible love. Maybe he would understand.

She took a deep breath and let it out slowly. "How did it feel when you thought you would lose Yue-ying forever?"

153

It was too personal of a question, even for a sister to ask a brother, but he owed her a debt.

"Everything hurt," he admitted. "It felt like daylight would never come. That I would never be happy again."

She bit her lip, forcing back tears. That was how she felt, whenever she let go of her anger even for a moment. The anger was better.

"But you were able to be happy again," she said. "We found a way, you and I."

"You know it's different for me," he said soberly.

Because she was a woman. A man could claim his own fate, even if it were one of scandal or ridicule. Her fate would always be tied to a father or husband or son.

Yue-ying was of a markedly lower class than Huang, but he'd fallen for her and wouldn't have anyone else. Their parents had eventually accepted the marriage and now they had started their family, but the future was not without obstacles. In their world among the scholar-gentry, servants were to marry servants. There would always be a hint of scandal to Huang's union. It could limit how high his children with Yue-ying could climb.

Huang hadn't cared about any of that, but Wei-wei couldn't be so stubborn. How could she not be concerned about being accepted by her family or the fate of her children? It was her brother who was the romantic between them. Despite her love of poems and stories, she had always been more pragmatic. A woman had to be.

She looked back to the study. A lamp burned from inside.

Gao was also pragmatic. They were the same in that way, always considering and planning. He'd told her from the start that he was unsuitable, and she'd known in her heart he was right. She had just wanted to dream for as long as possible.

～

GAO WOKE up the next morning on a bed where he could stretch out his full height. Instead of the creaks, groans, and voices of the tenement, there was silence. A servant brought a hot bowl of congee to him and, a little later, a wash basin filled with clean water. He'd known life was different up in the mansions, but he didn't realize how different.

Once he'd composed himself, he opened the study door to see Wei-wei seated outside in the garden. It was striking to see her in the morning, first thing. Her skin glowing in the early sunlight. She was looking at him now, unlike yesterday, but there was no warmth in her eyes. Something had changed between them.

As he came closer, her demeanor remained cold.

"You were the one who attacked my brother," she stated calmly.

He stopped short. At least that explained things. "It took a long time for him to tell you."

"You could have killed him, but you didn't. That doesn't make you heroic."

"It doesn't."

"You're a scoundrel and you always have been."

Pain flickered behind her guarded expression. It hurt him to see it. He'd always known she would come to her senses, but maybe he had started to hope.

"I should go," he offered.

"Why didn't you kill my brother?" She couldn't even look at him.

"That never was the job. You can't collect money from a corpse."

"A job. Just business then." She plucked at the floral pattern on her hanfu robe.

"Just…business."

She shook her head in disgust. "Maybe you *should* go now," she said faintly.

To explain himself would mean telling her about the darkest parts of his life. That he was hired out to the worst of people. He did what he was told to do. There were other men, more desperate than he was, who would take him out to have his place.

They called him brother and treated him with respect because he'd done unspeakable things. And even that respect was only temporary.

Gao didn't need to explain any of this to Wei-wei. She didn't know what his life was like, but she was clever enough to figure things out. From the way she avoided his eyes, she didn't want the details. She already knew enough and it sickened her.

He'd lost her. Not because of her family's disapproval or her betrothal to the wealthy, illustrious, and honorable Magistrate Li. Gao had lost her because of his own poor character. He could only hide the truth for so long.

"Before he goes, we should talk."

They both looked up, startled by Bai Huang's voice. "*All* of us," he added.

Inside the study, Huang took his seat behind the desk. He looked every bit the scholar-official, and not at all the dice-enthralled playboy Gao had come to know. Wei-wei lowered herself onto the wooden couch where Gao had slept. Gao remained standing with his back up against the wall. Something told him it was best to keep his distance.

"I thought over what Gao told me yesterday," Huang began. "And I requested some records from the magistrate's office this morning. The open case record on the body in the canal."

He pushed a book forward. Wei-wei reached for it and

leafed through the pages, her eyes scanning the columns of characters.

"What does it say?" Gao asked.

"Note the reported cause of death," Huang replied.

"Drowning," Wei-wei read off. She looked up at him. "The victim drowned?"

Gao met Wei-wei's eyes, and then Huang's. "He was struck with an arrow. At least twice."

Wei-wei sifted again through the pages. "It's not mentioned."

"You're certain he was shot?" Huang asked him.

"I know the one who found the body. If Li examined it, the wounds would have been unmistakable."

Gao was reluctant to name Fu Lin, especially when he'd have to go against the word of someone as powerful as the magistrate. Fu Lin had pulled the body out of the water. He'd clearly described the arrow protruding from the man's chest.

"But Li Chen's reputation has been faultless," Huang remarked, troubled. "He's known to be honest and dedicated."

Of course. Faultless. A perfect match for Wei-wei, except his actions told otherwise. The magistrate had a tiger's head with a snake's tail.

"What is it?" Wei-wei's question interrupted his thoughts. "You look angry all of the sudden."

Gao shook his head, "Just thinking."

"*Really* angry," she insisted.

"Li Chen had one of the killers in his custody, yet the man mysteriously died before he could be interrogated," Gao pointed out. He held Wei-wei's gaze. "He can't be trusted."

"If the death in the canal and Chancellor Yao's assassination are connected, there are two things that would tie them together," Huang surmised.

"The arrow," Gao finished for him. "And the jade seal."

Yet according to the magistrate's case record, neither existed. It seemed obvious to Gao. Two men, both high-ranking, were killed within hours of one another, and the county magistrate was interfering with the investigation.

"If the same men carried out the attack on the man in the canal and the assassination before the Yanxi gate, they would have needed to be able to bypass the ward checkpoints," Huang continued. "The Censorate is investigating all recorded entries."

"I fought one of the killers yesterday," Gao explained. "He and his companion were highly skilled. Magistrate Li must have known this. He assembled a team fit to take down an entire den of bandits."

Wei-wei stared at the pattern of bruises on his face and started to say something before biting back the words. Her brother continued to ponder the magistrate's role.

"What motive would Li Chen have for these actions? They seem out of character."

"Corruption," Gao offered impatiently. "Greed?"

It was clear Bai Huang was reluctant to accuse one of his peers even when his actions were clearly dishonest. Li Chen was being protected based on name and reputation.

"Maybe Li isn't acting alone," Wei-wei suggested. She'd been quiet through most of the exchange, absorbing the information. "The magistrate could allow the assassins to move freely across the city and also protect them from getting caught, but someone else could be responsible for planning the attacks."

She was always thinking. Another woman might have shrunk away from even the thought of death, but Wei-wei was relentless when it came to the righting of wrongs.

"If only you could have been at the House of Heavenly Peaches last night, Elder Brother."

Huang's frown deepened at that, but Wei-wei went on

regardless. "The chief imperial censor was there investigating General Lin Shidao's son. It would seem that Li Chen and the general's son are associates."

Huang looked surprised. "You spoke to Lin Yijin?"

"He offered us a drink and thinks we're the best of friends now. He doesn't think very much of you."

"There was…an incident." Huang looked downward, smoothing a hand over the front of his robe, and said no more.

"Maybe it was both of them. General Lin Shidao *and* Magistrate Li Chen," Wei-wei suggested. "The general pulling strings from afar with the magistrate supporting from within the capital."

Huang thought for a moment before reaching into his desk to take out an official-looking paper. "There's a gathering at the East Park tonight to celebrate the full moon. Both Lin Yijin and Magistrate Li Chen will be in attendance."

"Another banquet?" Gao asked. "Captivity seems harsh for the sons of noblemen."

"We're a spoiled lot," Huang admitted, the corner of his mouth lifting. He placed the invite in front of him. "Twenty or thirty guests in attendance. Easy for one to lose themselves among them." Huang gave the invite a few taps. "A chance to get some answers."

A knock came on the door. Zhou Dan stuck his head in. "Your escort is here, Lord Bai."

Bai Huang certainly seemed to have risen up in the world.

His hand lingered over the folded paper for a moment longer before he rose. "I'm expected at the administrative offices."

"When will you be back?" Wei-wei asked, rising with him.

"The banquet will go on until late tonight. There will be a lot of people there. Many people to attend to."

Huang paused as he passed Gao at the door. "Watch over her."

Gao glanced at Wei-wei who narrowed her eyes at the suggestion. "I'm not so sure she wants me to do that."

"You know why it has to be you," Huang replied. "We'll need all of our strengths to resolve this."

The room was quiet once Huang left. Gao and Wei-wei stood facing one another, uncertain. She broke away to look to the invitation.

"Was it obvious to you?" she asked stiffly.

He frowned. Obvious? "No."

"My brother wants us at that gathering."

Gao wasn't entirely sure that was the case.

Wei-wei picked up the invitation. "Huang said we'd need all our strengths. He wants us there tonight. Both of us."

CHAPTER 15

That day, Gao received an education on what the life of the wealthy looked like. Steady meals and prolonged, unbroken stretches of time. And quiet. The walls of the Bai mansion shielded the inhabitants away from the noises of the street. Away from any interruption, actually.

There was enough time to indulge in whatever one wanted. For Wei-wei, it appeared to be books. He saw a glimpse of her through the round moon gate that separated the outer courtyard from the inner one. She sat upon a bench, reading. He moved past the same gate an hour later to still find her there, a faraway expression on her face.

Gao would have given anything to be able to go to her. Sit down beside her. Say something inconsequential when she looked up at him, her face bright and expectant.

There was no barrier in the circular passageway, but there might as well have been iron bars. The inner courtyard was a private place for Wei-wei and her family. The servants moved in and then quickly out of the back part of the resi-dence when needed. They also moved quietly around Gao, giving no indication there was anything strange about his presence other than the occasional sideways glance.

Perhaps his life would have looked similar, if only...

Of course, his family only had a fraction of the wealth the Bai family possessed. They didn't have servants, but Gao remembered a house, the rooms. A roof to sleep beneath and the sound of the market gong in the morning and evening. He could only picture the place where he'd lived with his family in pieces.

At midday, food was brought to him. He ate quietly in the study, surrounded by books he couldn't read.

Eventually, he left the house to wander though he remained close.

You know why it has to be you.

He still didn't know what Bai Huang had meant. Gao supposed he was the only person the young Lord Bai was acquainted with from the back alleys. The bad streets. How did the saying go? Combat poison with poison.

By evening Gao found himself in a carriage opposite Wei-wei as they headed to the East Park. Wei-wei was relentless when she had a plan in mind. She was dressed in another of her brother's discarded outfits. It was part of his flower prince persona—which Gao was certain was a persona now that he'd seen Bai Huang outside of the pleasure quarter. Gao would have to say the clothing looked more appealing on her than her brother.

The carriage ride was oppressively silent, just as most of the day had been.

"Is it bad?" Wei-wei asked, staring at the bandage. It was the first thing she had said to him during the carriage ride.

Gao curled and flexed his fingers. The bandage restricted movement, but at least it was only his left hand. He only needed his right hand to wield a knife. "It's not bad. This one was worse."

He lifted the other sleeve to reveal the dressing on his arm. He was probably showing off.

"Your face is still swollen." She stared at him with a grimace. "Can you see out of that eye?"

"I can see you."

She grew quiet.

"I don't understand why my brother thinks you should be here," she said after a long pause.

He was seeing another side of Wei-wei. One that was cautious and cold. Cutting. But he also saw that even from within the walls that she'd put up, she still cared for him. It meant something.

He still cared for her.

"You and your brother have your own way of understanding one another. Well, he and I also have a language," Gao tried to explain. "The reason I'm here with you is that there are killers on the loose. And Bai Huang only personally knows of one person who's also a killer."

She paled at the mention of death. They might as well have it all out now.

"I've done things, Wei-wei. Some of it was to survive, some of it was just in the course of life."

Her fingers twisted in her lap. The knuckles whitened.

"You don't ever have to be afraid of me."

"I'm not afraid of you," she replied, and he could see at least that was true. "But you almost killed my brother. And you're saying you've done worse—"

"Never for money."

He didn't know if that mattered to her, but it did to him.

"You think your magistrate hasn't made any life and death decisions?" he asked.

Wei-wei shut her eyes, summoning patience. "Not *my* magistrate," she sighed.

"Men send other men to death. They make decisions that

leave women defenseless, children orphaned. Then there are men who have no chance to decide, for good or bad. They just have to act."

"Would you ever do it again?"

"Stab your brother? No."

"Would you ever do that again to anybody?"

If the money was right. If the circumstances were there. If the person particularly deserved it. Like if he was threatening. Or irritating.

Gao had gotten to the place where he could make some decisions, but that hadn't always been true and it might not be true forever.

"Wei-wei, I'm not a good man."

"But you've risked your life to try to solve this case. It can't be just for the bounty."

"It's for you."

"That doesn't make any sense—"

"How else would I ever see you?"

At least they were speaking again.

"Don't you want to see justice served?" Wei-wei asked him.

"Nothing so lofty as that."

From where he stood, justice seemed like a luxury. He only wanted to see that those he cared for were unharmed. And there weren't many people he cared for.

He could see Wei-wei wasn't satisfied with his answer which threw her back into silence.

"What's in the box?" he asked.

She had been holding a long, expensive-looking wooden case in her lap. It was covered with dark lacquer and inlaid with mother of pearl.

"A scroll." She opened it partway to show him a roll of paper. "This will get us into this gathering."

"What's on it?"

"It doesn't matter. I'm here to give this very important thing to my elder brother who promised to show it to some very important person."

He regarded the box skeptically. "No one will question that?"

"No one." She was perfectly confident.

The party was already underway when the carriage arrived. Lanterns were lit around a central pavilion and he could hear a melody playing from a pipa.

They disembarked from the carriage and followed a path in the grass toward the pavilion. Gao noticed immediately the number of armed guards stationed at the perimeter. Surely the assassins wouldn't be bold enough to attack here. Regardless, Gao resolved to stay on alert.

"Is this typical?" he asked.

"I wouldn't know," Wei-wei said. "I've never been invited to something like this."

Her eyes were bright with the lantern light reflecting in them. The challenge of being disguised and sneaking in to where she wasn't permitted seemed to excite her. She spoke to the functionary who came to greet them at the perimeter, apparently saying the right things and bowing at the right moment.

To him, Wei-wei was barely passable as a male scholar. Her smaller stature made her seem younger, a youth of sixteen or seventeen. Apparently the right demeanor and sense of entitlement was all one needed. He'd never be able to pull off such a feat. They'd know he didn't belong the moment he opened his mouth.

Gao followed behind her into a gathering the likes of him was never meant to attend, but Wei-wei found a way inside. She was a schemer. She plotted and planned and had enough audacity for ten men. From the first moment he'd met her— when he realized she wasn't Bai Huang's younger brother—

Gao had sensed how relentless she was. Like endless water flowing over rock. Bai Huang had a reputation for scandal, but Wei-wei would be an absolute terror if she'd been born the eldest male child in the Bai family.

There was an archery field set up where a small group had gathered at the outskirts. Wei-wei headed immediately there.

"Do you know how to use a bow and arrow?" she whispered over her shoulder.

"Not at all."

"That's a shame. It might be a way to fit in."

Guards all around, but archery permitted within the perimeter. And a story and a scroll of paper would gain entry. If one had the right manner of speaking, Gao supposed. These people truly believed they were safe among their own.

When they reached the party, Wei-wei tugged on his sleeve. At the far end of the field there was a lone archer surrounded by a small entourage. It was their newest friend, Lin Yijin.

"I'm going to try to speak to him."

She darted forward, obviously with a plan in mind. Wei-wei always had a plan. She met the world head on with her chin held high. He had to admire it, the utter lack of caution. Some might call it fearlessness.

Gao followed a few paces behind. At their approach, Lin Yijin's entourage came to attention. Gao recognized a few of them from the night before at the pleasure house, including the man who had shoved Wei-wei apart from the general's son when they'd gotten too close. His party had thinned out to only four men who stood back watching as Lin nocked an arrow and took aim.

Wei-wei stopped a respectful distance away, presumably not to disturb the shot. She was focused on Lin Yijin. Gao turned his attention to the entourage. Two of the men were armed and likely acted as bodyguards. There was an older gentleman and a younger one who seemed to serve as attendants.

Lin released the arrow and it sang neatly into the center of the target. At least he wasn't inebriated this time. They might be spared an uncomfortable bout of poetry.

It was the older attendant who came forward meet them. "Lord Lin Yijin is occupied at this time. Is there a message this servant can convey to him on behalf of the young master?"

"Bai Chang-min wishes to send greetings. We met not so long ago."

"Bai?" Lin spoke from the archery field. "Let him come forward. I can use some interesting conversation for the night."

His focus remained on the target. The younger attendant hurried forward to place an arrow in his waiting hand.

Gao and Wei-wei stood back while Lin once again took aim. The long bow was nearly as tall as he was, requiring all of the young man's strength to pull. His shoulders and back tensed with the strain as he stilled himself before letting fly. The arrow landed into the target next to the first one, close enough to splinter the wood.

Wei-wei clapped appreciatively. "Such skill, Master Lin."

The rest of the attendants remained silent. Gao had to admit, in such moments Wei-wei affected a young nobleman eerily well.

Gao estimated the distance from the target to be half a li away. Perhaps it was a feat any skilled archer could manage, and Lin Yijin was, without a doubt, highly skilled.

～

Lin Yijin handed his bow to the attendant and ordered wine with a flick of his wrist at the serving girl. Then he started heading toward the covered viewing pavilion. Wei-wei made a line toward him.

"Well, friend. I'm glad to have someone to talk to after all." He spared a glance at Gao. "What happened to your bodyguard's face? It wasn't those two, was it?"

He indicated the two armed guards who were already moving toward them.

"No, young master Lin. It was some street incident."

Lin laughed as he seated himself at the stone table. "I wish these two guard dogs would wander away sometimes."

She glanced at the men. They remained just outside the pavilion. Gao did the same on her side.

The wine arrived, brought by a young courtesan who poured two cups for them with an elegant tilt of her wrist. Lin Yijin waved her away impatiently before taking his cup.

"To good wine."

She drank when he did, but apparently not with enough enthusiasm.

"Why so polite, Bai? Come on."

She finished the cup, while it seemed like the entire world watched on, waiting. The liquor burned down her throat and settled warmly in her stomach. Her brother had told her his primary talent was having a slightly higher tolerance for drink than everyone around him. He was still able to use his wits when everyone else was drunk—or at least use them slightly better than the rest of the crowd. Wei-wei wasn't so sure she shared that talent.

"Ancient Well Tribute Baijiu," Lin boasted. He poured more for both of them, thwarting the courtesan from her task. She stepped back quietly. "This comes from a famous well in Anhui province, do you know? Originally sent as a tribute to the Han Emperor. Now, hundreds of years later, the distillers keep up the tradition. Very expensive. Drink up."

She steadied herself before downing it. The second cup went down easier and seemed to burn hotter. Her fingers and toes were pleasantly warm.

"If you're going to be the Emperor's prisoner, might as well drink the Emperor's wine," Lin said gleefully, pouring again. Wei-wei wondered how many cups that flask could hold.

"Are those your father's men?" she asked, nodding toward the guards.

Lin snorted. "Those are the Emperor's men. Have to keep watch on the hostage. It's not so bad. I get paraded around at gatherings like this to show that the warlords are under control."

He beckoned for the courtesan to bring more wine while the cup was still raised to his lips. Then he good-naturedly nudged Wei-wei's cup forward with a knuckle. She was falling behind.

"Your bodyguard is scowling at me," Lin remarked, looking over her shoulder.

"That's how he always looks—" Heavens, it took effort to control her pitch. Huang was definitely more suited to this sort of discovery. "Your guards don't look so pleasant either."

The general's son grinned at that. "Then I've accomplished a goal."

She tried to put herself where he was, which was difficult, in part, because she was a woman. But not so difficult in others. He was a third son. Cast away as expendable sacrifice by his powerful father, a man who must deal in strategies of wins and losses. Did the general consider Lin Yijin an acceptable loss? She wasn't so different, the middle daughter between precious sons, but her father would never offer her up as hostage.

"To forgotten heirs," she toasted.

Lin nodded emphatically. "I like you more than your brother, Bai. You and I should be lifelong friends."

"Happily." Wei-wei was glad the wine had temporarily run out. "Have you seen Bai Huang?" She craned her neck to look toward the main pavilion. The moon was full and large, glowing yellow overhead.

"He's among those old, simpering fools. Why would I go there? It's that way in the Emperor's court all the time. Old eunuchs whispering in one ear trying to turn me away from my father. Dusty politicians in another ear trying to ally themselves with my father. It's so exhausting. Better to be known for this—" He picked up the empty ewer and tapped it against the table. "—And be above it all."

Wei-wei braced her hands against the table and leveled her eyes onto his. Lin Yijin, for all of his staggering at the pleasure house, seemed to remember every detail of his meeting with her and with Gao. Was he like Huang—able to handle his drink a little better than everyone thought?

"Tell me, friend. When we first met, you seemed to be expecting someone."

Lin's gaze sharpened on her. "I don't remember..."

"You weren't expecting an old eunuch or dusty politician, but certainly someone. You were waiting for a message," she reminds him. "Are you still waiting?"

His look intensified on her. A slow grin spread over his handsome face. He leaned forward gamely. "Are you the one that I'm waiting for, Bai?"

A large hand suddenly clamped over Lin Yijin's shoulder. It was one of the stern-faced guards. At first Yijin stiffened, set to rebel against the grip, but then he seemed to relent. He sank back in his chair willingly before brushing the hand away. The guards really did keep a close watch on him.

"Maybe you should go find your brother, Bai," he said coolly. "I'm sure we'll get a chance to talk later."

Wei-wei fumbled for her lacquered box and stood, bowing as she took her leave. Gao came forward to place a steadying hand on her elbow, but she shook him off.

Lin Yijin remained seated to watch their departure.

"Until next time, friend," he sang lightly.

CHAPTER 16

They didn't get far before Wei-wei pulled Gao off the path and into a cluster of trees.

"He's more intelligent than he leads everyone to believe," she declared. "And not as innocent as I thought."

Her eyes were bright and her cheeks flushed. Wei-wei was smaller in stature than the general's son and Gao wagered she'd had less experience drinking.

"And I think he's expecting some sort of message. Maybe from his father? Those guards don't let anyone come near."

Gao steadied her with his hands over her shoulders. "Slowly."

"I think he'll talk to me if we can find some privacy. He likes me."

Gao had certainly seen evidence of that. To him, the two of them had looked like a pair of bored rich heirs bantering and flirting.

"Can you think of some way to distract the guards?" Wei-wei asked.

"You mean like goad them into a fight while you pull Lin Yijin away into the shadows for a clandestine meeting?"

Her eyes brightened. "Do you think that would work?"

Gao stared back at her and shook his head firmly, no. At least the alcohol seemed to have made Wei-wei forget that she was upset with him.

There was the sound of footsteps up ahead. Wei-wei pressed two fingers to her lips to urge quiet. They peered through the brush to see Lin Yijin standing alone.

"He got away from them," Wei-wei whispered. "This is our chance."

She started forward before Gao clasped a hand around her arm to hold her back. "Wait."

Someone else was approaching. It was one of the guards. Lin turned to say something to him.

"We don't have much time," the guardsman said.

Lin reached up and dragged the taller man's face down close to his. "There's never enough time," Lin said huskily before pressing their mouths together.

Wei-wei stilled, her arm tensing within his grasp. For a moment, she stood transfixed by the sight of the two men. Then she backed away.

"We should go find my brother," she said once they were far enough away not to be heard. She turned to head toward the main pavilion, but not before he saw the blush of color high on her cheeks.

Gao remained a step behind her. It seemed proper for the role he was playing as her bodyguard, but it was also pleasing to be able to watch Wei-wei. She moved quickly, with a sense of purpose. Her head swiveled this way and that like a bird's, always watching its surroundings in case a hawk circled overhead.

"It's not uncommon," he remarked after a pause. "Men with other men."

"I know."

"You just seem...shocked."

"I'm not shocked. I just feel…" She struggled for the next word. "Embarrassed. On their behalf. It was a private, personal moment."

He regretted having to have this conversation with the back of Wei-wei's head. She was sure to be blushing fiercely by now, which was something he didn't mind seeing.

"I'm also trying to figure out what this could mean," she went on.

"Could mean for what?"

She turned around. Her cheeks were flushed, but she also looked deep in thought. "If Lin Yijin seduced his minder, then he could have the freedom to move around, go anywhere. Do anything. Without worrying about his guards reporting his activities to the Emperor."

"Maybe the guard seduced him," Gao suggested.

"Lin would still exert uncommon influence over him."

"Maybe it was mutual."

Wei-wei frowned at him. "What does that matter?"

Gao stepped close. Closer than would be proper should anyone wander onto the path and see them. "I don't know if it matters. But maybe you have a point. A man infatuated might do anything, unreasonable things. Forget his duties, forget promises."

She was so close. Close enough to hold, close enough to kiss. Maybe she hated him now, but it was very easy to forget when they were like this. Able to talk about anything, be anywhere and yet make it feel as if it were only the two of them.

"You like spinsters," Wei-wei noted. "And women disguised as men."

He had to smile at that.

"You have odd tastes," she said.

"Not really so odd."

Her lips started to curve upward, before she clamped them down. "Let's go find my brother."

~

THEY DIDN'T MAKE it far.

A pathway led from the archery field up to the pavilion where most of the guests had gathered. Once again, Wei-wei took the lead while Gao followed behind.

The moment they reached the top of the hill, she veered to the right.

"It's Chief Censor Zheng," she said, heading to the river. "He'll recognize me."

"He'll recognize me as well," Gao pointed out.

The difference was he wouldn't be scandalized if the censor saw him. His reputation wouldn't be destroyed.

"Go and wait beside the lake," he told her. "I'll find your brother."

He handed her the lantern and watched as she made her way down to the water. Then he changed directions to climb back up to the pavilion.

The gathering was separated into several low tables. The guests were seated on rugs and pillows on the floor. Wine was flowing freely between them and he could hear the hum of conversation. Small plates with various delicacies had been laid out before them.

Everyone was filled out and well-fed, with faces that glowed with good health and vigor. They probably dined on meat every day. Gao imagined he looked like a beggar in comparison. Not to mention, half his face was the color of a ripe plum. Despite this, no one seemed to notice him. Anyone who did notice didn't spare him any thought.

Gao stayed on the outside edges of the gathering, where other servants had gathered to wait on their masters. Unlike the noblemen, the attendants took note of him immediately, casting a few questioning glances his way.

He searched the gathering for Huang and saw him at the other side of the pavilion, deep in conversation. Magistrate Li was nowhere to be found. He maneuvered closer until Huang glanced up and noticed him. It was only a matter of time before the young Lord Bai extracted himself to come to him.

"Wei-wei is by the lake," Gao explained. "She managed to get some information from General Lin's son, but I'm not certain how useful it is. How were you planning to confront the magistrate?"

Huang appeared preoccupied. "About that...there's been a change of plans."

Gao's misgivings were correct. "You didn't mean for us to come, did you? Your sister insisted."

"I did mean to have you here. Something just—" Huang looked over Gao's shoulder and stopped mid-sentence. "Let me talk," he said beneath his breath before taking a step forward to address someone immediately behind Gao. "Chief Censor."

By the time Gao turned, Zheng was already upon them. "Are we ready?" he asked.

"Yes, Chief Censor."

Zheng's gaze fixed onto Gao for a brief moment as he passed by, but he said nothing more. Huang indicated they were to follow.

"What is this about?" Gao asked as they moved toward a tent set up on the grass, just clear of the pavilion.

Again, Huang shook his head and urged silence. Gao did not like this arrangement one bit. It felt like an ambush.

He looked toward the lake, where Wei-wei was supposed to be waiting to him. Huang detected Gao's concern. "She'll be fine," he assured.

They had reached the tent. A pair of guards stood at the entrance, and one of them reached out to pull aside the canvas for Zheng. The censor disappeared inside. Gao was next, but he halted.

"You'll be fine as well," Huang said.

He wasn't so sure about that. Maybe Huang had been planning his vengeance all along.

"It's safe," Huang assured.

Shaking his head, Gao stepped past the canvas flap into the tent. Huang entered immediately behind him.

Lanterns burned inside and a large painted screen spanned the space. Gao expected to see the imperial censor, but the official had disappeared somewhere behind the screen. Additional guardsmen stood like statues on either side of the tent.

A shadowy figure moved behind the silk panels and appeared to take a seat.

"The Emperor has arrived," a voice announced.

Huang dropped to his knees. Stunned, Gao did the same beside him.

"Lower," Huang whispered, tapping his forehead to the rug.

Gao glanced at the shadowy figure once before lowering his head to ground. He turned his head sideways to watch Huang for cues on what to do next. For right now, they were to stay right where they were.

It wasn't the Emperor who spoke, but rather the caller.

"His Majesty has been informed that this humble subject has performed a valuable service. For this, His Majesty owes this subject a debt of gratitude. He is to be commended and rewarded."

Gao frowned at Huang. He started to open his mouth to respond, but Huang shook his head.

The shadowy figure finally spoke. "What is the subject's name?"

The voice that spoke wasn't nearly as booming or commanding as Gao imagined the Son of Heaven would sound. He was just a man.

Apparently, Gao was supposed to answer. "I'm called Gao."

Huang was looking at him with a panicked expression. *Your Majesty*, he mouthed.

"Your Majesty," Gao added.

"The one who was killed in the river was the Emperor's nephew. The subject risked himself to catch the killer."

The long, drawn-out silence told him he should perhaps respond.

"Much thanks…Your Majesty."

"Do rise."

He and Huang rose to their feet but kept their heads bowed.

The exchange seemed unreal, as if someone were playing an elaborate joke. Common street hoods did not come into the presence of the divine ruler of the realm.

"The Emperor was told the subject's ruse was very clever. How did the subject devise such a strategy?"

"I—this humble servant just thought—" He glanced at Huang, who wasn't able to provide any assistance on this point. The shadowy Emperor was just going to have to bear his coarse conduct. "The guilty have a habit of revealing themselves. This humble servant just imagined the murderer, if he was still around, would be afraid or at least suspicious enough to reveal himself if he was convinced someone had seen him."

"Unexpected, and clever indeed," the Emperor said with a note of approval. "Casting a brick to attract jade. Do accept the Emperor's gratitude."

The crier announced the Emperor's withdrawal and, once again, Huang and Gao prostrated themselves, foreheads to the floor. Eventually the guards departed as well and they were left alone. They rose to stare at one another.

"You did this?" he asked Huang.

"All I did was submit my reports. I never mentioned you."

When they emerged from the tent, an attendant was waiting for them holding a small wooden chest. He presented it to Gao with a bow.

"The Emperor sends his gratitude."

A hundred taels of silver? Gao didn't dare to look.

Without batting an eye, Bai Huang gave instructions for the silver to be taken to the carriage.

"You would let that much money out of your sight?" Gao asked once the attendant moved to obey.

"He'll see that it's tended to."

Gao blew out a breath in disbelief.

"You're a man of some means now," Huang said.

He didn't even know what one could buy with that much silver, other than a knife in his back.

"There's a problem." It had been bothering him since the Emperor's pronouncement of his success. "This matter isn't finished. The man I captured took poison. He had an accomplice who was never caught."

"We did find the accomplice," Huang replied.

"How—"

"He was found dead," Huang said in a low voice. "Killed by someone else's hand."

"This isn't over."

They had uncovered a plot with deeper roots than he'd ever imagined. The two he'd chased down were dangerous, but they couldn't have managed both assassinations by themselves. They had other accomplices.

179

"The Emperor considers this case closed," Huang said soberly.

"What about Magistrate Li leaving details out of his report—"

Huang was already shaking his head. "He was ordered to do so to avoid scandal. I have word from the Chief Censor that the matter is closed."

"You know it isn't."

Huang regarded him with a grave expression. "The inquiry will continue quietly, in a more private fashion."

Private fashion? Gao had an idea what that meant. The man who had been killed was an imperial prince and the Emperor had given orders to close the investigation to avoid scandal. To save face.

Wei-wei's question came back to him. *Don't you want to see justice served?*

Why would Gao care about justice when the ruler of the empire himself cared more about appearances?

Huang clasped his shoulder. "The inquiry into the incident at the Yanxi Gate will continue. You've performed a great service to the Emperor, Gao. Leave the rest to imperial authorities."

Gao didn't know what was worse. Becoming entangled in a murder investigation that had nothing to do with him...or being cut out before it was complete.

He may not care about so much about justice, but he wanted to know the answers. The Emperor had declared the case a triumph, but Gao felt far from it. A wound was still open, and he had just been told to ignore it and walk away.

While better men took the reins.

CHAPTER 17

The lake looked like black glass in the night, with the gleaming white disk of the full moon reflected on the surface. Like a perfectly round pearl. Suddenly the mirror broke into a series of ripples. Someone had tossed a stone into the water.

That was Wei-wei's first sign that someone else was beside the lake. She searched along the bank until she could discern a lone silhouette. Whoever it was stood by the water in long flowing robes, cloaked in darkness.

She started to back away to avoid discovery, but it was too late. The surface of the lake had settled enough for the figure to see the reflection of Wei-wei's lantern in it.

"Are you enjoying the full moon, young master?" came a feminine voice. The tone was soft, but there was a backbone of culture and confidence behind it.

Exhaling slowly, Wei-wei came closer. The light of the lantern revealed a finely shaped face with skin faintly pink like a rose. It was the courtesan Song Yi from the House of Heavenly Peaches. Magistrate Li had come to see her the other night when Wei-wei had tried to spy on him.

"The night is not as enjoyable when one is alone," Wei-wei replied.

"Just because there are so many people around"—she waved an elegant hand in the direction of the pavilion —"doesn't mean one isn't alone."

Song Yi sounded melancholy. She must have been hired tonight for entertainment, but she was far from fulfilling her duties while hiding out down here.

"Does the young master have a name? Or does he wish to remain mysterious?" Song Yi asked gently.

"Bai Chang-min," Wei-wei replied, thankful for the darkness.

"From the illustrious Bai family," she murmured.

At first Wei-wei thought Song Yi was just trying to sound impressed to be flattering, but then Song Yi said, "You have a sister."

"Usually people ask about my eldest brother," Wei-wei replied, in a bit of shock.

"Lord Bai Huang is quite distinguished as well, but your sister is said to be a great talent."

Huang had built a reputation for himself in the Pingkang li, especially the pleasure quarter where the House of Heavenly Peaches stood. Wei-we couldn't imagine how anyone would have formed any impression of her.

"I hear she is very well-read and educated."

She realized then how Song Yi knew about her. This was the courtesan Li Chen was besotted with. He'd spoken to Song Yi night after night. She could guess what had happened. Li Chen had informed the courtesan about his impending betrothal, mentioning her name.

And now Song Yi was mourning silently by the lake, presenting a lonely picture.

How much had Magistrate Li confided to her? Was it possible Li Chen had revealed some details of the case?

"We have a mutual acquaintance," Wei-wei ventured.

Song Yi raised her perfectly shaped eyebrows in question.

"Magistrate Li Chen is a friend of our family. He speaks well of you."

The courtesan frowned. "That is a surprise to hear."

Wei-wei wished she weren't in disguise at the moment. Perhaps it would have been easier to get Song Yi to speak to her woman-to-woman. Instead the courtesan was wary, taking great care with her words.

"Being a magistrate must be a great burden on one's shoulders," Wei-wei said. "Just the other day he spoke of a very difficult case. It involved the death of a wealthy noble-man. Such a tragedy."

Song Yi's face was a mask. "The magistrate doesn't speak of such important matters to one like myself."

Wei-wei was doing a poor job of getting information. She hadn't yet gained Song Yi's trust, and a gossipy cour-tesan willing to spill secrets left and right would lose patronage rather quickly. Wei-wei considered switching topics, maybe reciting a poem about the moon bringing forth thoughts of separated hearts. That was something a young scholar trying to impress a talented courtesan might attempt.

Unfortunately, there was no chance. Another lantern had shown up, also reflected in the water.

"Please excuse me, young Lord Bai. I've neglected my duties for the night," Song Yi said after looking over Wei-wei's shoulder.

The courtesan glided past her. As Wei-wei turned, she saw Song Yi pass by the newcomer while making a concerted effort not to make eye contact.

With Magistrate Li Chen.

Li was momentarily distracted by Song Yi's departure, but once she was gone, his focus returned to Wei-wei. He took one look at her before his eyes grew wide. She stared back at him, caught.

Her disguise might fool someone who had never met her before, who would assume that she was younger than her age based on the slightness of her build. They might sense that something seemed not quite right, but would be too polite to bring it up.

To someone who knew her face, Wei-wei always suspected the disguise would not be convincing at all. And she was right.

"Lady Bai," he stated.

"Magistrate Li." She sounded a lot calmer than she would have thought.

He cleared his throat. "Perhaps we should talk somewhere more private."

～

THEY FOUND a bench surrounded by a cluster of trees a short distance away from the gathering, though they both remained standing. A lantern hung from the branches.

"So...uh. Do you do this often?" Li Chen began.

She had a picture of how he must conduct interrogations in the yamen, and it wasn't like this.

"Only once in a while," she replied.

"Oh."

Wei-wei was disappointed he didn't sound outraged or scandalized or even disturbed. What sort of family would allow their daughter to run about in such a way? But he didn't say anything like that and she doubted he would. Li Chen folded his hands together and bent his head down with a thoughtful expression.

"Do you think this practice is likely to continue? What I mean is, after?"

If there were anyone who liked to speak in pauses. After she was married, perhaps even to him is what Li was saying. It was a lot for a pause to say.

"It's not something that I plan for so far ahead," she replied awkwardly.

"It certainly must require some planning."

"Well, yes. There's indeed some planning involved." This was not the conversation she expected to have at all. "You don't find this to be at all…outlandish?"

"Not really." Li Chen smiled slightly. "In a way, it makes sense for you. Like the legend of Liang and Zhu."

She blinked at him. The magistrate had named her favorite story, the tale of tragic love between two scholars, one of them a woman who had disguised herself as a man to be allowed to study.

Li looked nervous standing across the bench from her. In this light, all her plots revolving around how they would confront him about his sinister plots faded away. She could see why her brother would think Li Chen was a suitable match for her. He was a man of learning and books and poems. Most importantly, he wasn't frightened away by her misbehavior as much as she wanted him to be.

"I understand we don't know each other well," he said. "But perhaps we know each other better than most before becoming betrothed. You are of an age to know your mind. And I have also had time to give the matter of marriage much thought."

Meaning she wasn't a bride at the tender age of fourteen or fifteen. She was a spinster. Maybe he didn't appreciate spinsters like Gao did, but Li Chen didn't seem to mind her being one either.

With a sigh, Wei-wei sat down at one end of the bench. A wave of sadness struck her, like a child whose game had come to an end. It had been exhilarating to play, but she had just been prolonging the inevitable.

"Please sit," she said. He did, taking the opposite end of the bench. They were as far away from each other as they could possibly be. "You're going to ask my parents to marry me."

"Well, my mother will make the official proposal—"

"I know how the process works," she said, agitated. A spinster and a shrew and he still wasn't turned away. "Is there someone else you care for?" she asked in a gentler tone. "Someone who evokes passion in you?"

Li Chen swallowed. "You're…uh…very direct."

"Not usually." Finally, she turned to look at him. "Just tonight."

"There is someone," he admitted. "But matters of the heart are fleeting. One must be practical."

"One must be practical," Wei-wei echoed.

Just as Li Chen was likely thinking of someone at that moment, she thought of Gao. He was exciting to her. He was like an epic tale of the impossible. A story of dragons and tragic lovers and faraway lands. But he was an outlaw and unsuitable.

She and Li Chen would raise children who would become distinguished scholars and officials. It was a journey of generations, of the lives of her ancestors before her leading up to the present. Not a singular journey she was meant to make on her own.

"I don't think I would be a jealous sort of wife," Wei-wei said. "Men are known to have companions."

She didn't love Li Chen, and he didn't love her. Why would she begrudge him his happiness?

"I think this is getting rather personal. We don't have to plan this all out tonight, Lady Bai."

She nodded. He was a gentleman, wasn't he? Studious, cultured, and polite.

But not completely honest. His demeanor was so amiable, she'd almost forgotten.

Wei-wei turned to him, so quickly that he was taken off guard. "If I'm to be your wife, there's something I need to know. You lied about the man found in the canal. Why?"

He straightened. She could sense him putting on a layer of armor, but they had come to an understanding that night. On a personal level. That had to mean something.

"I was asked to hide the truth," he confessed. "To protect the Emperor. It's in the hands of imperial authorities now. That is all I can say."

"But you omitted the seal on the report and lied about the manner of death—"

Li sprang over to her, taking hold of her wrist. Startled, she tried to pull away.

"*Quiet*," he whispered, in alarm. He lifted a hand to her mouth, not quite touching her lips. "I never mentioned your name, but you've been seen coming to my office. Don't say anything. Please trust me on this."

She was in shock. He still held onto her wrist. The magistrate had never done anything so forward.

"Who told you to lie on the report?" she demanded.

His eyes had a troubled look in them. Emotion warred beneath the surface.

"*Lady Bai.*"

An iron-hard voice sliced through the silence. Wei-wei looked up to see Gao standing over them. His gaze fixed onto Li Chen.

It was the first time she saw a glimpse of what her brother had talked about. What Mingyu had warned her away from. Gao didn't have to say or do anything. Magistrate Li kept his eyes on Gao as he released her arm, moving slowly as one would do when facing an unpredictable and wild animal.

"We should go," Gao said.

She rose, her heart pounding, and left the grounds with him.

CHAPTER 18

"I had just asked him about the report," Wei-wei explained once they were in the carriage.

Gao swallowed, trying to rid himself of the bitter taste in his mouth. "So, that was what you were talking about."

The carriage had left the guarded perimeter of the park and there was no one to hear their conversation but Zhou Dan.

"The magistrate confessed that he was instructed to hide the truth," she said.

He cared little about that at the moment. The image of Wei-wei and Li Chen, hidden away together among the trees, had wormed its way into his head. No matter what he did, he couldn't let go of it.

"He was afraid," she went on.

"I didn't threaten him." Hardly. Even though Li Chen had his hands on her.

Wei-wei frowned, searching his face. "I don't mean he was afraid of you," she said, finally understanding. "He didn't want me speaking of the jade seal or any details of the case. I tried to find out who instructed him to lie. It had to be someone higher than him in rank."

"I could have told you. It was the Emperor."

Her mouth dropped open.

"The man who was killed was the Emperor's nephew. Magistrate Li only did what he was told. Your brother informed me this matter will be taken up by imperial authorities from now on."

"That was what Li said as well," Wei-wei murmured.

He could see the questions in her eyes, but they weren't the same questions he had. She and Li Chen had looked too familiar sitting beside one another, sharing private thoughts. It was like a knife twisting inside him.

"There's nothing more for us to do here. I'm done with this."

Wei-wei was taken aback. "Do you really feel the investigation is over, Gao? There are so many unanswered questions."

"There will always be unanswered questions," he spat, his tone harsher than he intended. "There are many murders in the city that go unpunished. You have to realize that this crime may never be over. It may never be resolved—especially if certain people don't want it to be."

"What do you mean by that?"

"What use is it for me to chase assassins through the streets or for you to scour records for evidence? There are men with influence and power, deciding what is a crime and what isn't. What is true and what isn't."

"Truth is truth," Wei-wei argued. "If there are men abusing power, then they need to be stopped. There's an entire branch of the imperial government dedicated to fighting corruption."

He did spit this time—at least over the side of the carriage. He slumped back in the seat in frustration, glaring. Wei-wei regarded him with an appalled look on her face.

"What happened tonight?" she demanded.

Zhou Dan glanced over his shoulder briefly, before snapping his attention back to the road. The things that young man must have seen and heard.

What had happened that night? He'd been brought before the Emperor and commended, rewarded even. He had more money in his possession than he had ever dreamed. The chest of silver rested on the floor of the carriage. Gao shoved it beneath the seat with his foot.

"I was reminded of my place," he retorted. "By the most powerful men in the empire."

There was the stench of double-dealing about the entire evening. Someone was in a rush to declare the case closed and done. Gao wasn't one to care about what made an honest living versus a dishonest one, as long as it meant living, but here he was obviously being manipulated.

It made all the Emperor's praise ring hollow, and the rich reward look like nothing more than a bribe.

～

GAO WOKE up early that morning to bury his stash of silver in the corner of the garden in the Bai mansion. He couldn't imagine there was any better place to put it. The place had walls as thick as the magistrate's yamen and they were rich enough to have no interest in his silver. Bai Huang had tossed the chest around at a whim as if it were nothing.

He took one ingot and tucked it into his robe before he started digging. In the midst of his task, on his knees with his hands in the dirt, Gao had realized the absurdity, the complete absurdity of his predicament. Wei-wei was sleeping peacefully in the next courtyard. Clever, well-fed, well-educated, beautiful Wei-wei who he burned for, and here he was, clawing up her garden like some rodent. He smoothed the dirt back over the silver, and covered the patch with a rock.

Then he left.

If he'd been able to write a note, Gao might have left one. As it was, he'd have to explain when he saw them next. There was an hour until the ward gates opened, so he walked around to pass the time. He was becoming quite familiar with the grand mansions of the neighborhood. How many taels of silver would it take to live in one of those? One tael was at least enough that he could eat well for an entire month—or at least he thought. He'd never had reason to do such calculations.

It was a ridiculous fortune. More than he had any sense of what to do with. It was the sort of fortune that could drive a man of no means to ruin. He'd seen it happen. Bad fortune too often followed good fortune, especially when silver fell into weak hands. Such was the case of his father, a corrupt tax collector. Their family had lived comfortably for a time, before ruin found them.

As ridiculous of a fortune as he now possessed, the Bais were wealthier than that. The ward gates finally opened near sun up, and Gao headed back to more familiar ground. It took hours on foot, but he had time. It gave him space to think.

Back in the north lanes of Pingkang li, Gao went to the bathhouse. He even paid to have his clothes laundered. He was still living off the bounty he'd gotten for capturing the man with the machete.

As Gao paid the coin to the proprietor of the bathhouse, he remembered he'd planned to share half that bounty with

Fu Lin. That hapless fool. If he hadn't stumbled upon the body in the canal and the jade seal, none of this would have happened.

The decision came to him as he soaked in the steaming water with the morning light just coming in through the slats in the walls. Gao laughed at the thought of it.

He would split his entire reward with the boy. Fu Lin and his entire family were crammed into the tenements. They could make some use of the Emperor's silver. Fu Lin could pay off his gambling debts and be free of Headman Hui. Hopefully, he would finally learn his lesson and stay away from the gambling dens. Then again, probably not, but that wasn't Gao's problem to solve.

Gao closed his eyes and leaned back in the bath, relaxing as his muscles loosened. He let his mind drift to Wei-wei, trying to picture whether he preferred her in woman's clothes or men's...or maybe none at all.

It was a fantasy only. They'd left off last night with him steeped in his nameless, faceless anger and Wei-wei coldly quiet. She still hated him for being a knife-wielding lowlife, and he'd have to admit the sentiment was deserved.

By the time he left the bathhouse several hours later, the sun had risen high into the sky. His clothes had dried enough to wear. The summer heat would have to do the rest.

Gao went to call on Fu Lin's family in the tenements. Gao realized then he didn't even know the boy's actual name, but the family seemed to recognize his street name. They reported their son hadn't come home the previous night, though no one seemed to think anything of it.

Fu Lin came and went as he pleased. Gao left a message that he had something for the boy, giving several locations where they could meet. Then he sought out Fu's usual haunts — the teahouses, gambling dens. Even the pawn shop.

"Been missing you around here." Headman Hui cornered

Gao as he was asking around the lottery dens about Fu Lin. The boy would sometimes peddle game slips around the streets for a little extra money.

"Collections have been lagging."

"It's only been a few days, Hui," Gao replied noncommittally.

"Ever thinking about getting back to work?"

"I'm taking care of some things right now."

Gao tried to extract himself as delicately as possible. It served no purpose to anger Hui, who still had many street connections. Keeping the peace or at least a neutral stance seemed a good strategy in general. Unfortunately, Hui seemed to have come to him with something in mind.

"I hear you've turned thief-catcher. Good money in that?"

Gao shrugged. Gossip about the dramatic arrests had inevitably spread through the streets. Hui was rightfully curious, that was all. Still, Gao thought it was worth exploring the possibility that the gambling den boss might know more.

"Have you heard anything about those men? The killers?" Gao asked.

"Only that they're both dead," Hui said dismissively. "Take care. Thief-catching can be dangerous work."

As Hui walked away flanked by his henchmen, it was unclear to Gao whether he'd just been threatened or warned. Or Hui could just be making conversation. One thing was clear, crime bosses did not like thief-catchers.

Without any idea where Fu Lin was, Gao decided to settle down at one of the meeting places he'd left with the boy's family. Maybe Fu Lin would receive word and show up.

An odd sense of being out of place followed him as he moved through the streets. He realized what was missing—it was the constant watchfulness and scheming. He didn't need to hustle for the next coin. He wasn't wondering whether he would end the day with food in his stomach or not.

And Gao didn't exactly know what to do with himself after such a sudden turn of events.

CHAPTER 19

I t took Wei-wei a long time to fall asleep after the gathering. For the second night in a row, Gao was sleeping in her house, separated from her by only the division between the inner and outer courtyard. Even though he was untrustworthy and a cutthroat, Wei-wei felt safer with him there. Had her brother asked Gao to stay? What did it mean that the very person who had threatened Huang's life was now the person Huang asked to watch over her?

All those questions didn't matter. He was gone before she even woke up the next morning.

"Did Gao say anything before he left?" she asked Zhou Dan, who only shook his head wordlessly, avoiding her eyes. As a servant, Zhou Dan wasn't supposed to see things, but he saw things.

Wei-wei wanted to apologize for subjecting him to the heated argument she and Gao had had in the carriage. She had hoped to speak to Gao as well, but now he was nowhere to be found. It was unfair of her to assume Gao would be there that morning, waiting to do whatever she expected him to do.

So much had happened the night before. Gao seemed angry at everything. Li Chen was still acting suspicious. She couldn't even talk things over with Huang because he hadn't yet returned.

With her brother and Gao gone, Wei-wei could do nothing but wait. She was too distracted to even set the lesson for Chang-min. Her younger brother had settled in the study on his own to read over passages from the Classics.

Chang-min really was dedicated. Much more dedicated than Huang had been at that age. She hoped she hadn't ruined the poor boy's reputation venturing all over the city in his name.

It was past noon when someone came calling at their gate for Bai Huang. The servants gave the usual answer that Lord Bai was not present and asked to take a message, but the visitor was adamant.

"She's a woman," Zhou Dan told her, with great interest.

Wei-wei went to the gate and was surprised to see who was standing there.

"Lady Song Yi?"

The courtesan stared at her with a frown of almost recognition.

"Yes, we met last night," Wei-wei acknowledged impatiently, drawing the woman into the courtyard. "My elder brother isn't home. What's the matter?"

"You're very beautiful," the courtesan said, not entirely happy with the observation. "Just like your brothers. I should have known."

"Well, I *was* one of my brothers," Wei-wei reminded her. "Did Bai Huang ask you to come here?"

"He came to the pleasure house several days ago," she

explained. "He told me to come find him if I heard anything or saw anything. But the Imperial City was barricaded so I couldn't get to the records office."

The imperial offices closed off? When did that happen?

"I managed to find your family's mansion by asking around," Song Yi continued. "If you know how to reach Lord Bai, there is something he should see."

Song Yi looked genuinely concerned, and Wei-wei felt helpless not being able to do something for the other woman, but there was no telling when her brother would return. "If it's an urgent matter, can you not go to the magistrate?"

The courtesan shook her head. "I can't go to Magistrate Li. I'm afraid it will put him in danger."

That put a halt to Wei-wei's questioning.

"Are *you* in danger?" Wei-wei asked. She had learned that the pleasure quarter could be a treacherous place, and courtesans, even the ones who were praised and celebrated, were too often expendable to the men of power they served.

"I don't know." Song Yi tried to explain what had happened. She was flustered and shaking. "Someone's been watching us. It's a warning."

Wei-wei didn't want to send Song Yi back alone, as frightened as she was. "I know someone who might be able to help."

She summoned Zhou Dan to fetch the carriage and convinced Song Yi to show her this warning first. Zhou drove them both, bringing a wooden club up beside him in the seat though Wei-wei assured him it was probably unnecessary. This didn't sound like the work of street rabble.

The quarter looked like a different place in the daylight without its swaying lanterns and ladies in colorful silk. Even though it was past noon, the pleasure houses were quiet and asleep. Perhaps to prepare themselves for the late evenings they were known for.

There was a girl with a broom at the front of the House of Heavenly Peaches. Wei-wei almost didn't recognize her. It was Sparrow, looking child-like without her painted lips and shaped eyebrows. The young courtesan didn't recognize her either, giving her barely a glance as Wei-wei and Song Yi walked by.

If they were truly being watched, as Song Yi feared, then there was little to raise any alarm with just Wei-wei visiting. They were just two women, walking into a courtesan house before business hours. The inside was quiet as well. There were a few girls cleaning the floors. Cooking sounds came from the kitchen in the back.

There was a routine and ritual that played out every day in the House of Heavenly Peaches, Wei-wei realized. It was very much like the theater. Every night was a performance.

"In my chamber," Song Yi said in a low voice.

Song Yi's quarters were in the back corner of the house. She had a private sitting area and sleeping room to herself. There was nothing amiss in the front room. A low table was set in the center and tasteful scrolls hung on the walls. It looked to be a place to entertain guests.

Song Yi directed Wei-wei through the curtains into the chamber in back. An older woman in a gray robe was situated there, scrubbing at a large black character on the wall.

"Auntie!" Song Yi chastised.

"Need to get rid of it," the woman insisted in a gruff voice. "It's scaring the girls."

Wei-wei assumed Auntie was one of the former courtesans who remained with the house after retiring from her role as hostess.

"Is that it?" Wei-wei asked, looking up at the character on the wall.

Song Yi nodded, biting her lip anxiously.

A single character, 'Li'. Exactly as Song Yi had described.

"I imagined it would be more...sinister," Wei-wei admitted.

"Is this not sinister enough?" Song Yi cried.

The character was painted in what looked like black ink. It spanned nearly the entire wall in the small space. Auntie's scrubbing had transformed part of it into a dark smudge.

"It's probably some jealous patron," Auntie said. "You've been spending too much time with that magistrate."

"He pays for my time, I have no choice in the matter," Song Yi replied stiffly.

Auntie snorted.

"When did you find this?" Wei-wei asked. She had figured Li Chen and the courtesan were involved. She didn't need to know the lurid details.

"I didn't leave the gathering at the park until nearly sunrise. I found this when I returned this morning."

Song Yi hadn't even been allowed to sleep. She'd probably been paid to stay all night, playing music and conversing until the last guest left.

"Most of the girls were at that gathering or upstairs with patrons," Auntie added. "I tell you, once in a while an admirer gets possessive. They think something like this is a sign of devotion. Just ignore it. Now you've barely had any rest. Go sleep in my room for a few hours so you can get ready for tonight."

"I'm fine, Auntie," Song Yi snapped. She turned back to Wei-wei. "What do you think?"

Whether it was an overzealous admirer or an enemy of Li Chen's sending a warning, both were too disturbing to ignore.

"Can you take leave tonight?" Wei-wei asked. Song Yi looked exhausted and frightened on top of that.

Auntie made a rude noise at that suggestion.

"We'll go together to the magistrate," Wei-wei went on, ignoring the garrulous old woman. "I know you're concerned for him, but he's a man with power and influence. It's his duty to address injustices like this."

"Injustice." Auntie turned back to the wall and continued scrubbing. "She calls it injustice. I call it a stain on the wall. Your magistrate will call it two fussy women who are not worth the trouble."

Song Yi directed Wei-wei back out to the sitting room and presumably out of earshot from Auntie. Or at least Auntie was no longer invited to comment on the conversation.

"You said you knew someone else who might be able to help?"

Wei-wei let out a breath. She was less confident about this than she had let on, but the man was practically family now since Yue-ying had married Huang.

"He used to be head constable in this county," she explained. "His name is Wu Kaifeng."

～

HEAVEN AND EARTH, black and yellow. Space and time, vast and limitless.

Sun high or low, moon full or parsed; with stars and lodges spread in place.

Gao held the pages open over the teahouse table, palms flat over the paper as if that would keep the characters from swimming together before his eyes.

"It is impossible for you to learn enough in this lifetime to impress her. You must know that."

Gao looked up to watch as Mingyu poured hot tea into

his bowl. He should feel flattered that she always took the time to grace him with a remark, even if it burned of acid.

"I know that," he replied coolly.

He'd found the tattered booklet at the pawn shop a couple days ago. The *Thousand Character Classic* was commonly used to create lottery slips, but it was also used as a primer to teach children. The first lines were still familiar. He'd memorized them years ago as a child learning how to read. The rest he'd tried to recall in bits and pieces, but never managed more than a few minutes before tossing it aside in frustration.

Mingyu's eyes flickered across the page, probably holding back laughter at the tiny sketches above the characters. She was known to recite poetry and debate philosophy with scholars. Gao, on the other hand, had paid the letter reader on the corner to read these nonsense lines to him while he drew in little pictures to help him remember the words.

Maybe another man might feel shame with those shapely eyes looking down on him, but Gao was who he was. If he had any shame, it would be for a multitude of other sins.

"You do it because it makes you feel closer to her," Mingyu remarked, realization dawning.

A sharp pain needled him in the chest. Gao set his elbow onto the table, propping his head against three fingers. The position served to partially hide his face. "It gives me a headache," he complained.

Mingyu lowered herself onto the stool across from him. "You're pining after her." Her tone had softened considerably.

He found her sudden kindness more grating than her cynicism. His first thought was to rudely chase her away, but no one ever dared to say a cross word to Mingyu in the teahouse. Here, she was Queen Empress and even those who didn't know of her prior reputation were in awe of her. Those who weren't in her thrall knew enough to be mindful of her intimidating husband, the infamous Wu Kaifang, who cast a long shadow and was always hovering nearby.

But it was Gao's rule not to ruin the road he'd just tread on. "Do you have any advice, Lady Mingyu?" he asked.

"Well, Mister Gao. If I were a brothel madam, I would tell you to make the acquaintance of another girl. Despite what the lovesick may say, that distraction does sometimes work."

There could be no other girl. It wasn't just that he found Wei-wei beautiful, he also found her difficult. And he liked her way of being difficult.

"That's bad advice, Lady Mingyu."

She flashed him what may have been her first genuine smile. "There's no possible good advice for what you're suffering."

He wasn't suffering. He was just sitting here, trying to read lines from a nonsense poem that Wei-wei probably memorized when she was five years old, that was all.

The sudden beating of the signal drums from outside interrupted them. All conversation in the teahouse ceased as the drumbeat continued. It was the city drums sounding from the guard towers throughout the city. They were used to signal the closing of the ward gates, but the hour was too early for that. It was long before sundown.

Wu Kaifeng came to Mingyu's side. She reached out to him, taking hold of his arm as if to steady herself and him as well. "What's happening?" she asked.

He moved in quick strides to the entrance with Mingyu following closely behind. Gao looked out the window to see a messenger on horseback coursing down the street.

"Curfew!" the messenger shouted. "Curfew is in effect. Clear the streets!"

"Emergency measures," Wu explained, drawing his wife

back inside. "Go home," he instructed the patrons. "The magistrate is enacting early curfew."

Either due to his past authority as head constable or his commanding presence, the customers immediately began exiting the teahouse. The streets were far from clear, however. Everyone milled around outside, asking strangers what was happening.

"Clear the streets!" The rider was making a return trip through the lane. "For the safety of the city!"

Typically, the ward gates would close at dawn, but activity could continue freely inside the ward. For them to be clearing the streets as well, something big had to have happened.

Gao stood to go, intending to hunt down several contacts to see if they knew anything. He was stopped by the sight of Magistrate Li riding up to the teahouse. Li wore his dark green magistrate's uniform and was accompanied by several constables, all visibly armed.

"Is Lady Bai here?" he asked Mingyu.

"No, I haven't seen her," Mingyu said. Inexplicably, she looked toward Gao which prompted the magistrate to do the same.

"Her family is worried for her," Li said. "They said she left to come here hours ago."

Hours. Gao fought to keep his expression neutral, but inside his mind was racing.

Wu came to stand beside his wife. "What has happened, Magistrate Li?"

The two men had worked together not long ago. Li ran a hand over his neck in agitation. "Wu, I can really use your help with this."

"What's happened?" Wu Kaifeng repeated.

The magistrate's gaze swept the teahouse, making sure the room was empty. His eyes lingered on Gao, but he made the decision to continue. "It's Constable Ma. They got him."

The head constable. Gao didn't have to ask what Magistrate Li meant. Head Constable Ma had led the party to hunt down and apprehend the canal killers. Whoever "they" where, they had already gotten rid of Machete Man and his accomplice, Double Knives. Now they had also murdered Head Constable Ma as a warning.

"Have you seen Lady Bai?" Li asked again, looking directly at Gao now.

"I have not."

But if Wei-wei was out and unprotected in the Pingkang li right now, he was going to find her.

~

OVER THE NEXT HOUR, confusion ruled in Pingkang. The city's criers continued to ride through the streets, announcing early curfew and urging everyone to get inside. All the vendors in the marketplace were forced to close up early and the lanes became clogged with carts and wheelbarrows as everyone struggled to get home. The patrols moved through teahouses and restaurants, warning that arrests would start.

Amidst the turmoil, Gao heard rumors that there was some big announcement to come in the morning. For now, clear the streets.

He checked with several informants asking around for Wei-wei. She wasn't known in Pingkang li, unlike her brother, but if anyone had seen her, she'd definitely be remembered. One contact indicated that she might have been seen at the House of Heavenly Peaches. Gao hurried there and once again encountered Magistrate Li with his posse.

"Have you found her?" they both asked each other.

The answer was no and no.

"You should be careful," Magistrate Li warned as they started to set out in different directions. "This lot, whoever they are, they've sent warnings to the magistrate's office, to the constable stations. No one is safe."

Gao was the one who had captured the machete wielder. Did that make him even more of a target than Constable Ma?

"Get inside," Li Chen said as a parting warning. "We're sweeping the streets."

He didn't comply. Instead he circled back toward the teahouse. If Wei-wei was stranded in this ward, she'd go somewhere familiar to her, and he couldn't think of any other place. On his way there, another one of his informants caught up to him.

"Go to the canal," he said, out of breath.

Dread sank its claws into him. "What do you mean?"

"Go to the canal," the informant repeated. He hurried away, disappearing into the alleyway.

On his grave. The waterway was in the dark northwest corner of the ward. Gao shouldn't go there alone, but he couldn't not go.

His heart pounded and Gao could barely breathe as he made his way there. He slipped his knife into his hand. As a rule, he never brandished it out in the open, but this was a day for rules to be suspended.

There was something near the water. A gray bundle huddled at the bank. Gao's mouth went so dry he could no longer swallow. He forced his feet forward, his body going numb when he saw that it wasn't something, but someone. The body was turned away toward the water with one shoulder jutting in the air.

It couldn't be Wei-wei. It couldn't be. The size, the clothes. Nothing matched what she would look like, his mind insisted wildly. He didn't know how to pray, but he tried it anyway as he crouched down and pulled the shoulder toward him. The body rolled onto its back.

It wasn't Wei-wei, but Gao's stomach sickened nonetheless. It was Fu Lin.

CHAPTER 20

Wei-wei was on her way to the teahouse when the drumbeats started to signal curfew.

Zhou Dan pulled the carriage to a halt and looked back at her. "What do we do?"

"I don't know."

Nothing like this had ever happened before. When the city crier rode through the streets, it finally occurred to her that there was a larger crisis at hand. She directed Zhou Dan to go toward the ward gates at the north end. There was a crowd gathered there, but the gates were shut and barricaded. The guards were not letting anyone through.

There was only one option.

The doors of the Spring Blossom teahouse were closed, but Mingyu opened them when Wei-wei knocked.

"There you are!" Mingyu said, ushering her inside.

"What's happened?"

Mingyu sat her down as Wu Kaifeng went with Zhou Dan to stable the horse and carriage.

"The magistrate has declared a state of emergency," Mingyu barred the door behind them. "There's been at least one other death—the head constable. A formal proclamation will be made in the morning. In the meantime, the city guards are enacting curfew and clearing the streets."

"In all the wards?" Wei-wei asked.

"I think so." The drums were the same ones that signaled the closing of all the gates. "The entire city is on watch."

Chang'an had faced several sieges in the past, some more devastating than others. None of the major rebellions were in their lifetimes, but the city remembered. There was another reason the capital would shut down like this. Wei-wei waited until Wu Kaifeng returned with Zhou Dan before she revealed her suspicions.

"I think the Emperor is in danger." She recounted the news of Chancellor Yao's assassination on the same night as the Emperor's nephew. The news hadn't yet reached the rest of the city, but that could be what was being announced in the morning.

"There was also the character 'Li' written in courtesan Song Yi's chamber in the House of Heavenly Peaches," she reported. "It looked like a threat."

"From the assassins?" Wu asked.

The former constable considered the possibility, but didn't concede anything. Wei-wei was already convinced. Gao had told her another suspect was poisoned.

"I won't be able to go home while the gates are locked. My family will be worried."

"Magistrate Li came looking for you. Perhaps he'll come back," Mingyu soothed. "He'll be able to get through the barricades."

"It would be safer to stay where you are." Wu went to position himself near the door, taking a moment to look out the window. "And for Li to get off the streets himself."

"You were his head constable. Do you trust the magistrate?" Wei-wei asked.

He thought on it. "Li Chen is overly careful with his words at times, but I've known him to be trustworthy."

"His behavior has been"—she had to be careful here—"less than honest at times with this investigation. Important details were removed from the record. Suspects have passed away under his custody. Now he's closed off the wards without warning."

Wu's brow furrowed as he absorbed the information. "While I was in his employ, Li Chen performed his duties impeccably."

"All the more reason this behavior is so suspicious," she insisted.

He pinned her with a severe look. It would have intimidated most people, but Wei-wei had come to know this was just the way Wu Kaifeng always looked. Finally, he nodded. "No man is above corruption," he agreed.

What if Li had closed to gates to allow co-conspirators to move unimpeded through the city? The city guards were occupied at the gates and clearing the streets.

She could be arrested for falsely accusing an appointed official, but there were too many coincidences. One of the last things Li Chen had said to her last night was a warning, wasn't it? He'd warned her not to speak of the case.

"*Gao.*" How could she have not thought of him until now? Gao was also in the middle of this case.

"He was here earlier as well," Mingyu said gently. "Also looking for you."

He could be in danger.

"Gao," Wu Kaifeng echoed, interrupting her thoughts. "Now, there is someone who is not to be trusted."

∼

MAGISTRATE LI NEVER DID RETURN. Neither did Gao. After an hour, the streets grew quiet except for the occasional foot patrol marching by to ensure the streets were clear. Wu Kaifeng set up a pallet in the main room downstairs for Zhou Dan while Mingyu brought Wei-wei to the extra room upstairs.

"We rent this out to the occasional traveler," Mingyu explained, rolling out the sleeping mat and blankets.

She wasn't used to seeing Mingyu doing something so mundane. Mingyu had always seemed otherworldly, so elegant and ethereal. Wei-wei knelt to help her set up the sleeping area.

"Thank you for allowing me to stay."

"Of course. Aren't we family now?" Mingyu patted her hand affectionately before rising. She closed the door gently behind her, leaving Wei-wei alone.

She removed her outer robe to prepare for bed, leaving on the pale-colored tunic and trousers of her undergarments. She folded the robe into a neat rectangle and laid it in the corner beside her shoes. Then she opened the shutters on the window before blowing out the lamp.

The moon was still round and bright, reminding her of the gathering the night before. She and Gao had returned home last night beneath the full moon, but they hadn't left on good terms.

As she leaned against the ledge, an evening breeze swept in, whispering her name.

Her name?

Someone really was calling out her name. Wei-wei looked down to see Gao standing down in the alleyway.

"What are you doing down there?"

"Making sure you're safe."

There was a haunted look in his eyes. He looked ready to fight demons for her and her heart broke.

"Come up," she urged. "The patrols are sweeping the streets."

Wei-wei expected him to go around to knock on the front door to be let in, but Gao reached up, found a handhold, and started climbing steadily up the side of the building. Her heart pounded, nervous on his behalf. One slip and he'd plummet to the hard ground. When his hand closed around the ledge, she was flooded with relief.

She stepped back, letting out a trapped breath, as he climbed inside. Then looked up and their eyes met. His were dark and fathomless and some kind of madness flowed into her. She reached for him, pressing her mouth against his.

His arms circled tight around her waist to return the kiss. His mouth was so warm, and his skin heated. She could feel his heat through his clothes, and beneath that, the hard, corded strength of his muscle.

"I was afraid they'd come for you," she said when they pulled apart.

"They?" Gao looked at her, searching her face. His jaw tightened, his expression starker than she'd ever seen.

She reached for the part of his robe, her fingers slipping past cloth to follow his heartbeat. Her palm pressed against bare skin. There was something dangerous in that first touch. His chest rose and fell. There was an audible catch in Gao's throat.

"Wei-wei." He trapped her hand beneath his. Longing mixed with alarm in his voice. "We can't."

"I don't care."

She kissed him again, sensing resistance even though Gao returned the kiss. She pressed closer, deepening the kiss until he yielded. Gao reached for her hungrily, threading his fingers through her hair. Gao had said this touch was meant to confuse yet she'd never been more certain of anything in her life. She'd never been more afraid either, but she liked this fear. She liked how it tasted, her pulse racing the way it was. Like she was falling with no end.

"I care," Gao insisted.

His voice was thick with desire, but he broke apart despite that. Then he looked at her for a long time, as if second guessing his decision. The hard lines of his face entranced her. She wanted to trace them with her fingertips. She wanted to trace every part of him. Warring emotions flickered across his face as he let go.

The bruising on his face was more pronounced now, making his appearance even more striking. She could feel it down to her toes when he looked at her.

"What's wrong?" she asked him. The darkness she'd sensed in him had returned.

"I don't want anything to happen to you." He turned to look out the window, scanning the alley below. Then he sat with his back against the wall. "I'll just watch this window while you sleep. I won't touch you," he insisted, his voice hoarse.

Something was different. He was always calm, even in the face of danger. Wei-wei had never known Gao to be easily agitated, but he was agitated now.

"Try to sleep," he urged, before forcing his gaze outside into the night.

Wei-wei sank onto the mat and pulled the blanket over herself. All the while watching him.

Her body remained awakened and restless with arousal. Gao didn't turn toward her, but she could sense the same awareness in him. Every muscle in his body pulled tight with barely restrained desire. His throat rose and fell as he swallowed.

For a long time, they remained like that, Wei-wei laying on her side and Gao sitting by the window. The room was so small that if she reached her hand out, she could touch him. He was that close.

"You should rest too," she said finally.

Gao shook his head. "No, Wei-wei."

She sighed, squeezing her eyes shut. "Just please come here so I can say something to you."

He was slow to move, but he finally did. Gao stretched himself out at the edge of the bamboo mat. He lay flat on his back and looked up at the ceiling. She mirrored his pose, also looking up. Maybe that would make it easier for both of them.

"I don't hate you for what happened with my brother," she began. "It was in the past. You're different now."

"I haven't changed," he insisted.

She wouldn't accept that. "I think you have. And Huang told me you how you spared him."

Whether or not he admitted it, Gao appeared to feel a sort of kinship with her brother.

"I just didn't want him dead."

"I'm glad for that."

They were quiet for a long time until Gao broke the silence.

"I didn't like seeing you with Magistrate Li last night."

"I don't feel anything for him." Not like what she felt for Gao. Why was it so hard to admit it out loud?

"But that doesn't matter, does it?" Gao pointed out.

"My family is convinced that we should be married."

There was something about speaking to Gao that was comforting. She would miss this when it was gone.

"I used to plot that instead of marrying, I'd run away to a temple and become a nun," she confessed.

There was a long pause before Gao's reply. "You'd look strange with your head shaved."

"Not a Buddhist nun, a Taoist nun."

"Well, that's much better. You get to keep your hair."

She listened to his breathing for a few moments and tried to match her rhythm with his. His was ahead of hers. It was hard to match the pace.

"There have been several imperial princesses who have done the same. They became nuns and converted their residences to convents rather than marry."

"What would you do for the rest of your life as a nun?"

"Meditate. Read books. Write essays."

"You dream of writing essays."

"I do. Famous ones. What do you dream of?"

Silence. Then, "You."

Her heart felt the word like a sharp blow.

"I used to dream of my family, sometimes," he continued. "But not much anymore."

"What happened to them?" She had no right to ask, but she was greedy for every last drop of him.

"My father was disgraced. We left the city with nothing to our names. Then my father died. We begged in the streets for a while, but there was never anything but scraps. I'm not as good at telling stories as you are," he interrupted. It was the first time he turned to look at her since they'd kissed.

"I don't mind."

His tone was flat and factual. It was the way he always sounded when speaking of the past. Like recounting a tale that had happened to someone else.

"My mother, she actually did bring us to a Taoist temple," he said. "She begged for them to take her in, but they couldn't while she had a son with her. Certainly not one who was nearing manhood."

"How old were you?"

"Nine years."

She fell silent, feeling selfish with her grand plans to run away to temple as if it were some idyllic retreat.

"Eventually my mother decided the only way we would survive was at the mercy of others. She left me at a Buddhist monastery. The monks would feed a motherless orphan, she told me. And then she was gone."

"Were you sad, being left alone?"

"Mostly I was angry with the monks. I was too old and didn't take to temple life. There were so many rules. I did have to shave my head."

"I never knew any of this."

"It was a long time ago."

Wei-wei tried to imagine what Gao had been like as a young boy losing his home and then his family.

"What happened then?"

"I broke too many rules." His eyes were directed at the ceiling above, his gaze distant. "I always ran away or was expelled. I stole, got caught. Was sentenced to penal servitude—which turns out is one way to get fed. And then eventually, back to Chang'an. At some point I learned how to no longer get caught."

"People like the two of us, we shouldn't know one another," she said, not meaning it as an insult. "It's fate that we're here together."

"Fate indeed," he said softly.

But not destiny. Their lives were so far from one another. Hopelessness grew within her, hollowing her out until her skin felt like the thin shell of an egg. Like she would break apart any moment. She wished Gao would at least hold her.

"I met the Emperor," he announced quietly.

She turned her head to him and he did the same. His face filled her vision.

"How? When?"

"Last night, at the banquet."

Her brother was in the Censorate, yet he'd only ever seen the Emperor from a distance.

"He wanted to commend me for catching the suspect."

"What did the Emperor look like?"

"I didn't get to see him; I could only hear his voice. He was behind a screen."

"This is an important moment, Gao. Most subjects will live their entire lives and never even come close to the Son of Heaven, and you sound as if this was nothing. Just another night."

"Seeing the Emperor and listening to him speak made me realize something," he said soberly. "We have no place trying to solve this crime."

"But we've made such progress. You caught one of the killers."

"What use are all our efforts when some powerful shadowy figure can simply make all evidence disappear?"

He'd mentioned something to that effect the night before.

"The Emperor's seal was outside of the palace. Someone could have used it to order whatever they wanted. Maybe the tower guards saw nothing because they were ordered to turn their backs."

Wei-wei tried to imagine it. The watchtowers standing empty that morning as the guards were called away. Assassins lying in wait along the way to the Yanxi Gate to ambush the chancellor's entourage. It was possible with a false order bearing an imperial seal. The ward gate records would show no one suspicious entering the ward, night or day. All the barricades and searches would turn up nothing. No one was there who wasn't supposed to be there.

"Maybe it was the Emperor himself who issued the order," Gao considered. "And he threw out that seal to cast suspicion on someone else. These men can do anything, and we'd never know."

What had happened to him? Gao seemed cynical and defeated all of the sudden.

"An Emperor can't issue any command on a whim," she protested. "Imperial decrees are reviewed and approved. Then they're archived in the records office. It's one of the functions of my brother's position."

"In the end, it doesn't matter if this is the work of the Emperor or some chancellor or warlord. Let the bureaucrats fight among themselves."

"Why are you so ready to give up now?"

He exhaled and redirected his gaze overhead. "I wanted to find these answers because they mattered to you, but I can't keep doing this."

Something had changed in him.

"You'll be married soon. To a magistrate, of all people. I need to stop coming to you." He sat up and refused to look at her. "And you need to stop coming to me."

"Did something happen?" she asked, raising herself up beside him. Gao had an edge about him tonight. He was harder and harsher than she'd ever seen him.

His jaw locked. "Not to me," he replied cryptically. "Something happened to a person I should have protected. I won't let anything happen to you."

She watched as his chest rose and fell. "Is this really the last we'll see of one another?"

Gao wouldn't look at her. Wei-wei reached for him, her fingers twisting into the front of his robe. He covered her hand firmly with his, and she waited, heart pounding, for him to push her away. Finally, he turned to her and something flickered behind his eyes. Tenderly, he caught her face in his hands. His long fingers wound into her hair as he kissed her, then kissed her again. His tongue slipped past her lips, invading her mouth in a shocking caress and she pushed all caution aside.

"Show me more," she pleaded against his mouth. "Show me everything. Tonight."

She pressed against him. Gao's arms folded around her to drag her fiercely against his hard body. His breathing grew uneven. She made a sound of protest as his mouth pulled away from her.

"You don't know what you're asking," Gao ground out.

"I do." She did and she didn't.

Suddenly Gao shifted, and she was pinned beneath him. The full weight of him against her was shocking, but then he was kissing her again. Breath to breath, nothing else seemed to matter.

"You don't know," he whispered gravely, but his hand was unfastening her tunic, pulling folds of pale cloth aside.

It was just one night, her mind insisted. And it had to be tonight. He palmed the soft weight of her breast and she jerked, her back arching into his hand. When he ran his thumb over the hard peak of her nipple, an invisible thread of desire tugged between her legs. She could feel herself growing damp.

Before she knew what was happening, his other hand had slipped down below the waist of her trousers to press against her sex.

Her lips parted. "Oh!" she gasped, startled.

She may not have known what she was asking for, but he seemed to. Gao parted her folds to slide one fingertip intimately against the tiny knot of flesh at her center, sending waves of sensation through her.

"If we do this and anyone finds out, you'd be ruined. You wouldn't be able to marry the magistrate or anyone you'd consider respectable. Is that what you want?" he asked harshly.

Maybe that was exactly what she wanted. The only answer she could manage was to strain upwards, seeking his touch. Whatever was happening, whatever Gao was doing to her, her body wanted more of it.

"I can be yours tonight," she whispered in his ear, her voice shaking.

"Just tonight," he said darkly. He stretched himself over her so that he had her pinned, hip to hip. "If you truly want this, then stay with me."

She blinked at him through her lashes, confused. His long, deft fingers stroked against the tender flesh at her center. Then, when she thought she couldn't bear any more, he slipped his fingers inside her. Her body grew rigid. She grabbed onto his shoulder, nails digging deep.

"If you'd risk everything for a night together, your life, my life, then marry me," he urged, his voice rough with desire. "Be my wife."

Emotions warred within her. She never imagined he'd ever ask. Wei-wei wished more than anything that she could answer, but what he was talking about was impossible.

Gao kissed her, swallowing her cries as his fingers circled and stroked. Faster. Deeper. His words were forgotten as the pleasure inside her grew at a frantic pace, so acute that it neared the point of pain. She buried her face against the crook of his neck. The earthy scent of him assailed her. Deep and masculine. She longed for release, but it eluded her, floating just beyond reach.

Then the moment came, one of pure ecstasy, when she finally broke free.

Her next breath was a long time coming. She had to force herself to take it. Remind herself to inhale and exhale.

Gao lay still against her. She could feel the male part of him rigid and pressed against her hip.

When she moved slightly, Gao freed his hands and clamped them onto her hips, holding her still. "Don't," he pleaded, releasing a ragged breath. "Don't move."

They lay still for a long time. Long enough for rationality to return.

Gao laid his head against her shoulder, his face pressed against her neck. Wei-wei could still feel the echo of his touch deep within her.

His question still hung in the air between them, unanswered.

"I wish I could," she told him in a small voice, squeezing her eyes shut against the pain that seized her.

He raised his head to look at her and she started tearing up.

"It's alright," he said.

"I wish I could say yes."

Gao rolled away from her, leaving her bereft and cold in his absence. They lay side by side once more. The only sound she could hear was his breathing and the pounding of her heart.

"I never thought you could possibly be mine, Wei-wei," he said, his voice heavy. "I just wanted to ask."

CHAPTER 21

Gao stood by the window the next morning, looking out over the streets. The drums hadn't sounded that morning to signal the opening of the gates, and the streets remained empty. It seemed curfew was still in effect.

Wei-wei was still sleeping in the center of the room.

Her hair was unbound. Her silk underclothes were enticingly modest, revealing a slip of soft skin at her throat and a hint of curves at her waist. He could feel his blood warming.

Last night, he'd managed to stop before stripping away Wei-wei's clothes and making love to her, but he wasn't far from it. He'd lost restraint in other ways, asking her to be his wife. Acting as if were even a possibility.

Gao had never imagined a life with Wei-wei beside him before. Just as he'd never imagined he'd one day become Emperor. He didn't waste time on fantasies. He could barely feed himself, let alone a family.

Still, if she had said yes...

Wei-wei stirred, raising herself up and looking around the room until she found him. She blinked at him with dark bedroom eyes that made his lower body tighten. "I spent all last night thinking you would be gone this morning before I woke up."

Even her voice did things to him this morning. Their gazes locked. It was impossible to look at her now and not know what it was like to feel her tremble and climax in his arms. His throat went dry at the memory.

"I need to go, Wei-wei."

She nodded. He could see the same knowledge in her eyes. Her pupils darkened as he came close. He took her face in his hands once more and kissed her, his mouth moving tenderly over hers.

He pulled away to move to the window. When he looked back, Wei-wei was watching him.

A thought came to him. It was something he'd been pondering for a while now. After what he'd asked her last night—he had no reason to hold anything back.

"I was wrong," he said. "About Magistrate Li. He's not well-matched for you."

She remained where she was, listening.

"A man shouldn't be allowed to have everything purely on name and birth," he told her quietly. "He should have to fight and scheme and risk ruin for what he wants. Then he'd be a match for you."

Wei-wei regarded him with a look of surprise. Her lips parted, as if she meant to say something, but she bit back the words.

"Be careful," she said instead.

Gao nodded, his heart in his throat, as he eased out of the window and climbed back down.

There was nothing more to say. He knew there was no way for her answer. It hurt to want her that way.

The streets were still empty. He had business left unfinished. Gao glanced once more up at the teahouse window, before heading toward the canal.

≈

GAO WAS GONE SO QUICKLY, leaving her in the grip of things she should have said.

Wei-wei hurried to the window only in time to see him disappear around the corner. Her heart sank and a wave of loneliness swept over her.

He'd told her she needed to stop seeking him out, but in the next breath he'd asked her to be his wife. It was all so overwhelming.

Then there was the emergency curfew, killers on the loose, and her hair. Her hair had come completely undone.

Wei-wei straightened her clothes, a flood of memories coming to her from the previous night. She set the back of her hand to her lips, pressing hard enough to almost bring back the feeling of Gao's mouth crushed against hers.

Would Mingyu take one look at her and just *know*?

She dressed herself and then quickly sorted out the bedding, hoping she was doing it correctly. Mingyu came in with a basin of wash water shortly after, her eyes doing a brief sweep of the room. Heat rushed up the back of Wei-wei's neck.

How loud had they been? She didn't remember. There might have been moments. *That* moment. Now her entire face was hot.

"Did you sleep well, Lady Bai?"

"Well enough." She ran her fingers through her hair nervously, which only brought it to Mingyu's attention.

"You can wash up. I'll get a comb," Mingyu said pleasantly.

Breathing deep, Wei-wei splashed water over her face and

dabbed it dry with a towel. Mingyu returned with a wooden comb and immediately went about pulling it through Wei-wei's hair.

"You seem thoughtful this morning," Mingyu remarked.

"There's so much happening right now."

"Hmm." Mingyu made a soft and all-knowing noise. The motion of the comb was soothing, even though Wei-wei's thoughts were in turmoil.

"Have you ever had feelings for someone who was…who was unsuitable for you?" Wei-wei asked.

"Some would say a constable and a courtesan are not suitable for one another."

"Why not?"

"I was indentured to the Lotus Palace at the time," she replied as a matter of fact. "My den mother owned me."

Wei-wei pressed her lips tight. She was about to lament about arranged marriages and her lack of freedom. It would have probably sounded a bit spoiled in comparison.

"I should be grateful," she said instead, and hated it.

"You are fortunate in many ways, Lady Bai, but everyone has their own sorrow as well."

Mingyu's fingers worked deftly through her hair, coiling and looping. And then she was done.

"That was fast."

Her long hair was pinned into a loosely elegant crown.

"I grew up surrounded by many other girls," Mingyu said, with a gleam in her eye. "We spent a lot of time practicing."

Wei-wei had always looked up at Mingyu with a sense of awe. She was talented and famous, but sitting here beside her, Mingyu seemed so approachable.

"You were able to gain your freedom, follow your heart," Wei-wei remarked with admiration. "Own this teahouse."

Mingyu's lips curved into a smile. "You make it sound so easy."

"Oh no! I didn't mean—"

"No woman is free," Mingyu said. "But there are ways to exert influence. No matter how small it may seem."

Wei-wei thought about that. She knew how to get her way on the small things, but what power did she have over her family? It was selfish of her even to consider it. If she was fortunate, if she was advantaged, it was all because of her family. Every member, in turn, was expected to repay in kind.

Her parents had allowed her to study, but it was for the purpose of helping her brothers and bringing honor to their name. Mother had sacrificed her own happiness for the sake of the family, and she'd been grooming Wei-wei to do the same. That was how they cared for one another—through self-sacrifice. True happiness was not something she could seek on her own. It was woven inextricably into the family's well-being.

Mingyu also knew about self-sacrifice. She also valued family, shown by how much she cared for her sister. But Mingyu seemed to believe there was room for something else. Some glimmer of self that didn't have to completely be surrendered.

"There's someone," Wei-wei began tentatively.

"Someone?" Mingyu asked gently.

Wei-wei could still feel Gao's touch on her. She could hear the impossible things he'd dared to say. Yet here she was, too afraid to even speak of him aloud.

"He's unsuitable in every way, but I care for him."

She felt a surge of longing. Something had changed between them. Not just because of last night, but rather a feeling that had been growing day after day. It made her eager to tell Mingyu everything. So at least someone would know and what she and Gao shared could be real, in some small way. Even if it was hers only for a brief moment.

Wei-wei started to speak when a pounding came from the door down below. She jumped at the sharp sound.

Mingyu rose. "It's quite early," she said with surprise.

The pounding came again, increasingly urgent. Wei-wei followed from behind as Mingyu hurried down the stairs. Wu Kaifeng was already at the door. He opened it and Wei-wei froze as a deep and all-familiar voice resonated through the empty teahouse.

"I'm looking for my daughter."

The blood drained from her. It was her father.

He stepped into the teahouse, and even as imposing as Wu Kaifeng appeared, her father was a hundred times more so. At least to her.

Father's gaze swept upwards and immediately locked onto her. "Wei-wei."

"Father," she rasped.

All the blood in her body rushed to her head. Had he seen Gao climbing down through the window? Could he see how flushed her face was at this moment?

The city, the entire world changed whenever her father returned. Their home revolved around Father. All of their daily patterns and routines became centered around his needs. Never in a hundred years would she dare to take the horse out at night while her father was home. She only feared two things and foremost was her father.

"What were you doing here? Your mother is worried."

Wei-wei was acutely aware that she wasn't where she was supposed to be. She was similarly keenly aware of all the things she'd done over the last week that Father would surely disapprove of.

"Curfew was enacted early. I couldn't get home."

"Daughter." He stopped her hasty string of explanations. "Come down."

Swallowing, she gripped the wooden rail of the staircase

to keep her steady. Of all the things she'd done, she knew what would be the most objectionable to her father. As she descended, she kept on telling herself not to think of that one most objectionable thing, but now she could think of nothing else but that. And Gao. And how she hadn't found it objectionable at all.

Zhou Dan appeared from wherever he'd been sleeping and stood quietly at the side of the room. Father acknowledged him with only a glance before returning his attention to her. His expression was unreadable, but she knew her father. He would want a full accounting of what she was doing in Pingkang li. Why had she come out alone? Who had let her go?

Her pulse quickened. She was in trouble. There was going to be a long lecture and very hard stares. Father would…She had no idea what her father would do. She'd never been in trouble before. It had always been Huang who'd done something unacceptable.

At least they wouldn't talk here. Father was a private person. He'd taught them that matters of family were to remain amongst themselves.

The door opened behind him and Huang stepped inside. His eyes met hers and she was reminded that there were larger, more important things happening in Chang'an.

"The imperial messenger is about to read the proclamation," he told their father.

Wei-wei looked between the two of them. "What proclamation?"

"The Emperor is announcing the news of Chancellor Yao's death, and that the perpetrators have been discovered," Huang explained. "It was General Lin Shidao."

She had suspected the general at one time, but the proclamation seemed so quick. "How do you know?"

"His son and several of his associates were brought before the Censorate. They confessed to the conspiracy."

She'd spoken to Lin Yijin just days ago. Her impression was that he drank too much and spoke too loudly. He was an unfortunate soul in an impossible situation, but he didn't strike her as a traitor.

"This doesn't feel right. Lin Yijin was kept under close watch as the Emperor's hostage," she protested. "How could he have done these things?"

She saw from the tick in her father's jaw that she had overstepped her bounds, being so quick to speak, but this was too important. She turned to her brother.

"Are you going to say anything to Chief Censor Zheng about your suspicions? There had to be someone inside the imperial court, remember?"

"Daughter." Father stopped her with a word. "It is not your brother's place to question imperial decisions, and it is hardly yours."

"But, Father—"

"It is time to go home, Wei-wei."

Her father raised his tone enough to tell her the conversation was over. Not only had she contradicted him, but she'd done so with outsiders present. She glanced over to Wu Kaifeng and Mingyu, who'd remained silent throughout the exchange. Even though they were family by marriage, Father still considered them outsiders. Theirs was a close circle. What her father would tolerate between the two of them when they were alone was not the same as what he would allow in public. She knew that so very keenly—but there was no time.

"You know Lin Yijin," she said to Huang in a smaller voice. "Won't you say anything on his behalf?"

"The Censorate is convinced of the evidence."

At that moment, Huang was like their father. Duty above everything.

She was close to insisting that Huang was part of the Censorate. That it *was* his place, at least in part, to question imperial authority. She wanted to tell her father that she wasn't meddling in something that didn't concern her. She was the one who had first cast suspicion on Lin Shidao. It was her fault an innocent young man had been questioned and possibly tortured into confessing.

"There's nothing I can do, Wei-wei," Huang told her gently. "This is above my station."

She was putting him in a difficult position. Even Father didn't know her brother had been recruited into the Censorate, and that he, in some small part, had the Emperor's ear.

"Father," she pleaded. "Even if his father plotted against Chancellor Yao, Lin Yijin could still be innocent. They've only suspected him for the last few days. Shouldn't they spend more time making sure? Won't you reach out to Chief Censor Zheng?"

She could see the question in Father's eyes. How did she know of Lin Yijin or the Chief Imperial Censor, let alone have a care in imperial politics? She'd tell him everything, including all of her indiscretions great and small, if she could get him to understand.

"There is nothing to be done," Father told her gravely. "The Emperor must act quickly when it comes to treason. General Lin Shidao's son is sentenced to be executed at noon."

~

GAO WAS STILL THINKING of Wei-wei as he headed toward the canal. He'd slipped away like a thief. That was what the moments felt like with her, stolen time. At the beginning, he'd accepted that. He didn't know if he could accept it now. Not after what had happened between them.

The drums signaling the opening of the ward gates hadn't sounded even though the sun had risen. The wards were still locked down. As he emerged onto the main street, it appeared everyone was gathering at the center of the ward. There was to be an imperial proclamation.

Gao moved in the opposite direction. He had other business to tend to.

He'd been forced to leave Fu Lin lying by the water. Perhaps the patrols had found him when they were sweeping the streets, but Gao couldn't be certain. The canal was in a drainage area, sparsely populated with little foot traffic. Gao needed to see that Fu Lin's body was taken care of and that his family could be notified. Fu had always tried to be helpful, and had even tried to fight by his side when they were both outmatched.

The boy might be alive if it weren't for him.

The lanes surrounding the warehouse area were empty as Gao approached the strip of land beside the canal. From a distance, he could see there was no body on the bank. The entire area was clear. Gao moved closer to stand over the spot where Fu Lin's body had lain.

Yesterday, he hadn't been able to inspect the ground beneath Fu Lin. Now he could see the dirt was clean of blood. Someone had cut Fu Lin's throat, then taken the trouble to bring him here to the same place where Fu had found the body of the Emperor's nephew.

Along with the cursed jade seal.

"He was moved to the ward station for examination."

Gao swung around to discover Magistrate Li behind him.

"Sometimes the guilty are known to return to where a wrong was committed," Li offered mildly.

"I didn't do it."

"The constables reported this young man was with you on the expedition to hunt down the assassins."

"Is that why he was killed?"

Constable Ma and Fu Lin in the same night. Both involved in apprehending the machete-wielding assassin. It didn't seem like coincidence.

"No one can say why your friend met his end."

Li's gaze was fixed intently on him. Gao was certain it was Li Chen who had commended him to the Emperor. No one else knew of his involvement in such detail. Was it also Li who wanted the investigation closed?

It was easy to underestimate the magistrate. He was young for such an influential post, his demeanor mild and unassuming. But Gao could see Li was the sort who watched and waited. He chose his words carefully, hoping to spur a reaction.

"He was my friend," Gao confirmed, feeling a pang of regret.

"I've spent a little time learning more about you," Li probed. "Some say you're a dangerous man."

He met the magistrate's gaze head on. This man controlled the county and had a team of constables working for him. He was the one that Wei-wei's family wanted her to marry on name alone.

"Between the two of us, who holds more power?" Gao challenged. Who was the greater threat?

There was a flicker of movement from behind the magistrate. Gao dove at Li Chen, toppling him to the ground just as two knives sliced through the air right where he'd been standing.

Gao twisted to his feet and threw an arm up just in time to take a small, thin blade in his forearm. It had been meant for his throat. He grabbed his own dagger and whipped it back in response, cursing his stupidity a moment later. He knew better than to throw his weapon away. Now all he had was this tiny throwing blade. He pulled it from his arm, clenching his teeth as pain radiated from the wound.

The assailant broke into a run and disappeared among the warehouses. Gao moved to give chase.

"Leave him!" Li shouted.

Gao ignored him. His arm was throbbing now that his body had finally figured out he'd been injured.

He was pretty certain his dagger had hit its target. There were no more throwing knives flying at him and their assailant was retreating down the alley.

From behind him, Gao could hear the flap of Li's footsteps, trying to chase them down in his silk shoes. Then the sound was overtaken by a heavier thud of boots. Two constables appeared at the end of the alley to cut off the assailant's escape. More men surged into the alleyway from behind Gao. The magistrate hadn't come alone after all.

As his men closed in on the assailant, Magistrate Li came up alongside Gao and started to say something.

"He has my dagger," Gao muttered, the realization just coming to him.

Gao rushed forward as the constables tried to subdue the man. At the sight of Gao, the man freed the dagger from his midsection and attempted to plunge it into his own throat. Gao grabbed his wrist to wrestle it away.

By that time, the assailant had weakened from the loss of blood. The constables were able to tackle him to the ground and clamp shackles around his wrists.

"If you want to interrogate him, you better do it quickly," Gao remarked, watching as the captive crumpled to the ground. His stomach wound was bleeding out quickly.

Heaven and Earth. Whoever these killers were, they were dedicated. Determined to die rather than reveal any information.

To his credit, the magistrate acted quickly. He moved to the injured man's side. "We have to stop the bleeding."

"Press hard against the wound." This part he knew, but that was the limit of Gao's medical knowledge.

"Wu Kaifeng," Li Chen said.

Gao thought he had misheard.

"Wu Kaifeng has knowledge of medicine. His teahouse is nearby."

Gao, of course, knew exactly where Wu's teahouse was located.

CHAPTER 22

One moment, her father was telling her that Lin Yijin was to be executed at noon. In the next moment, the earth split open beneath Wei-wei's feet.

The earth didn't truly split, but the door was kicked open and in came a group of men carrying a fourth. Gao was at the head of the party, and there was blood everywhere. Blood and shouting.

Her father immediately positioned himself in front of her and Huang, his arm outstretched in a defensive position. With his other hand, he reached for his sword.

"Wu, I need you!" Li Chen came out from behind the intruders. He searched the teahouse for Wu Kaifeng, his gaze settling first on Father, then Huang, then maybe her. "We need this man alive," he said finally to Wu.

Gao and the two constables lay the injured man onto one of the tables. When Gao straightened, she could see he was bleeding as well. His sleeve was soaked and his hands were stained red. She started toward him only to come against the immovable wall of her father.

Wu Kaifeng faced no such impediment. He came forward and the constables backed away to give him room.

"Needle and thread," he said to Mingyu. Then, after a closer look at the man sprawled over the table, "And opium."

Mingyu disappeared up the stairs, looking not too pleased.

"Who is he?" Father asked as Wu pressed a fresh cloth to the wound. It was immediately soaked through with red.

Magistrate Li looked up from the proceedings and broke away to come to them.

"Forgive me, Lord Bai," he began with a slight bow. "This man was involved in the death of an imperial prince."

"And the chancellor's assassination," Huang added. He moved to join Li Chen. "We knew there were more than two men responsible."

Wei-wei was still focused on Gao. He had come to attention at the mention of her father's title. Gao reached deep into her with a mere look. The memory of her lying beneath him and the wicked pleasure of his touch crashed into her.

It was only a moment before Gao averted his eyes, but she sensed the shift in her father's attention.

Mingyu returned with the needle and thread along with a sheet of cloth to use for bandages. By that time, the color had drained from the suspect's face. Wu lifted the blood-soaked bandage to inspect the wound before pressing it back in place. Mingyu offered him the needle, but he shook his head, refusing it.

"We need to bind the wound tight," Kaifeng said, the dark look in his eyes indicating it would only delay the inevitable. He addressed Li Chen. "Do what you need to do quickly."

"He won't talk." Gao came forward with a hand clutched over his forearm. "They're hired killers. He tried to take his own life so we couldn't question him."

Wei-wei took hold of her father's sleeve. "This man

knows who's responsible for Chancellor Yao's assassination," she pleaded. "Lin Yijin could be innocent. You have to stop the execution."

Huang turned away from the suspect to face their father. His expression was grim. "There are others out there, Father. We will find them in time, but wrongly executing Lin Yijin now will start a war."

Father grew quiet. Wei-wei knew he was examining all the details, but there was so much to consider and not enough time to tell him everything. The man in front of them was going to die and take his secrets with him, and an innocent man would be executed in only a few hours' time.

When she looked back to the table, the man's labored breathing had quieted. His eyes were half-lidded, and whatever intention was left in his body was directed at Gao. Gao returned his stare. There was something chilling about their stand-off, unrelenting even moments from death.

"Huang," Father began, coming to a decision. "Come with me." Then softer, to her. "Get yourself home, my girl."

Her father provided her with a pass to get her through the blocked gates, then moved with a purposeful stride past the bloodshed and confusion. Wei-wei hoped there was still enough time to stop the execution as her father left the teahouse with Huang beside him.

With her father gone, she let out a breath and went to Gao. Magistrate Li's gaze flickered toward them, his expression unreadable, before he turned back to the prisoner.

Li Chen wasn't ignorant of her association with Gao any more than she was ignorant of Li's connection to Song Yi. It was something they would both have to swallow silently and hold inside for the rest of their lives. At least they would have that in common.

Gao's attention was also focused on the man they'd captured. The injured man's eyes had fallen shut. His breath came in slow, shallow gasps. Gao continued to watch him, only breaking away when Wei-wei touched her fingertips lightly to his arm.

He turned to her, his expression cold. There was blood between these two. And it wasn't just the blood that flowed from their wounds.

"Are you hurt?" she asked.

The hard steel look in his eyes faded. "It's nothing."

It wasn't nothing. There was blood and death, and Gao was at the center of it, but he was looking at her as if she was the only thing that mattered. Wei-wei wasn't afraid of Gao, she was afraid for him. He was the one who had taken the risk while she and her brother and even Li Chen remained protected behind their wealth and walls and armed guards. They called Gao dangerous, but he was the one who had drawn the danger to himself.

His gaze flicked toward the door. "That was your father?"

She nodded wordlessly.

Zhou Dan came out of the shadows to interrupt them. "Lady Bai, we should go."

He had heard Father's command as clearly as she had. They didn't have time to linger any longer.

"Take care of yourself," she said to Gao.

"I'm sorry you had to see this," he replied quietly. His eyes remained on her until she left the teahouse.

~

MOTHER MET her just inside the gate when she returned home.

"We've been so worried! Where were you?" Her mother touched gentle fingertips to her hair, to her cheek before embracing her.

"Huang thought you would go to Mingyu's teahouse." Yue-ying stood just behind Mother.

Mother released Wei-wei and that was when the scolding began. "A lady shouldn't be running around to who knows where. Haven't I taught you well? What would your father think?"

Wei-wei wasn't upset about the lecture. She knew a lady shouldn't be running around in all the shady corners of the city. She had been taught well, and, above all, her mother wasn't incorrect. Mother was just saying all the things now that she'd been unable to say while she fretted and worried all night.

"Where's your father?" Mother asked, looking behind her. "Your brother?"

"They had important matters to attend to."

Mother nodded, accepting her answer. It was typical for her mother to not ask too much into what Father did outside the home.

"Did you hear that a chancellor was murdered?" Mother asked. "It's a good thing that the Emperor has captured the killers."

The household knew little of what was going on beyond the imperial proclamation. For them, it was a distant drama, and, now that Wei-wei was home, nothing that would affect them directly. Only Yue-ying thought to ask more into what was happening.

"Huang is somehow involved in this, isn't he?"

Wei-wei told her how Huang and her Father were going to petition the Emperor. "They're not in danger," she assured.

"Are you certain?" Yue-ying searched her face for the answer and was not convinced.

Wei-wei hoped they would return soon. With news.

Exhausted, she retired to her room to change into clean clothes. She didn't think any blood had gotten onto her, but just the memory made her want to scrub herself clean. As she put on a fresh robe, Wei-wei felt something tucked within her sleeve. She reached in and pulled out a crumpled piece of paper.

It was the corner of a public bulletin, but there was a squarish smudge stamped onto it. She'd ripped the paper off the wall after inadvertently imprinting the imperial seal onto it. That had started it all, finding that jade seal.

The jade seal.

She went to Huang's study. Chancellor Yao's papers were still there, in the neat stacks she had separated them into. She regretted her impetuousness now. She'd spoken of things she didn't know enough about and, one thing after another, it had somehow led to Lin Shidao and his son being implicated for treason. Maybe they were guilty, but she didn't feel it in her soul. Lin Yijin wanted to stay out of politics.

Chief Censor Zheng had warned her about such instincts, about assuming that things fit together so neatly. And Father had always warned her about speaking before thinking things through carefully.

She lay out the muddy imprint on the desk, flattening out the edges of the paper with her hands. She'd been frightened upon seeing the imprint for the first time because she knew the power the imperial chop potentially carried. With it, one could forge imperial orders.

She sorted through the papers again, busying her hands and hoping to keep her mind occupied. The execution was supposed to take place at noon and then the curfew lifted after. She wouldn't know if her father had succeeded until after the planned execution time.

Hopefully the Emperor would listen to Father. Father always urged caution. He was in the Ministry of Defense, but his position was meant to prevent war. He would counsel the

Emperor to take time to find the other suspects and review the evidence more carefully.

That was, unless the Emperor wanted war. She couldn't imagine an Emperor would, but Gao had suggested it.

Wei-wei sat back, trying to lay the pieces out in front of her. The Emperor's nephew murdered. The jade seal. The hired assassins.

She kept on coming back to the seal. There was too much activity around the seal for it to be unimportant.

An imperial prince shouldn't have been carrying that seal. The fact that the Emperor's nephew was killed with it on him carried a hint of conspiracy. Someone had smuggled the seal outside of the palace. Someone had planned to issue imperial orders and usurp the Emperor's authority.

It finally came to her. There had been two investigations, one into Chancellor Yao's assassination and one into the unidentified body in the canal. The assassins had targeted the magistrate's investigation, not the Chancellor's assassination. They'd murdered his head constable and attacked Gao. Magistrate Li had been ordered by higher authorities to cover up who had been killed, and, more importantly, what he had carried on him. The imperial seal.

As soon as the imperial seal had come to light, someone had tried to end the magistrate's investigation. Someone had silenced those witnesses. What they wanted to hide was that seal.

The imperial seal would allow someone to create an order that seemed to come from the Emperor. Huang was suspicious when the tower guards reported they had seen nothing—but perhaps they had been ordered to see nothing. And one man had taken custody of the tower guards for interrogation. The same man had also questioned Lin Yijin and his bodyguards.

Wei-wei fumbled through the desk, searching for paper

and ink. The last gong she'd heard had signaled the start of the Horse Hour. There wasn't much time left. Only enough for two lines and then a hard ride to the Imperial City.

She poured water and ground out some ink against the stone, before dipping her brush. Her message had to be brief and she prayed it would be brought to her father and Huang in time. Huang would understand.

The Censorate was responsible for investigating corruption and overseeing the conduct of imperial officials *including the Emperor*. An imperial order didn't simply go out unquestioned. Each one was scrutinized and officiated and archived. There was an entire records office dedicated to it.

She wrote hastily, not taking the time to consider her brush strokes. Her heart pounded.

Who is responsible for approving all official communications from the Emperor?

Imperial Chief Censor Zheng Shi.

Zheng had been so complimentary of her, so willing to listen to a naive young woman's assumptions about conspiracy and power when it served his purposes. Wei-wei finished the last brush strokes and waited for the ink to dry.

She didn't know exactly why the chief censor wanted Chancellor Yao dead. It was a power play she couldn't quite understand. All she knew was Zheng was the most likely culprit when she put the pieces together.

Accusing the chief censor could have dire consequences. Wei-wei was, so very much, out of her place.

CHAPTER 23

The assassin never spoke another word. The last breath left him before the hour was done.

Only four of them remained to witness the suspect's death. Gao and Magistrate Li were there along with Mingyu and Wu Kaifeng, the unfortunate proprietors who'd had a dying man dragged into their establishment. They looked upon the body, laid out and forever still, with a long silence.

Death itself deserved an air of respect. With his passing, the man was no longer an assassin or a killer or anything else. Only his spirit remained to atone for his actions in the next life.

"I need to send a message to the patrols and blockades," the magistrate said. "There had to be more in league with this one."

Li instructed his constables to transport the suspect to the morgue and gave his apologies to Wu and Mingyu for the unfortunate turn of events. Mingyu appeared relieved to be free of them. Wu Kaifeng looked perhaps even more unwelcoming than he typically did.

Gao found himself in the street beside Li Chen. Some odd fate had tied to the two of them together.

"Your friend's death was sudden," Li said after a long silence. "I hope that your grief is not overwhelming."

Li was so formal. So proper.

"The same for you," Gao said brusquely. "For Constable Ma."

The magistrate nodded slowly. They looked down the empty lane at nothing.

"I want to catch these killers," Li said.

"Not all killers can be caught."

"I know, but I want to catch these killers."

The magistrate had never stopped investigating the crime. Even when he had orders to withhold the truth and when the palace had tried to declare the case closed and the killers punished, Li Chen had never wavered from his duties.

Was it possible? Li Chen, who would soon be betrothed to Wei-wei, was an honest magistrate after all.

Li Chen and Wei-wei were alike in that way. Wei-wei cared about whether Lin Yijin lived or died and whether justice was served. To Gao, those were matters that were far beyond him. He was one to keep his focus on what was immediately in front of his face.

Gao wanted to think of Li as a rival, but to do that would mean he'd have to admit he was sorely outmatched. At least in the ways that mattered to Wei-wei's family. And family was everything to Wei-wei.

But he was something to her as well, his stubborn head insisted.

"With this curfew in effect, they know they're being hunted," Gao surmised. "The killers would be in hiding now."

"What do you imagine they'll do next?"

It wasn't long ago when he'd been advising Hui, the local crime lord, in the very same manner. Strange fate, indeed.

"If I were them, I'd flee the city. Or—" Gao considered what he knew of these assassins. "Mercenaries aren't loyal to their employers, but these assassins seem to be loyal to one another. They targeted Constable Ma and Fu Lin possibly in retaliation."

Li raised an eyebrow at Fu's nickname. Gao looked downward, digging at the dirt with his toe. He hadn't expected to be so bothered by the boy's death. Fu Lin's killer had just breathed his last, yet the boy's ghost remained.

"I would say if you truly want to lure these men out of hiding, you have to consider what they want," Gao suggested.

"What is that?"

"Your head." He looked up to meet the magistrate's questioning gaze. "Or mine."

"We can bring these men to justice," Li proposed.

Gao shook his head. He had no interest in pursuing justice. It wouldn't keep him warm or fed. Or win him what his heart desired.

He turned to walk away. Together, the two of them presented too obvious a target. The magistrate would be shielded by his constables and the thick walls that surrounded his compound. For Gao, there was only his wits and his knife. He knew better than to keep playing this game, and he wasn't impressing anyone.

He was tired of bleeding.

～

ZHOU DAN SADDLED their fastest horse and Wei-wei took to the road on her own, ignoring Mother's protests.

She was out in open defiance of curfew, of her parents, of all the rules of propriety. There was no one else to carry out the task, and the carriage would be too slow.

"Imperial business," she declared when she reached the first blockade.

She waved passes and letters and everything she had at them. None of it would withstand serious scrutiny in the light of day, but she had learned something important during her capers. The patrols were not there to stop the likes of her. She was of noble blood and beyond reproach. That was, in part, how Zheng had been able to push his plot so far unchallenged.

When questioned, she refused to waver. She had a message for Lord Bai in the Ministry of Defense who was in audience with the Emperor. There would be consequences for all if she didn't get there on time.

They let her through. She was either telling the truth or mad, and the patrolmen feared both enough allow her to pass.

The gates of the Imperial City were shut, but the guards at the front recognized her. She'd been allowed inside before. They refused her entry this time, but she managed to push her letter into the hands of one of the functionaries.

"Take this to Lord Bai," she instructed. "He's in audience with the Emperor."

She hoped her father and brother had made it that far.

And then she waited. The gong sounded for noon time and she squeezed her eyes shut. Lin Yijin was gone now, or he wasn't. She didn't know.

The curfew was lifted shortly afterward by imperial proclamation, but the message said nothing about the execution.

After waiting for a long time, she finally headed home.

Mother was sitting in the inner courtyard, waiting for her. "You're home," her mother acknowledged curtly.

She was livid, but Mother didn't show this by scolding or fussing the way she had when Wei-wei had first returned after the city was locked down. Instead, Mother slowly rose to her feet and retreated to her chamber, leaving a cold silence in her wake. This sort of silence cut deeper than the sharpest knife.

Father returned eventually in the late part of the afternoon, but without Huang. He went in to check on Mother before taking residence in the study. More silence.

There were times when Wei-wei could have had special tea brewed and used it to approach one or the other. Today was not one of those times. She remained in the courtyard, quietly reading or pretending to read.

It was her younger brother Chang-min who broke the silence. He came to her holding a notebook.

"I completed my commentary on Jia Yi's approach to state," he told her.

"A true king battles using righteousness," she quoted.

"A true emperor battles using virtue," he responded.

How fitting, considering all that had happened. Chang-min handed the notebook to her, his look tentative.

He wasn't really here to have her read his essay, just as she wasn't intent on ensuring Mother and Father had their special tea. It was the only way Chang-min knew to come to her.

"Come sit with me," she offered.

He took a seat beside her on the stone bench and waited patiently while she read through his writing. Her younger brother had brought a different element to the household when he came to them. Even as an infant, he'd rarely cried. It was as if he knew even then he was in the shadow of older, more statured siblings. Huang was metal and she was fire. Chang-min was water, the long and patient river.

"Very good," she remarked. "You should show this to Father."

"Bai *Furen* worries whenever you're gone," he said after a while.

She frowned at him. "Today was unusual."

"Not just today."

Did Mother know about her nightly excursions? Did Chang-min? Wei-wei was foolish to think they'd remain oblivious. Just the other day, she saw the robe she'd worn at the House of Heavenly Peaches being laundered. It had been taken from her room by her maidservant to be treated as just another chore.

Between her family and their servants, they were ten people enclosed in the same walls. Everyone knew everyone's secrets. Everyone had silently agreed not to speak of them too loudly.

Chang-min was breaking the pact to come to her. He was making an effort to make peace.

"You do very well in your studies," Wei-wei told him. "I'm proud of you."

He looked away, not at all comfortable with such recognition. And now she was uncomfortable for being so complimentary. Chang-min was, after all, only seventeen and somewhat her charge. She should be careful he didn't become self-centered. Like Huang.

And maybe like her too.

She was saved from the situation when Father summoned her. He was able to do so from within his study, his voice carried so clearly in this household.

Wei-wei handed the notebook back to her younger brother and went to her father. He was seated at the desk as she stepped inside.

"Sit," he bid her.

Long conversation, then.

She seated herself across from him, and it immediately made her feel smaller. Father was so much taller than her as it was, she preferred to stand when talking to him. Though she loved her father, he was intimidating. More intimidating, she realized, than the thought of knife-wielding assassins.

"Your elder brother and I received your message," he began. "Lin Yijin lives."

Wei-wei let out a breath.

"Wei-wei." Her father paused and it was not a good pause.

She waited, her nails dug into her palms.

"Your behavior over the last two days was reckless. You acted without thinking."

Reckless, but not disappointing. Anything but disappointing. She couldn't bear to disappoint her parents.

Counterarguments hovered on her tongue. For once, she was doing something important. She was helping her brother. She was helping the empire! And she had been reckless. Danger to her was being caught and scolded. She didn't know what true danger was.

Wei-wei knew better than to say any of this out loud. Even making her voice heard to say she was sorry would be out of line.

"Yes, Father," was all she could say.

"You have more than overstepped your bounds."

There it was. Boundaries. Place.

All of this had been spoken in Father's deep, even tone, but she wanted to shout back with her eternal question. *Why did you teach me all this, if you never wanted me to use any of it?*

She fought back tears. The boundaries. Always the boundaries.

"Wei-wei." His voice was gentler now. "You could have been hurt."

"I know, Father."

When Li Chen and Gao had come rushing into the teahouse, with blood and death in their wake, Father's first instinct was to throw out his arms to protect her. How disheartening it must be to know that one's arms would never be wide enough.

They were silent for a long time after that. Time for her to consider what was spoken, even as few words as there were. Time enough to choose her next words carefully.

"I wanted to do what you do. What Elder Brother is able to do."

Father's eyes shined. "I know."

But she wasn't meant to do such things.

"Will you tell me what happened to the chief censor?"

She could see how he hesitated. Father rarely discussed the details of his work with her, but in this case, she was entangled within it.

"Zheng Shi was removed from his position."

"For treason?"

Father shot her a disapproving look. Within this study, her question was considered an outburst.

"For issuing an imperial proclamation that proved false," he answered. "This morning's proclamation wrongly accused Lin Shidao."

Wei-wei made a face. An improper proclamation? How disappointing!

Her father saw her sour expression but tolerated it.

"General Lin and his son have been exonerated," he continued. "Reparations will need to be made for the damage to their family name, and Zheng has been banished from Chang'an."

"But what Zheng did was so much worse."

"Lin Yijin's life was spared, and Zheng has been stripped of power. Is that not the end that you desired?"

Wei-wei bit down on her lip to keep from blurting out her immediate thought. Zheng had harmed so many people. He'd abused his power and usurped the Emperor's authority.

She didn't wish death upon anyone—but that man had been responsible for so much death.

"Balance and compromise," Father told her. "One takes the victory he is given, not the one he wants. Chancellor Yao was a negotiator, Zheng Shi was not. He looked upon military governors, like General Lin, as enemies of the state who needed to be defeated one by one."

"So the chief censor did want to start a war," she observed, incredulous. "He wanted the General to retaliate after his son was executed."

"It's your father's belief that Zheng Shi's aim was to bring war to the warlords," Father said. "He saw them becoming more powerful and forming alliances among themselves. To Zheng, the time to negotiate was over."

Wei-wei listened carefully to her father's every word. Father was a negotiator as well. She was grateful Zheng hadn't thought to target him.

"Your position is dangerous, Father." She hadn't realized how much before.

"Nowhere is completely safe. You need to remember that, Daughter. For your sake, and for our family's sake."

She bowed her head. "Yes, Father."

He didn't need to say more. Every time she ran to the Pingkang li, every time she ventured out in disguise was a gamble. She'd always known she was courting disaster, but she'd ignored all reason for just the slightest taste of freedom.

"And you'll be married soon."

When she glanced up, Wei-wei was surprised to see her father didn't look completely happy with the idea.

"I suppose it's time," she said sullenly.

"It is." He appeared deep in thought. "Magistrate Li Chen showed himself to be a worthy match for you today. He remained calm and capable throughout the ordeal."

And proper. Li had stopped in the middle of a crisis to properly address her father by title. Their union would be a courteous one.

"I hear he comes from a good family," she recited.

"Who was that other man with him?"

She snapped to attention, heat rushing to her face. "The other man?"

"He was injured, and had a...rough look about him."

Father watched her face closely. When she'd seen that Gao was hurt, she'd wanted to rush to him and Father had sensed it.

"Just one of Elder Brother's associates," she replied, her throat suddenly dry.

He considered her answer for longer than he should have. Finally, he nodded.

"That is all for now. Send your younger brother in," he instructed. And then, as she neared the door. "You've done well with your brother's studies, Wei-wei."

She thought of Chang-min handing her his essay to seek her approval. There were few acceptable ways to receive commendation and acceptance in the Bai household. How many papers and poems and writings had she passed to her father over the years?

Today, she'd urgently passed yet another paper to her father through the gates of the Imperial City.

She looked back to see Father sorting through his letters. There were things she'd said and done over the past week that Father would never accept, but her father had trusted her when he needed to. It was the victory she would take.

CHAPTER 24

The next days went by as the city settled back into its regular rhythm. The drums sounded in the morning to open the gates and in the evening to close them. Most of the inhabitants of Chang'an would never know of the murder and conspiracy that upended the Imperial City for those ten days.

Wei-wei didn't dare leave home without permission while her father was in residence. All she had was the two courtyards of their mansion, the study, her books.

Her brother was able to come home now, even if it was late in the evenings at times. The family still didn't know of his position in the Censorate. It remained a secret between her and Huang.

One night, he returned close to the middle of the Rat Hour; late, late at night. Wei-wei was up, rocking the baby to give Yue-ying a chance to sleep. She was getting better at it. The little treasure was snuggled in her arms and Wei-wei was no longer afraid of dropping her.

Huang went directly to her. She knew something had happened from the dark look in his eyes. She feared that something had happened to Gao. They hadn't heard from him in the days since the city lifted the emergency curfew.

"Zheng Shi was killed by bandits on the road two days after leaving Chang'an," he reported. "None of his attendants were harmed."

She should have been shocked but was surprised to find she wasn't. Zheng had stirred up fear and violence and it had come back to him. They would never know whether it was truly the work of bandits, or the Emperor's form of mercy to allow a long-time bureaucrat to save face. His name was spared, while his crime was punished.

"Is there any other news?" she asked. Huang knew what she meant.

"No word from Gao." Huang took his daughter from her. The infant only stirred, but thankfully remained sleeping through the exchange. He continued in a lowered tone. "He might have gone into hiding just to avoid any unwanted questions. The imperial investigation and the county investigation are still open to complete the record."

"What about the assassins?" she asked. "The ones Zheng Shi hired. Have you accounted for all of them?"

He considered it. "The magistrate has been searching, but they seemed to have disappeared. Probably fled once Zheng was sent away. The head of the snake has been cut off."

"But you don't know for certain. Gao could still be in danger."

"Gao is cunning and he knows the streets better than anyone. His best protection is himself. There's nothing more we can do."

His dismissive answer was less than satisfactory, but Huang was right. There wasn't anything she could do. Certainly not while she was trapped at home.

She was tired and Huang was tired and she wouldn't find out any more tonight. They said their good-nights and sleep-wells, and Huang carried his infant daughter back to his chamber. Wei-wei retreated to her bed where she lay awake, staring up at the moon. It was waning now, a sliver of it had disappeared. Before it was full again, she'd be married. The official betrothal was to take place in two days.

She just wanted to know that Gao was safe. There would be no seeing Gao or speaking to him or even asking about him once she was betrothed. Certainly not once she was married.

Why did the word always make her feel a sense of loss? Except for when Gao had mentioned marriage. In that instance, she'd felt a bright flash of hope, before regret seeped in.

Wei-wei fell asleep wishing.

The next morning, it seemed the moon had heard her plea.

"There is someone outside the side entrance," Zhou Dan told her.

She hurried to the gate and found Gao there. He was waiting for her in the alleyway.

He stopped her, holding her away when she tried to fly into his arms. "Wei-wei," he warned, looking toward the house.

She was so happy to see him that she'd forgotten herself. She pulled him away from the gate and deeper into the alleyway. It was still reckless to be out there like this, but she wanted to see him too much to be cautious.

"How are you? You're well? You disappeared."

She supposed that from his perspective, she was the one who had disappeared.

"I wanted to come," he replied, looking at her so intently that her heart skipped. "You know it's not so easy. Even this, you talking to me. Here. This is enough to destroy your reputation."

She shook her head, wanting to deny it, but she knew it was true.

"My father is home now," she said soberly. "I'm to be betrothed tomorrow."

Emotion flickered in his eyes. "I know. I didn't know it would be tomorrow, but I knew it would be some day. I came to tell you I'm leaving."

"Leaving?" She couldn't keep the hurt from her voice.

"Yes." He fought to keep his tone neutral. "I couldn't stay, knowing,"

Knowing she was to be betrothed. Knowing she was marrying Magistrate Li.

It was too much to bear. She'd always imagined Gao would at least be out there, in a place she could at least imagine him even if she couldn't see him. How foolish she was. What difference would it make whether Gao was a few wards away, with walls within walls between them, or if he was a hundred li away? In either case, they'd be unable to see one another.

Wei-wei couldn't explain it, but there was a difference. Her eyes stung, but she blinked back the tears. She couldn't expect Gao to live his life for her.

"It's time for a change," he told her quietly. "The Emperor granted me a hundred taels of silver. This seems like a good use for it."

His next words lodged in his throat, and she summoned enough courage to reach for him, laying her hand against his chest. For now, he was still something she could touch and feel, but not for much longer.

"This is so awful," she whispered brokenly.

Gao took her hand in his, but it wasn't to take hold of it. He pressed something into her palm. It was the silk bracelet he'd woven for her. Her fingers closed protectively around it.

"You'll forget me, in time."

"No, I won't," she snapped, her vision blurring. "My memory is very good. I'll remember you when I'm eighty years old—"

Gao did take her in his arms finally, pulling her close to press his lips to hers. The kiss was full of urgency with a touch of defiance—but then Gao ended it, stepping away from her. She wanted more than anything to have him back, even though there was nothing but a brick wall keeping them from being discovered.

"I'm going now," Gao breathed, his expression one of anguish.

"You should know that you have…good qualities. You're a good person." It was difficult to find words, but this was the last chance she would ever have. She had to tell him everything there was to say. "Do good things."

"I'm glad for all of it, Wei-wei. Glad to have met you."

She tried to get a long look at him. A last look, but her vision swam before her. Her cheeks were drenched.

"I've fallen in with love you, Gao," she said before the next sob stole her breath. "I'll love you until I grow old and gray."

He went still, the stark angles of his face fixed and tense. She wished Gao would kiss her once more, but instead he turned to go.

She fled back into her house. It would have destroyed her to watch him fade into the distance. Not caring who saw her, Wei-wei fled to her room and collapsed upon her bed. It was still morning, and the household had just woken up, but she stayed where she was. Everything inside of her hurt and she curled up tight to try to banish this feeling—or was it to hold onto it? Once she no longer felt his loss, Gao would truly be gone. This grief was laced with her last touch and taste of him.

Nothing would ever be bright or adventurous or exhilarating again. Gao wouldn't be there to tease her or listen to her stories. Show her a world beyond these walls.

Wei-wei didn't know long it was before Mother entered her room.

"Are you not well, Daughter?" Mother asked gently.

She kept her back turned. Her eyes were swollen and the pain in her chest wouldn't go away. She looked and felt miserable.

"My head aches," she murmured.

Her head did hurt from crying, but really, she just wanted to be alone for a while.

Mother came to sit on the raised platform of the bed. "Do you want me to brew some wild ginger tea?"

Wei-wei closed her eyes as her mother's fingers combed slowly through her hair. "No."

"Change is always difficult, but you've always been so brave."

It wasn't so bad having Mother fuss over her. She lay quietly while Mother stroked her hair and felt a little bit better. Not much, but a little.

"Every woman is destined to leave her family one day. When I was betrothed to your father, I knew nothing about him. I hoped I would marry a kind man. A good man without too many vices."

Wei-wei was still so broken up about Gao leaving. It took her a moment to realize Mother thought she was upset about the upcoming betrothal.

"What happened when you finally met Father?" Wei-wei's nose was clogged and her voice sounded small to her own ears.

"He never said anything to me until our wedding night."

"What did you think of him?"

"He was kind. And well-spoken. I was very fortunate."

Yet her parents lived apart for months at a time. They

hadn't shared the same bed since she was born, and Father had a second wife, Chang-min's birth mother. Mother always insisted she didn't mind—that he deserved companionship and she didn't care to move to the provinces where Father's appointment required him to be for most of the year.

"I came to love your father in time."

Mother usually wasn't so open to her questions. Maybe it was because Wei-wei would soon be betrothed and then married. In the short time that remained, she was supposed to teach Wei-wei all the things she needed to do to be a proper wife. Things that weren't written in books.

Wei-wei thought twice before asking her next question, but the pact of silence was temporarily lifted. She may never have the opportunity again.

"Are you happy, Mother?"

Wei-wei held her breath waiting for the reply.

"Of course, I'm happy," Mother replied. "My children have grown. They're strong and clever. I'm very happy."

Yet she frequently retreated to her room with headaches. How many times had her mother done so to escape?

She turned around to see Mother looking at her with a mix of kindness and concern. Her mother was happy and she did love Father, but there was still something unfulfilled within her. So much that she would hide away in the dark for hours at a time, searching.

But there was no solution. The pieces of the puzzle had been locked in for so long, the missing key long gone.

"Are you hungry?" Mother asked, which told her it must be time for the mid-day meal.

"No," she answered. "I just want to sleep."

≈

EVENTUALLY WEI-WEI DID FALL ASLEEP. When she woke up again, it was dark outside. There was a light shining out in the courtyard in an odd location. She could see a faint glow through the rice paper window.

The light stayed there for a long time, piquing her interest enough for her to get out of bed. She emerged, disoriented, from her room into the garden and the light of the waning moon. Someone was in the corner of the garden by the fish pond.

Wei-wei squinted as she came forward. It was Zhou Dan, digging in the dirt.

With all the conspiracy she'd been entangled in lately, Wei-wei's thoughts immediately strayed to wickedness and wrongdoing.

"Zhou Dan!" she whisper-shouted.

He turned, shovel suspended in mid-air.

"What are you doing?"

He couldn't be burying a body. There wasn't enough dirt in that part of the garden.

Instead of answering, the manservant reached down and picked up a crumpled paper from the ground. He mouthed something she couldn't hear. She came closer.

"Your friend," he repeated.

"Friend?" she asked, confused.

He shot a look of disbelief at her. "Your *friend* left this in the stable. No one else has been back there."

Gao had left a note? Her heart gave a little squeeze.

Eagerly, Wei-wei took the paper from him. The writing appeared crude and uneven. *"Dig under rock.* How did you know which rock?"

"My father and I tend this garden every day. Only one stone had been moved."

"Oh." She bit down on her lip, feeling foolish for asking. The rest of the note was just a house number and street.

"Is your friend secretly a rich man?"

"What do you mean?"

Zhou Dan reached into the fold of his tunic and pulled out a silver ingot, molded into the shape of a boat. "The paper was wrapped around this."

Part of Gao's reward from the Emperor.

"I wasn't going to keep it," he insisted, holding it out to her. "It was left on your family's property."

"You can keep it. If Mister Gao left the note in the stable, he meant for you to find it."

Zhou Dan first looked surprised, but then the look transformed into a grin. "Thank you, my lady. This is the first time I've ever touched silver."

He stuffed the ingot back into his tunic and picked up the shovel again to resume digging. It couldn't have been buried deep. Just a few shovelfuls later, Zhou Dan hit against something solid.

Wei-wei peered over Zhou Dan's shoulder as he knelt down. There was a chest in the dirt, wrapped in cloth. Zhou Dan pulled the lid open to reveal an entire cache of silver ingots.

"Waa…" Zhou Dan made a sound of amazement as he dragged the chest up. "It's a fortune."

Wei-wei looked at the folded paper again. She didn't know where the address was.

Gao had talked about starting a new life, but he'd left his hundred taels of silver in their courtyard. Was Gao waiting for his money at the address? The thought of seeing him again, even just one more time, made her heart beat faster, but it didn't make sense for him to leave this note when he could have just asked her that morning to retrieve it for him.

Her wild heart was already whispering. The horse. The carriage. Everyone else would be asleep in just a few hours.

Her wild heart was urging her into disaster. Not this

time. She tucked the note into her sleeve. It was the only note she had from Gao, though its message was far from romantic.

It appeared there was one more mystery to solve, but it would have to wait until morning.

CHAPTER 25

The gates to the magistrate's yamen were still shut when the carriage arrived the next morning. Wei-wei stepped out and headed toward the entrance, to the brass gong situated beside it. She lifted the striker, looked around at the empty streets, then swung it against the brass.

The gong rang out through the still morning in waves. After a while, the sound settled back into silence, but the gates remained closed. It was said that anyone, rich or poor, need only ring the bell to request a hearing with the magistrate. The affect had been so dramatic that she didn't dare do it again. She looked back to the carriage where Zhou Dan sat guarding the knotted sack of silver. He merely shrugged as to their next course of action.

Fortunately, the gate creaked open a moment later and a servant peered out. Wei-wei asked to see Magistrate Li and the servant disappeared to relay the message. Magistrates lived in the residential section of the yamen and worked in the offices. Li Chen should be inside even though the gates were closed.

The gate finally opened again and Li Chen appeared dressed in his magistrate's uniform complete with his official black cap headdress.

He was surprised to see her. "Lady Bai."

"Magistrate Li."

"You rise early," he remarked, then immediately looked uncomfortable which, in turn, made her uncomfortable.

It was the sort of intimate observation a man and woman would only know about one another once married. Their official betrothal ceremony was to take place that afternoon, but they were already more than strangers. She'd come very close to accusing him of corruption—which certainly constituted some sort of relationship.

"I need your assistance."

"Yes," he replied, listening.

She handed him the note and explained the situation.

"Who lives there?" he asked.

"I don't know."

"Where does your family think you are?" he asked next.

"The temple," she replied.

He nodded, watching her warily. "This is the first time anyone has rung the gong."

Li Chen roused one of his constables to join them and they boarded the magistrate's wagon to ride to the address.

Wei-wei had stayed up half the night thinking of a solution. Venturing out to some unknown location on the day of her betrothal would be courting both danger and scandal. The only solution was to enlist her intended, the honorable Magistrate Li. She had protection against thieves who might try to snatch the silver as well as a way to avoid scandal. Li Chen couldn't unexpectedly find out about a secret excursion if he was in on the secret.

She looked over at Li now. He had a perturbed look about him, and she wondered if he'd only gone along with her request because they were to be married. Over time, would his troubled yet tolerant look change to a long-suffering one of frustration? And then to disdain?

Wei-wei was also acutely aware that sitting beside Li Chen didn't feel the same as being beside Gao. There was no sense of shared purpose and adventure. Li Chen tolerated her impetuousness, but he'd never question, tease or collaborate with her.

Li Chen, like her family, preferred the path of silence.

She had to stop hunting for flaws, and she had to stop searching for reminders of Gao.

The directions on the paper led them to a four-story tenement house beside Jujube Alley. Li Chen took the lead with her and Zhou Dan following behind. Zhou Dan carried the silver strapped over his back.

"It's heavy," he remarked.

As they moved through the cramped corridors, Wei-wei passed by open doorways that revealed squalid living conditions. Entire families were packed into small spaces. Gao's words weighed heavily on her. Her home, the one she frequently complained about being trapped in, *was* a palace.

Why would Gao want his silver brought here? Was it a debt he owed? Perhaps to some moneylender? She'd had an unpleasant run in with a gambling den boss once, though he'd been in a much nicer establishment than this one.

Gao's address had designated a room at the corner. There was no need to knock as the door consisted of a curtain hung over the entrance. Li Chen announced himself as he stood beside it.

The family peered out and looked them over with surprise.

"A man named Gao requested that this be delivered to you," Li Chen explained.

Zhou Dan untied the makeshift pack from his shoulders

and stepped inside to lower the sack unceremoniously onto the floor.

"Gao, you say?" the woman said. "Does Mister Gao know what happened to my son?"

He wasn't a bad son, she explained to Li. But easily influenced and he liked to gamble too much. Gao had taken him under his care. Tried to teach him.

"He hasn't come home. They say he was killed in the street." The woman's lip trembled and she pressed a hand to her face, overcome. "Just days ago," she wailed.

Wei-wei and Li stood at the door. She looked helplessly at him, then back to the woman.

"I know who this is," Li said quietly.

It was the friend Gao had spoken of. Something had happened to this friend the last night she had been with Gao, and it had affected him deeply.

Li Chen spoke to the woman as gently as he could, asking questions, and listening. He informed her that her son's body had been found. That he would be returned now to his family.

The mother staggered, collapsing to the ground and let out a wail of anguish. Wei-wei bit down hard on her bottom lip as it started trembling. It was hard to be witness to such raw pain. A family's deepest, most private moments.

The other members of the family came to comfort the mother. Li cast Wei-wei a glance and a curt nod that told her they should go. He'd remained calm throughout the entire exchange. His expression was firm but not harsh.

When they left, the family hadn't yet opened the parcel. It wouldn't dull the pain of losing their son, but it might help them in other ways. Gao had done this rather than take the silver for himself.

Her brother had once painted Gao as an opportunist and a cutthroat. She looked around at the rotted wood and rags.

Gao was also poor and hungry. Maybe he was all those things, but to the people he'd committed to, he was giving of himself. He knew no boundaries.

Both Wei-wei and Li Chen remained silent throughout the ride back to the yamen. There was a place for silences.

Once they returned, Li Chen helped her from the wagon with a steady hand on her arm.

"You're very patient," she told him once the constables had dispersed.

Zhou Dan had gone to fetch their carriage, and she and Li had a moment alone.

"You're a kind man," she said. "And well-read."

He frowned a little, confused by her sudden outspoken-ness, but willing to wait and gain more understanding. From how he'd interacted with the family who'd lost their son, she could see he wasn't just a capable magistrate. Li was a decent person. In time, they would become familiar and comfort-able with each other. They might even form close bonds. She'd have children who would grow up strong and healthy. Maybe they would also be clever.

But somewhere, deep down, there would be a seed of unhappiness. It was already planted, and it contained more than just her longing for Gao. The tiny seed was her attempt to hide away so much, all her dreams, inside something so small.

She suspected there was the same seed inside of Li Chen. "You shouldn't marry me, Magistrate Li."

He frowned. "I shouldn't?"

A marriage could be grown around whatever seeds they carried. Their union could be fruitful and years from now she might even be able to say that she was happy even if she wasn't at the present, but—

"There's someone you care for," she said. "Someone who

is in your thoughts and in your heart night and day. You should marry her, not me."

Li Chen appeared extremely uncomfortable now. "Let us talk inside, Lady Bai."

She went with him inside the yamen and to his offices. He brought her into the study and closed the door. After a deep breath, he finally faced her. Wei-wei stared at all the books on the shelves and at his desk.

"Chang'an is a large county. There is always more work to be done," he explained, perhaps grateful for something neutral to speak of.

She would live in the yamen with Li once they were wed. When he was reassigned to another county, as magistrates frequently were, she would go with him and settle in a new city. It wasn't a bad life. Li Chen wasn't a bad man. She wasn't doing this for herself.

Not entirely for herself.

"You have a chance at happiness," she told him.

He let out a breath and rubbed a hand over his chin. Back to unspeakable topics.

"She cares for you as well," Wei-wei insisted.

His eyes clouded with emotion. "It's not a possibility."

"Only because I'm here."

Everyone saw that they were well-suited for one another and couldn't see it any other way. Even she had thought the match was too perfect to deny. At the moment, Li's true love might seem impossible, but he was a man with wealth and influence. Even if Wei-wei could bear her own loneliness, how was she going to put up with his disappointment for the rest of their lives? It might make for good poetry, but she imagined very long days full of regret.

"If our marriage would be so objectionable to you, I won't push for it," he offered, though she could see how much this troubled him.

It was Li's mother pushing for their union. And her mother. Their families were supposed to have tea and exchange gifts just hours from now. Breaking their arrangement at this late of a stage reflected badly on both of their families. There was no way to escape this without scandal and, even worse, ill-will.

"You can claim I'm unsuitable," she suggested. "That I'm too spoiled and unmanageable."

Li was horrified. "I wouldn't do that to you."

"But how can we do this so your family won't lose face?"

"Or yours," he insisted.

An alternative would be for her to insult her would-be mother-in-law, and Wei-wei didn't think her reputation would ever recover from that. Her own parents might disown her.

"I don't know. This is not how I usually think," Li said.

Of course not. He was dedicated to upholding social order and mores.

"Surely we can think of something together." She was getting a taste for it. "It's a puzzle. Like solving one of your criminal cases."

Li frowned at her. "It's nothing like that," he said sternly.

"I can do this. I'm good at this."

Now Li looked truly troubled. And perhaps a little relieved he wouldn't be marrying her after all? "I can't see how it's possible to come away from this unscathed. If one of us has to sacrifice—"

She hushed him, squeezing her eyes closed to shut out everything around her so she could think. There had to be a way.

"We have to do it at the same time." Her eyes flicked open and she looked to Li.

"Bring everyone together?" he asked.

"No, we must do it separately. But *at the same time*. I must find a reason why we absolutely cannot be married, and tell my father and mother. A reason that doesn't question your honor. And you have to do the same."

"How can that help? Both our families will be upset then."

"No, listen." She grabbed at his sleeve to get his undivided attention. "I tell my Father I absolutely cannot marry you. He'll be angry. Then, what happens when your mother tells him the same thing about you?"

Li shook his head. "He grows even angrier?"

"At that moment, my father is suddenly *relieved*."

Magistrate Li fell silent. She gave him a long moment to think on it, something she'd learned from her parents.

"You are quite formidable, Lady Bai," he said eventually.

She had so few avenues where she could exert herself. It was important to master them.

"Our families are very similar, are they not?" she went on.

"Yes. It's one of the reasons we were presumed to be such a good match."

She shot him a warning look before continuing. "When the possibility of scandal comes up, each of them will worry for the other party. Each will be determined to act honorably toward the other."

"As the saying goes—In divorcing a wife, make it so she can remarry," Li Chen quoted. "In severing a friendship, make it so he can make new friends."

They were in agreement.

He blew out a breath. "If my mother ever knew we talked like this, she would never forgive me."

It was vindicating to see that a man older and more accomplished than she still held some fear of his mother. This was the closest Wei-wei had felt to friendship with Li Chen—the two of them plotting to dissolve their union before it ever formed.

"There isn't much time. We both need to act within the next hour," Wei-wei instructed.

He nodded to her, and she back at him.

Now Wei-wei had the difficult task of coming up with a story that would convince her parents.

CHAPTER 26

Gao was halfway through a bowl of noodles at a street stand when the shadow fell over him. He looked up to see he'd been caught.

"Magistrate Li. Although, you're not magistrate here."

Over the last week, Gao had relocated to the western part of the capital, which was considered to be a separate county with its own magistrate. Though within the same outer city walls, the western half was far away from Pingkang li as well as from the mansions of the northeast quadrant. Certainly far enough that Wei-wei couldn't find him if the impulse struck her. And if Gao had the urge to see her, it would take long enough that he had time to stop himself.

He'd already tried it once so far, but had pulled himself back at the Imperial Way which divided the city in half.

"I had a feeling you hadn't left Chang'an yet," Li said.

"I'm dirt poor. Who wants to starve out on the road?"

"Yes, I happen to know something about your situation," the magistrate murmured cryptically. "May I sit?"

"May I eat?" Gao indicated the half-finished noodles.

"Yes, please. Feel free. Before the food gets cold."

Gao did just that, digging into his noodles. He usually attempted some level of manners, especially in front of someone of rank like Li Chen. Disrespect drew unwanted attention, but Gao just couldn't muster the will at the moment. By now the man was betrothed to Wei-wei. Gao's time to act, if there ever was a time, was that narrow space after they'd kissed for the very last time. And he hadn't done a thing.

He slurped his noodles loudly out of spite, which was a pretty toothless gesture considering, but jealousy made men do stupid things.

Since Gao hadn't said no to Li's request to sit, the magistrate apparently took it to mean yes. He seated himself on the stool opposite Gao.

"I have discovered," Li began pleasantly, "that since you use only a single name of Gao, it's particularly difficult to track your movements."

Gao lifted the bowl to tip broth into his mouth. What was Li Chen doing? Making polite conversation before getting to the point was something gentlemen did to gentlemen. He set the bowl down and wiped his mouth with his sleeve for good measure.

"By the way, your thief-catchers were lousy," Gao informed him. He'd evaded one just yesterday, wondering why someone was attempting to track him down. "What is it? Some crime committed years back that you want me for?"

"Uh...No." Li frowned, thinking more on that statement. "But you're innocent of any wrongdoing, right?"

Gao bit back a grin. "Of course."

"I came to make a proposal. I may have a job for you."

"I already have a job."

He was to guard a merchant caravan that was supposed to leave Chang'an tomorrow. It would take him out of the city, and he very much needed to leave. If he stayed, Gao knew that sometime, somehow, he would forget the consequences and find a way to see Wei-wei. He wouldn't be able to help himself. Even if she was married to this fool. Even when she was old and gray.

"If you would consider it, I have need of a head constable," Li offered, oblivious to Gao's thoughts.

He stared at the magistrate. Li stared back, unblinking.

"No," Gao replied.

"You didn't consider it very long," Li remarked.

"It doesn't suit me."

"I believe it will suit you very well." Li made the motions of settling into his seat and folding his hands before him. Gao sensed this was how a man like Li Chen prepared for battle. "You have experience as to what functions a constable serves. You've tracked down and subdued dangerous criminals. You know the streets of the city."

"I know ten streets in Pingkang."

"You're being too humble, Mister Gao."

Gao scowled. He did not like being addressed by Li in that way.

"The position of magistrate is, by nature, a transient one," Li began. Gao propped an elbow onto the table. This was going to be a lecture. Li continued, undeterred. "A magistrate is meant to be an outsider in his jurisdiction, so as to not become entangled in any local politics or loyalties. He requires the service of people who can provide insight into the community, particularly the rougher—"

"You don't suit me," Gao cut in.

"What?"

"I'd be working with you," he replied more succinctly. "We are not a good match."

"Well." Li was taken aback. His brow furrowed. "I disagree. I've worked with two head constables who had two very different temperaments. Not only do I consider you qualified, based on the abilities you've demonstrated, but I've learned that an effective head constable is one who has what I would characterize as opposite qualities to my own."

"Your second head constable was killed."

Li exhaled slowly, taking the time to smooth out the sleeves of his robe one after the other. Gao didn't aim to make the magistrate angry, but the fact was, being head constable was dangerous, on top of the fact that all of Gao's previous associates would distrust him. He'd have to wear a uniform, putting a target on his back. Constable Ma had seemed disgruntled most of the time and Wu Kaifeng looked dour all of the time.

On top of that, the position was only barely respectable to those for which respect mattered. It was the lowest rung of the bureaucracy.

Why was he even considering it? Gao always considered all options. It had become key to his survival.

This option was easy to turn down. Li Chen would take Wei-wei as his wife, and she would come to live in the magistrate's compound, the very same place where Gao would report for duty every day. Gao didn't like the prospect of being tortured daily any more than he liked being knifed.

Magistrate Li was watching him, his gaze steady. "You're cunning," he said bluntly. "Quick. I need someone like you."

Gao sighed and pressed his fingertips against his temple before replying. "Did she ask you to do this?"

Li blinked at him. "I don't know what you mean."

The magistrate had to know. "The woman you're set to marry." Gao stopped himself from using Wei-wei's familiar name. "Did she ask you to offer this position to me?"

"There is no woman I'm set to marry."

Gao straightened. He searched Li Chen's expression.

"You and Lady Bai were to be betrothed."

Li shook his head. "It wasn't meant to be."

Gao's heart pounded as if it had just come back to life. "What happened?"

As Li considered his response, Gao suddenly regretted acting like such a pig to the man.

"Her family sent her from the capital—is there something wrong, Mister Gao?"

Gao ignored him for the moment. He dropped his head into his hands and tried to think.

Had her family learned about him and sent her away to avoid scandal? Was she in danger? How would he be able to find out what happened to her?

Finally, he lifted his head to face Li Chen. "When does the position start?"

~

GAO'S ROUTE to the Bai family mansion brought him past the place where he'd last seen Wei-wei. He lingered by the alleyway, the memory still so sharp that the empty air took on phantom shapes. Wei-wei in front of him, his heart beating hard at the touch of her hand on his chest. Her parting words that she wouldn't forget him.

He'd told her he was leaving Chang'an but hadn't gotten any farther away than the west end of the capital.

At the gate, he rang the bell and heard the clang of it deep within.

It was the manservant Zhou Dan who answered.

"Mister Gao," he greeted, surprisingly cheerful. The young man looked him up and down before correcting himself. "Constable Gao?"

He was outfitted in the head constable's uniform which consisted of a black hanfu robe and leather arm guards. He'd moved around in it long enough that the uniform no longer felt like a costume, but he still endured the occasional taunt from his former cronies.

His appointment had the opposite affect from the den lords. Instead of shunning him, they suddenly became very friendly. Hui invited him frequently for tea, eager to find out how much the new head constable could be influenced. Gao continued to refuse. Interestingly, the way he handled the crime bosses was the same as it had ever been. The delicate balance hadn't changed significantly from the street to the magistrate's office.

For the most part, the magistrate turned a blind eye on gambling dens. Gao kept his eyes open as he walked on by. There were greater crimes to chase down. Such as the one found in the wooden case tucked beneath his arm.

"I've come to speak to Lord Bai," Gao said.

Zhou Dan invited him inside and allowed him to wait in the first courtyard. Gao took in a view of the house from where he stood. The outer courtyard was where the studios and parlor rooms were located. He'd been brought here before and had even been allowed stay for a few nights. It looked the same, but felt flat and faded now. He'd pressed Li Chen for enough information to know that Wei-wei hadn't yet returned. The house seemed quieter with her gone. Empty, for all its lavish furnishings.

Li Chen had only been able to find out Wei-wei had been sent away by her family and that she was safe. Gao had tried to reach out to her brother, but Huang was evasive.

At this point, Gao didn't know where Wei-wei was or if she would ever return, which made him more determined to close this investigation. He told himself if he could ensure there was no threat to her from Zheng's hired assassins, then Wei-wei would finally be able to come home.

The study door opened and Zhou Dan emerged, coming forward to usher Gao in.

Wei-wei's father was standing as entered. He was as broad-shouldered and commanding as Gao remembered. Senior members of the Ministry of Defense appeared more like soldiers than politicians.

"Lord Bai," he greeted with a bow.

"Head Constable Gao."

No bow in return, but just the use of his title was something in his favor. A barely respectable position was still respectable.

"I've come with information," he began stiffly. The magistrate was the one who would typically handle something like this. Li knew all the proper overtures to make a case.

"We've been searching for the assassins responsible for the attack on Chancellor Yao. Magistrate Li was certain there had to be more."

The elder Lord Bai's eyes lit with interest though his face remained a mask. The incident at the Yanxi Gate was still talked about in the city. By his count, they had only caught three of the hired men involved. Zheng Shi had been exiled and killed under questionable circumstances and from there the trail went cold.

He and Li Chen had watched their backs as they worked to track down the remaining killers. Gao worked his informants in the street while Li searched through administrative records of the investigation. One month of effort and little to show for it.

"Chancellor Yao and his party were shot by arrows. There were five men in attendance, and they'd been quickly overcome," Gao recounted. "There were twenty-five arrows fired leaving no survivors in the entourage."

"Only a matter of minutes with trained archers," Lord Bai commented.

"The chancellor was spared from the initial attack, but he was dragged from his horse only a short distance away and stabbed through the heart. The killers were waiting nearby, giving him no chance to flee. This was the work of at least five men. And the tower guards saw nothing."

Lord Bai's expression darkened. "The guards are dead as well."

Gao nodded. "Ordered to commit honor suicide under Zheng Shi's custody. There was a chain of deaths in this case."

The hired killers Gao had lured out using the ploy of the night soil men. Constable Ma. Fu Lin. One murderous incident—the incident at the Yanxi Gate—would have been difficult enough to hide, but a string of deaths meant too many loose threads.

"Someone was attempting to silence anyone who was a threat," Gao said. "Someone might have been a court manipulator, but not so experienced at dealing death."

Lord Bai raised his eyebrows at that. Li Chen had warned him that Zheng Shi was not accused of this crime. According to records, he was exiled for improper protocol and issuing a false proclamation. It was one of the points that had made tracking down the last of the killers so difficult.

"It was the first death that was the most important," Gao concluded. "The Emperor's nephew. An imperial prince."

An imperial prince with a seal he shouldn't have had. Li Chen concluded that the prince had either discovered the plot or been a part of it, losing his taste for treason right before the end. He'd been killed, but the conspirators had been unable to retrieve the seal.

It was the reason Fu Lin was dead, Gao reminded himself, regret heavy in his chest. He'd found the body and the seal that needed to remain hidden.

"When the perpetrator lost control of the imperial seal, he knew he had little time left to act. The chancellor's assassination, as coordinated as it seemed, wasn't the one he truly wanted."

Gao lifted the wooden case. "This was found beneath the floorboards of Zheng Shi's mansion."

It had taken the magistrate to get him inside the mansion. The lock had been easy to pick. Gao opened it now and held it out to the nobleman.

The elder Lord Bai scrutinized the decree inside the case before picking it up. He unfolded it carefully, his fingers pausing when he saw the red stamped insignia inside.

"This is an imperial order for an execution," Lord Bai said gravely. "With my name on it."

Wei-wei had said her father was a negotiator. His job was to maintain peace, whereas Zheng Shi was through with compromise.

"It is my understanding that Lord Bai is stationed between the armies of the Hedong protectorate," Gao said, recalling Wei-wei's words.

"My death would easily spark a war between the imperial aristocracy and the warlords. And Zheng Shi had suddenly taken an interest in being a mentor to my son," Lord Bai remarked grimly.

Wei-wei's father had always been scheduled to return at the end of that week. With Bai Huang's involvement in the records office, any forged documents would have passed through his hands. A grieving son faced with tracking the death of his father's killers would have been easily manipulated.

"Zheng Shi was forced to carry out his plot earlier than he expected with a different target," Gao concluded. "The magistrate's office spent a lot of time looking for rest of the assassins. We wondered how they had infiltrated the rooftops along the main road to the Yanxing gate. How had they evaded the tower guards? We originally assumed an imperial order took the guards away from their post just at the right time."

Lord Bai looked down at the forged document in his hand. The one that called for his execution. "The tower guards were the killers."

Gao nodded. "Thinking they were following an imperial order."

Lord Bai took a moment to absorb the information. Slowly, he placed the document back into the case. "Good work, constable."

The man's eagle eyes remained on Gao as he closed the wooden case. "This is not the only reason you came to see me."

Gao met his gaze squarely. "It isn't."

Lord Bai waited, his look growing more intense. The conspiracy had been the easy part of the meeting.

"This humble servant—" How was he supposed to say this? "I don't have family to speak on my behalf," he began again. "So I've come here personally to ask the most honorable Lord Bai for permission to marry his daughter."

The man remained silent. A muscle worked in his jaw, tensing and untensing. Gao was grateful that Lord Bai didn't have his sword on him.

The stand-off broke as Lord Bai called for tea, skewered Gao with another sharp look, then invited him to sit. Up until then, Lord Bai had been cordial enough, but matters of state were apparently more welcome than marriage proposals.

The who of them stared at one another as they waited for the tea to come. Even when it did, Lord Bai continued to stare at Gao, taking in his every measure, while the maidservant poured the tea. Gao had no choice but to follow his lead.

Steam rose from the bowls. The leaves had already been added and the wispy cloud formed a thin screen between them. When Bai drank, he drank. When Bai set his tea down, Gao did the same.

"I've seen you before, Constable," Lord Bai said finally.

"Yes. Once, Lord Bai."

The morning after he'd spent the night with Wei-wei in his arms. Gao kept his expression neutral.

"You've been promoted quickly since then."

"The last head constable was killed."

Wei-wei had mentioned her father didn't speak when he had nothing to say, but she didn't tell him he could use silence like a weapon. All the while, those sharp, iron hard eyes stayed fixed on Gao. No wonder Wei-wei was afraid of her father. Gao, however, was only afraid he would be refused. By all rights, Lord Bai should refuse him.

"It appeared that my daughter knows you. How is that?"

Gao paused. To reveal anything would be to reveal too much. He would compromise Wei-wei's reputation and destroy any chance he had of gaining Lord Bai's approval. But to lie or say nothing would also be damaging.

"I protected her whenever I could."

Lord Bai spent a long time weighing his response.

"You said you had no family to speak for you. Where is your family?"

Gao felt a pain deep inside his bones. "Passed away or long gone."

"Were they from Chang'an?"

"Yes. My father was a disgraced tax collector sent from the city. My mother and I were separated after his death."

Wei-wei's father let out a slow exhale, looking over Gao's uniform. "What did you do before you were appointed constable?"

"Whatever it took to keep me fed."

Lord Bai did not appear impressed.

As painful as the process was, this was what Gao

knew he should have done after Wei-wei had told him she loved him. He should have walked into their house and made his case. He might have fared just as poorly then as he did now, but he wouldn't have given up his chance.

"My daughter is very precious to me."

It was the only time Lord Bai had revealed any part of himself, and Gao seized on it. "Wei-wei is precious to me as well. More than gold."

The aristocrat fixed a hard, disapproving stare onto him. Gao realized, too late, where he had mis-stepped.

"Wei-ling is precious to me," he quickly corrected to her actual name, which was also out of line.

"Lady Bai," he corrected for a third attempt. He was about to be executed.

The elder Lord Bai looked like he'd had enough. "So, Gao is a family name?"

"Yes, my lord."

"What is your given name?"

Gao hadn't used any other name in years. He wasn't even sure if it was correct.

He swallowed past the sudden dryness in his throat. "It was Shen, sir."

Lord Bai took in the information, nodded, and then methodically set the bowls of tea aside. Picking up an ink stick, he ground out some ink, and then dipped a brush into it. Wei-wei's father had obviously done this ritual of thousands of times.

Over the last few weeks, Gao had been trying to improve his writing. He hadn't been aware that the head constable was expected to turn in reports pretty frequently. Currently, Gao paid a letter writer to do them while he dictated, which ate into his wages.

Gao wished he could understand what the man was writing, but upside-down and with Lord Bai's elaborate brush script, there was no chance.

"I have a request, Head Constable Gao Shen." Lord Bai let the ink on the paper dry before handing it to him.

Gao recognized a place name among the characters. Huashan.

"Bring my daughter safely home," Wei-wei's father commanded. "Then we'll talk again."

CHAPTER 27

Wei-Wei set her book down and closed her eyes. Crisp, cool air filled her lungs and seeped into her skin. After her betrothal had dissolved, she'd retreated to a Taoist convent tucked into the mountainside of Huashan. It was a place to seek peace and purity—and occasionally served as a refuge from an unwanted marriage. She had been there for a month now, and every day she grew more restless. It was the opposite of what she was supposed to strive for in this sanctuary.

At first there was the thrill of a new adventure. Huashan was a sacred mountain, and the view from its heights was truly breathtaking. From the ethereal mist that covered the peak to the vibrant green of the valley below. She wrote poems inspired by the surroundings, learned how to find the edible plants that grew along the trails, created paintings of the landscape.

Though she hadn't been ordained, Wei-wei lived alongside the Taoist nuns who ran the convent. She dressed in the same simple gray robes and pinned her hair in a simple knot to blend in among them. She was given chores like tending to the convent garden and taking on kitchen duties on a rotating basis. At first even the little tasks had been interesting due to novelty. For instance, Wei-wei had never cooked anything in her life. Learning how to boil and stir and put salt on grains and vegetables to season them was fascinating. Unfortunately, most of their meals consisted of boiled millet and pickled radishes. Eventually those tasks became routine and weren't enough to distract her.

That morning, she'd gone to forage for herbs and wild mushrooms. Afterward, she decided to retreat to one of the natural alcoves in the mountainside instead of returning to her cell. The rocky formation was just off the grounds of the convent. The nuns used the alcoves as places of meditation and reflection, but Wei-wei had thought to read instead. The book of poems she'd brought was one she'd read before several times.

It had been written by a distant relative who shared the family name of Bai. He'd also lived in Chang'an for a time, moving in and out of favor with imperial authority. During various periods of isolation, he wrote poems. This one was about a pipa player who'd once been celebrated, but had eventually fallen so far from grace that she was forced to marry a lowly merchant. The poet similarly lamented his own fall from grace.

Partway through the preface and she was already agitated. The pipa player was considered on her own merit and accomplishments only until she was married. Then her worth and happiness was to be measured solely by the match she made.

It was Wei-wei's own fault for reading maudlin poetry. She missed her family and Chang'an. And she missed Gao every day. She had been correct about the strength of her memory or maybe she was too stubborn to let herself forget.

Wei-wei rose to return to the convent. Maybe she would see if one of the sisters wanted to explore one of the mountain trails with her. They could collect wild yams for dinner and she could expend some of her pent-up energy. The nuns distinctly did not like it when she paced within the grounds.

As she started down the path, she saw a stranger coming in the opposite direction. It was a man, which was a rare sight. Over the last month, there had been occasional visitors and pilgrims, even one woman who'd been recently widowed who came to stay at the convent. Those who came to this nook of the mountain were usually women.

The stranger came closer, and she saw that he was in uniform with a dark hanfu robe and black cap. Something about his gait seemed so familiar. When he came even closer, she could see that he wasn't a stranger. It was Gao. Gao looking more serious and austere than she remembered him, but still him.

His expression intensified when he saw her, and he lengthened his stride to climb up the path. Her heart flooded with emotion as she fell into his arms. He felt so solid and warm and *there* as she pressed close to him.

"I thought I'd never see you again," she said, radiating with joy. And then, "Why are you disguised as a constable?"

～

IT DIDN'T TAKE LONG for Wei-wei to retrieve her belongings from the convent and to say her farewells. The journey down the mountain trail had to be by foot. Wei-wei took the lead, moving with confidence down the slope while she chattered away.

This was the Wei-wei he remembered. She was full of stories and questions, wanting to know what was the news from Chang'an. Where had he gone, what had happened to him.

He loved hearing her voice again. Wei-wei laughed when he retold the story of how Li Chen had come to offer him a job and the sound resonated through every part of him like the purest of music.

Wei-wei appeared radiant in the clean mountain air, with the kiss of mist around them. She was the Wei-wei he'd remembered and thought of night and day, but also different in so many small ways. He could see her more clearly now than he had before. What he saw made his heart beat faster and his body grow warm.

The last time they'd spoken, he'd tried to commit as many details as she could to memory, thinking it would be his last chance. But now he could see that the memory would have never been enough. He needed to have her with him to capture all of her, each feature and flaw. He wanted to be there to see every moment, every little change as the days went by.

"How did Huang know I was ready to leave?" she asked, teasing.

"It wasn't your brother who sent me to come get you. It was your father."

She came to a full stop, eyes widening. "You spoke to my father?"

"I spoke to your father."

Wei-wei bit down on her lower lip. He could see the questions flashing in her eyes. Her hair was pulled up, exposing the smooth, pale skin of her throat as well as the delicate area at the back of her neck. The urge to kiss her there came to him unexpectedly, like a clap of thunder on a clear day. He was aroused by the thought alone. His mouth against bare skin.

"What did Father say?" she asked.

"That he expected me to return you home safely."

Not in so many words, but that had to have been Lord Bai's intent. This was a test. He was to protect Wei-wei, escort Lord Bai's precious daughter home as a gentleman would. There was nothing in the world that could make Gao into a gentleman, but he could do this one thing.

The problem was as soon as he dared to ask Wei-wei's father for permission to marry her, his head seemed to have broken all walls and lifted all boundaries—at least the ones in his imagination. Gao wanted her more than he ever had. More than he wanted anything.

He could say it was love, and it was. But he would also honestly have to say it was lust.

"What else did he say?" she asked.

"Not much."

Gao hadn't told her that he'd asked to marry her. Her father hadn't said yes.

But he didn't say no.

"Well, did you talk about anything else?" she pressed, unsatisfied.

"You should walk faster," he replied, moving past her. "We need to get down to the foothills before dark."

"Did you come to him?" Her footsteps quickened to catch up to him. "Or did he come to you?"

"Quickly. Before dark," he reminded, increasing his pace down the mountain.

The faster he could get Wei-wei home safely, untouched, the faster he and her father could continue their conversation. And he could finally have his answer.

～

THE HORSES HAD BEEN STABLED at a roadside inn at the foothills of the mountain. Gao had also paid for two rooms there where they would sleep for the night.

They shared a small meal in the common room as night fell. Wei-wei sat across from Gao, and she couldn't stop looking at him. So much of him was the same, yet different. Sun-darkened skin and loose-limbed confidence. His angular features didn't seem as stark to her now. Had familiarity softened her eyes? His spare, rawboned look had refined somewhat into a lean virility that took her breath away.

She'd dreamed of him so often while they were apart. If she blinked now, would he disappear?

"You look so differentfor in the uniform," she said.

"Less frightening?"

She smiled. "I wouldn't say that."

"Li said the clothes would keep bandits away. I'm afraid they'll have the opposite effect."

Subtle changes aside, Gao had the same relaxed, yet watchful posture as he scrutinized his surroundings with hawkish gaze. No one would ever mistake him as harmless.

"You changed your fate," she marveled. "Like you said you would."

He started to say something but stopped himself. His expression as inscrutable.

Here they were. She was still dressed in the gray robes of the convent while Gao was in uniform. Neither one of them looking like themselves.

The innkeeper brought two bowls of bone broth with greens and dumplings to set before them. Wei-wei's mouth watered at the fragrant steam rising from the soup. She was excited to taste something that wasn't radish.

"I asked your father if he would allow for us to be

married," Gao revealed right as she spooned a dumpling into her mouth.

She froze, staring at him. He looked serious.

His fingers curled over the edge of the table. "I was told we would discuss it further once you returned."

The dumpling was lodged in her mouth. She bit down, chewed and swallowed, all the while staring at him in disbelief.

"If you'll have me," he added, his voice cracking. His eyes were opaque as he watched her reaction.

She was too stunned to answer. She didn't know if she was supposed to answer or if she *could* answer. The decision belonged to her father.

"It's good that you asked Father," she said finally.

He nodded in agreement. After a pause he added, "I brought some of your things from home for you."

"Thank you."

"If we start out early tomorrow, we should be back in the capital in three days' time."

"Good."

Something had gone wrong, but she couldn't place it.

Wei-wei finished her soup without tasting a single mouthful. Across from her, Gao didn't seem to have much of an appetite. They retired to their rooms once supper was done. It wasn't a large inn and they were situated in adjacent chambers. Gao waited until she was inside her room before heading to his.

Her room was tidy and serviceable with a sleeping mat rolled up in the corner. A satchel with her belongings had been placed inside the door just as Gao had mentioned. The first thing she did was change out of her pigeon gray robes into night clothes, trading the feel of rough hemp against her skin for the smooth feel of silk.

She unrolled the sleeping mat and then laid out her hanfu

robe beside it. The silk was pale blue like a clear sky, and embroidered with a cloud pattern. It had been a month since she'd worn anything so elaborate. She'd brought few luxuries to the convent besides her books and ink brushes. Even having the few personal items in the room felt extravagant.

As she started to lower herself onto the mat, she realized something.

She hadn't given Gao an answer.

He'd spent the entire meal waiting for her response. No wonder he'd been so quiet. Grabbing her robe, she pulled the silk over her shoulders. It settled over her like water. She tied the sash around her waist with quick fingers and blew out the oil lamp before slipping out the door.

She opened the door to the adjacent chamber and slipped inside.

The lamp was still lit. Gao was lying on the sleeping pallet, reading from a tattered book with a dark blue cover. He turned his head as she entered and then pulled himself up into sitting position.

"Wei-wei."

She spilled into his arms. "Yes. I'll have you," she replied.

"I didn't mean right now—"

She pressed her lips to his, cutting off his protest, but it couldn't have been much of a protest because he returned the kiss, his mouth hard and hungry. It was only then that Gao seemed real to her. Earlier, at the convent, he had been so formal, so reserved. There was nothing reserved about him now. She clung to him, feeding on the raw, rough-edged essence of him that she remembered. Wei-wei longed to press against him, so much closer than they were, until they absorbed one another.

Somehow Gao ended up on his back on the sleeping mat while she leaned over him, her hands tugging at the knot in his belt. Gao gazed up at her with a look of awe, his breath ragged. "So beautiful," he murmured.

"Mmm-hmmm." She was too busy trying to loosen the knot to appreciate the compliment. Her heart was pounding so hard. A mixture of anticipation and nervousness was making her fingers clumsy.

Gao reached behind his neck to pull out the booklet he'd been reading. There was a deep crease in the already worn cover.

"What is that?" She'd abandoned the knotted sash to slip her hands into the fold of his robe, stroking until she found skin. His heart beat forcefully beneath her fingers.

"The *Thousand Character Classic*," he replied, his eyes dark on her. "I'm reading it to try to impress you."

She frowned. "It's a primer given to children."

His lips quirked. "I know. Are you impressed?"

She fell on top of him, her mouth over his. She could feel the curve of his smile against her lips as he rolled her over. Gao fared much better than she did with knots. Her sash yielded to his hands in a whisper of silk. He slipped her robe from her and removed her underclothes, bending to place a heated kiss against her bared shoulder. Wei-wei shivered as the evening air chilled her skin, but Gao undressed quickly and returned to gather her into his arms. His eyes were deep and black as they remained locked on hers.

"Now?" he asked.

She nodded, her throat dry. As certain as she was of the moment, she was inexperienced in the how of things. Gao captured her mouth in a kiss again, removing any need to speak. For the next moments there was only this, mouth to mouth, skin to skin. Her breath caught up with his. Gao was the same Gao she knew, but different. The hard, bared angles that she remembered had been filled in, smoothed over, but the hard lines were still there. Tempered.

His hands molded over her, as if Gao was remembering her too. And discovering new places as well.

The urgency grew inside her as his long fingers stroked over her breasts, then lower. She remembered this touch so acutely. There had been so many nights when she tried to conjure the same sweet desperation. The intense way Gao watched her face as the world shrunk down to a single point of heat between them.

She clung to him now, pulling him closer. She didn't have to imagine Gao any longer. He was here.

"I thought I would never see you again." She gasped as he touched her intimately, rough fingers with a gentle stroke over the most sensitive part of her. She felt the caress deeper than in her flesh, darting straight to her heart.

"I thought the same," he said.

She arched her hips helplessly toward him as his fingers stroked, circled, doing things to her until she was flushed, heated, liquid. This was as wonderful as she remembered. She could feel the male part of him pressing against her hip and reached downward to search for him. She couldn't see, but what her fingers slid over was silken smooth. Unexpected when the rest of him was all heat and hardness. Gao clenched his jaw, letting out a ragged breath.

"I'm doing poorly on this test," he muttered through his teeth.

She was so confused. "I think...I think you're doing quite well," she said breathlessly.

Gao made a choked sound and shook his head. His expression was either one of anguish or amusement. Maybe both.

He curved a hand around the back of her neck, tilting her head up to kiss her passionately. Then he broke away and bent to press his mouth to the hollow of her throat, her neck. Each caress sent shivers down her spine. Then his gentle lips were replaced by the sharp rasp of teeth, and her body jerked up, pressing restlessly against his male member. A sound of unrestrained pleasure escaped her throat.

She pleaded, crying out as she clung to him. Gao's gaze captured hers as he repositioned his body over hers.

"Wei-wei," he murmured. He laced his fingers through hers, holding on tight, and she waited breathlessly for what would come. Fleeting visions of caves and springs, yin rain and yang essence came to mind. The books on the matter were so cryptic.

His other hand dipped again between her thighs, parting her with gentle fingers. She blinked up at him, her heartbeat thundering in her chest. Wanting and anxious. A deep furrow etched itself into his brow. He looked deep in concentration.

The first sensation of penetration stole her breath. Then the fear came along with a feeling of being slowly invaded and altered, but Gao held her through it. His hips continued to thrust and she closed her eyes to focus on the feelings. Gao exhaled sharply and groaned. Her pulse was rushing too fast in her ears. The sensation between her thighs intensified as he pushed deeper, sending a wave of sensation through her that she could feel all the way to her toes. Gao was inside her, flesh to flesh. It was unfathomable and miraculous.

When he began to move, his thrusts became a second pulse. Her breath followed each pull, his body urged hers into the same rhythms. There was no more wondering of how or why. Her knees curved upwards, bending to fit around his hips. When she touched a hand to his cheek, his eyes were lost.

The feeling was beyond pain or pleasure. She was too overwhelmed with the knowledge of being joined with someone else. Gao shifted, hooking a hand beneath her knee.

There was an odd sense of being moved, mastered, but the altered angle changed everything.

She cried out as his every movement became pure pleasure, a tide rising higher until it broke.

They continued like that, ending, beginning again. Learning each other with each minute as if they could regain the days lost between them.

Sometime near morning, they slept.

CHAPTER 28

I t was dark in the room. The oil lamp had long guttered out and the light filtering from outside was the dim orange of the new dawn. Wei-wei was still sleeping amidst the pile of their discarded clothing while Gao watched her. The feel of her was imprinted on his skin. Her scent surrounded him. He hoped her sleep was as peaceful and contented as it outwardly appeared. His own thoughts were in turmoil.

When she did wake, the first thing she did was search for him. It set a crack in his heart when she gathered the blanket around herself and moved to him, curling up in his lap.

"You look fearsome sitting here in the dark," she said

"Do I?"

Wei-wei nodded, closing her eyes again as her head settled against his shoulder. "What are you thinking about?"

That he would never, ever be able walk away from her again.

"I asked your father's permission for us to marry."

She made a soft sound of agreement. It seemed so simple,

so easy when it was just the two of them and she was warm in his arms, but nothing was simple.

"If he refuses, I will have to do something very rash."

Her eyes flicked open, large and luminous. "Please don't stab my father."

He bit her neck, feeling the ripple of pleasure that moved through her.

Wei-wei. He loved her, he loved her, he loved her.

"I'll have to steal you away."

Again, she made a sound to indicate assent and tried to curl up once more.

"If your father hasn't killed me by then."

Wei-wei was clever, and she'd proven her ability to move mountains when she set her mind to it. Gao could certainly use her help with his plotting at the moment, and he told her so.

"My father won't refuse you," she asserted.

"How do you know that for certain?"

She lifted her head from his shoulder. "Sending you here was his answer."

He regarded her skeptically. "He doesn't even know who I am."

"My father knows who you are," Wei-wei said, growing serious. "The day that Li Chen and I were supposed to be betrothed, I told him I would obey him and honor our family's promise if that was what he decided was best. But that I hadn't slept and I hadn't eaten. And I wouldn't be able to sleep and I wouldn't be able to eat because I was sick with love."

"Sick?" he questioned.

She blushed and hid her face against the crook of his neck, rendering him defenseless.

"I told my father exactly what was in my heart," she murmured against his skin. "I told him if I married Li Chen, I would never be more than half a wife. I told him bringing such unhappiness into a marriage from the very first day would doom it to failure. I hated failing my family more than anything, but one couldn't force sorrow away with a command."

Gao was stunned. "I can't believe your father found any of that acceptable."

"He was furious with me. I'd never been so unreasonable. So unseemly and emotional. Mother cried and lamented how she hadn't taught me well enough. It was the worst thing I'd ever done, not biting my tongue and remaining quiet." Her voice flooded with emotion. "Our two families never met that day. Instead, Father sent me to Huashan to avoid gossip and heal from a broken heart. By then, I thought you were gone forever. None of it mattered because I was already yours. Every part of me."

They held each other as daylight crept in.

"In the end, you just told your father the truth," he said quietly. She had risked everything to admit her feelings to her family, even if nothing came of it.

Wei-wei nodded, settling herself closer into the crook his arms. "And he listened, as hard as it was. So, he must have known who you were the moment you stood before him."

EPILOGUE

The ceremony of moving into a new home was an elaborate one. It had started three days earlier when she and Gao had come to bring light into the house. They'd walked through each room, placing oil lamps and shining lanterns in each corner. There were four rooms and two floors in the tidy residence and a kitchen in the back part of the ground floor. It was much smaller than the Bai family home, but Wei-wei was excited to finally have a place to call their own.

They had been living within the Bai mansion since their wedding a month ago while the necessary petitions for moving into the ward were approved. During that time, Yue-ying had tried to teach Wei-wei how to cook her own dishes to prepare her for having a kitchen without servants to take care of it.

"I can boil millet and pickle radishes," Wei-wei insisted. It might be a little while before there were more interesting flavors at the dinner table, but at least she and Gao wouldn't go hungry.

The entire purpose of the house moving ritual was to

cleanse away the energy and spirit of the previous inhabitants. That way, she and Gao would move into a home free of any ill-fortune and negative energy. And any ghosts. No one wanted old ghosts wandering around when moving in. Wei-wei had sprinkled rice and salt around the perimeter the day before to draw them outside in case any were lingering about.

Today was to be their first night in the home. They'd thrown open all the doors and windows when they'd arrived in the morning and had begun all the prescribed tasks.

"Go away now, old spirits," she called out to the walls. "Wei-wei and Gao are here now."

Gao laughed. "Do you believe all that?"

"You tell them," she urged. "You're the master of the house. They'll be afraid of you."

"Go away, old spirits," he said gamely, grinning at her the entire time.

If any of the ghosts refused to leave, it would be his fault.

Together, they lit incense before the altar and said a prayer for the Gao family ancestors.

Then Gao went upstairs to finish moving the bed while she tidied the downstairs rooms. She would be up later to sort through the books for the study. The furniture had been brought in earlier, but tradition dictated that they only finish adjusting everything into its final position today.

Wei-wei started sweeping the floor. This chore of house cleaning was novel enough to be an adventure of its own.

There would be many changes for both of them. Their house was right up against the neighbors to the left and the right. Instead of the wide double courtyard house Wei-wei was accustomed to, there was a small enclosed garden behind the kitchen. When they stepped outside, they would immediately be in the street.

The house was located to the west of the East Market, not

far from the magistrate's yamen. That was where Gao reported at the start of each day. He'd be able to go there on foot now instead of taking a carriage or horse all the way from the mansions in the northeast.

There were still people who said that Lord Bai's daughter had married a lowly constable. They wondered what scandalous things must have occurred for her to have settled for someone beneath her class. If the gossipers had asked Wei-wei, she would have told them scandal was just the start of it. There was subterfuge and disguise, murder and treason. But of course, the gossipers would never say anything so directly. They preferred to whisper. Wei-wei was glad to be far enough away from the mansion ward not to hear them.

She'd just finished sweeping when she heard a sound at the door. Li Chen stood there, holding parcels of tea and salt.

"Magistrate Li, you're early."

"I won't be able to attend the housewarming party, but I wanted to come and wish you both well." He held out the parcels and Wei-wei thanked him as she took them. "From my mother, though she told me not speak of it."

Another area where a hint of scandal remained. Lord Bai's daughter ended up marrying Li Chen's constable, the gossipers whispered with wicked glee.

Let them whisper. It was true, and she was quite gleeful about it herself. She was writing a tale about it.

"It's a good place," Li said, taking in the surroundings. "Good light."

"The study will be upstairs. We only have a small collection of books to start."

"That will certainly change over time," he remarked, wandering to the back toward the kitchen. "I've noticed the quality of Constable Gao's reports have improved quite a bit lately," he said casually, while peering out into the garden.

Wei-wei had hoped the papers she'd written would just be

filed away after a quick glance, but of course Li would dutifully scrutinize every report. He was a dedicated official.

"I've assisted my husband, from time to time," she admitted. By this, she meant every time. She looked forward to Gao's retelling of the day, and it was hardly any effort at all for her to record them. One never knew when Gao would recall something pertinent he hadn't thought of initially, or she might notice a detail that he hadn't.

"No matter. I didn't hire the constable for his calligraphy," the magistrate assured, still focused on the garden.

"May I ask you something as well, Magistrate Li?"

He returned his attention to her. This was the first time she'd spoken to him personally since the pact they had made inside his office.

"What did you tell your family in order to dissolve the betrothal?"

"I told my mother that I was caught in a dilemma. If I honored our promise to the Bai family by marrying their daughter, I would forever be unable to repay a great debt that I owed. Either way, our family would face dishonor."

She frowned at him. "That implies I was being courted by the man to which you owed a debt."

"Well, I didn't realize you were going to get yourself sent to a convent. That was much more dramatic than my play," he said with admiration.

Wei-wei started to correct him but decided it wasn't necessary. The overall details still worked out.

"In any case, I didn't lie. Your husband may not admit it. I don't even suppose he thinks of it this way, but Constable Gao saved my life the morning after the extended curfew."

She remembered how Gao and Li Chen had come rushing into the teahouse with a man who was believed to be one of the assassins at the Yanxi Gate. There had been blood everywhere, but none of it had been Li's.

"I owed Constable Gao a great debt from that day," Li Chen concluded. "And when I saw how he'd given away his reward from the Emperor, I knew he was the better man."

Her chest swelled with emotion. It was when she'd known as well. If Gao could risk so much, without any benefit to himself-—she could risk telling her truth.

There was a loud crash from overhead, followed by cursing.

"Better in some ways," Li amended.

"My husband is moving the bed upstairs."

"Can I offer any assistance?"

Together, Gao and Li Chen were able to move the heavy wooden bed into the correct orientation prescribed by the feng shui master. Then Wei-wei brewed tea and poured out two bowls while the magistrate and Gao discussed county details. The first tea she poured in her own parlor. She poured out a third bowl for herself and seated herself beside Gao, listening.

Li Chen eventually took his leave. Once they were alone again, Gao put his arms around her and they stood together in the center of the parlor. In their new home.

He stroked his thumb over the loop of red silk around her wrist, taking the time to adjust it so the eternity knot was centered.

"Am I dreaming, Wei-wei?" he asked.

"Yes." She pressed closer, finding all the places where they fit together as she leaned into him. "I'm dreaming with you."

~

AUTHOR'S NOTE

The Hidden Moon continues about a week after the events of "The Liar's Dice" novella, though the two can certainly be read separately.

Even though I can say I've been researching the Tang Dynasty for over a decade now, each new book sends me off on a new research adventure and there's always more to discover.

First of all, the title comes from a quote that is often attributed to Siddhārtha Gautama Buddha (and which, I learned after the book was finished, appears frequently in *Teen Wolf*). It's frequently cited as a misquote so I simply attributed the quote to antiquity. There's also a Chinese idiom that refers to someone being so beautiful that they "hide the moon, and put the flowers to the shame". Given that "The Shameful Flower" doesn't fit Wei-wei at all, *The Hidden Moon* won out as title.

Wei-wei is perhaps my favorite character I've ever created. She depicts the stereotype of the bookish, over-achieving, picture-perfect daughter. I admit that I was one of those—and have many memories of crawling under the garage door to get back into the house after the front door was locked and bolted at night. Someone who is dedicated to studying everything so diligently would reasonably be very good at misbehaving, don't you think? *wink*

The character of Wei-wei is inspired by several female literary figures in ancient China, most notably Ban Zhao, who co-authored the historical treatise on the Western Han Dynasty, *The Book of Han*, as well as *Lessons for Women*, an instruction guide for women used in China for over a thousand years after Ban Zhao's death. Legend has it that she assisted her brother, Ban Gu, in passing the imperial exams.

I was also inspired by the tragic story of courtesan Yu Xuanji, one of the most famous poets of the Tang Dynasty. She composed a poem about going to view the list of names of candidates who had passed the examinations, and lamenting: "How I resent this silk robe which hides the lines of my poetry."

For me, this poem embodies Wei-wei's frustration of having a lifetime of learning, but never being able to shine on her own merits.

For any who might consider Wei-wei's attitudes too modern, Yu Xuanji (840 A.D. - 868 A.D.) lived at the same time period as *The Hidden Moon* and her sentiments resonated enough to survive to this day. Author Justin Hill penned a gorgeous fictional account of Yu Xuanji's life in *Passing Under Heaven* which, much like the tale of Madame Bovary, reads like a cautionary tale of a woman who dared too much. I wanted to write the story of a woman who dared and wasn't punished for it.

As to other places in society where women were able to exercise agency, I've always been fascinated by the role of Taoist monasteries. There was a surge of high-born women, even princesses, who became ordained as Taoist priestesses during the Tang Dynasty. Westerners might think of monasteries as places that are restrictive and pinned down, but monasteries in Tang society were outside of societal and government control. They present an interesting counter-point to the pleasure houses, both of them being places where women could achieve some measure of autonomy and empowerment. Interestingly enough, Yu Xuanji was both a courtesan and a Taoist priestess at different points in her life.

The central crime in the book was modeled after the true events surrounding the assassination of Chancellor Wu Yuanheng in 815 A.D. He was attacked in Chang'an early in the morning by assassins hired by a rival in the imperial court. His entourage was fired upon and his head cut off. Quite a public execution, yet no one was immediately arrested. The killers publicly threatened all who would investigate and proceeded to attack another official as well. I changed the perpetrator and the motive in the book, but the elements of the original assassination and the investigation into it make for a fascinating read.

Historical record of secret censors is non-existent. Though I can imagine they would be hard to find—much like historical record of secret societies.

The original working title of the book was *Ten Days in Chang'an* styled after the mini-series *Longest Day in Chang'an*. If you want a visual feast, check this series out. It's an immersive and historically detailed depiction of Tang Dynasty clothing and architecture. I was only able to get one episode in before running off to pen this story.

ACKNOWLEDGMENTS

For the first time, I would like to thank my readers for this book.

It's been over five years since the release of *The Jade Temptress,* during which a series of disappointments put me in a tailspin. I'd always intended there to be third story with Wei-wei as the third "sister" to complete the trio that started with *The Lotus Palace.* Between life and contract issues, the possibility of a third book drifted further and further away.

An author's biggest fear is that if we don't publish, we'll simply disappear and readers will forget. But every so often, I would receive another letter asking me if I would one day write Wei-wei's story. I realized that even though I was holed away in my hermit cave, the *Lotus Palace* stories were still out there and new readers were coming to them. No matter what the publisher might do with them, these stories and what was created within belonged to me.

And to my readers.

Thank you for sticking with me. Each wonderful comment and lovely note you sent kept this story alive.

OTHER BOOKS BY JEANNIE LIN

THE LOTUS PALACE MYSTERY SERIES

The Lotus Palace - Book 1

The Jade Temptress - Book 2

The Liar's Dice - novella

The Hidden Moon - Book 3

THE GUNPOWDER CHRONICLES SERIES

Gunpowder Alchemy - Book 1

Clockwork Samurai - Book 2

The Rebellion Engines - Book 3

Tales from the Gunpowder Chronicles - anthology

Steampunk short stories:

The Warlord and the Nightingale

∼

Sign-up for Jeannie's mailing list to receive updates on new releases, appearances, and special giveaways.

Made in the USA
Las Vegas, NV
29 November 2020

11682259R00175